# LOVING DELILAH

He drew her near. Her skin was cold from the water. He kissed her softly, wove his hand through her hair, and held her head still so she would look at him. "It was hell working with you all day, wanting to kiss you but having to keep our relationship all business."

"I was thinking the same thing."

"You're going to have me moving to this island full-time, woman."

Other books by Candice Poarch

Bargain of the Heart
Tender Escape
The Essence of Love

The Nottoway Series:

The Last Dance
Intimate Secrets
With This Kiss
White Lightning

The Coree Island Series:

Loving Delilah
Lighthouse Magic
Shattered Illusions

The At Your Service Series:

Courage Under Fire

Candice Poarch

# Loving Delilah

BET Publications, LLC
http://www.bet.com
http://www.arabesquebooks.com

ARABESQUE BOOKS are published by

BET Publications, LLC
c/o BET BOOKS
One BET Plaza
1900 W Place NE
Washington, DC 20018-1211

All Kensington Titles, Imprints, and Distributed Lines
are available at special quantity discounts for bulk purchases for sales promotions, premiums, fund-raising,
and educational or institutional use. Special book ex-
cerpts or customized printings can also be created to fit
specific needs. For details, write or phone the office of
the Kensington special sales manager: Kensington Publishing Corp., 850 Third Avenue, New York, NY 10022,
attn: Special Sales Department, Phone: 1-800-221-2647.

First Printing: December 2004
10  9  8  7  6  5  4  3  2  1

Printed in the United States of America

*To my family for their continued support through the years. My husband, John; my parents, Alfield and Ethel Poarch; my children, Gerard, Shevonne, and Rachel; and my sister, Evangeline Jones.*

# Acknowledgments

My sincere thanks go to readers, book clubs, booksellers, and librarians for their continued support.

Special thanks to Therome Spivey and Carole Thompson. Thank you, Kicheko Driggins and the BET team for making the military tour such a success. I am grateful for my editor, Evette Porter. As always, profound thanks go to my critique partner, Sandy Rangel.

# Chapter 1

Delilah Benton was the bomb. Her new mauve St. Johns suit flattered her well-toned brown skin, skin that had been kissed by the North Carolina sun. A wide belt cinched her narrow waist and the short slim skirt and three-inch heels displayed the heart-stopping shape of her long legs. She'd spent a fortune on the Gucci purse to match the shoes, although she didn't make designer money. Not yet anyway, but that was coming. Daddy had always said it never hurt to splurge once in a while. Well, truthfully, she splurged often, but who was counting?

Delilah tossed back her shoulder-length black hair and headed to the far corner of the room. Her high heels clicked on the white tile floor. She reached the gunmetal-gray desk that her boss had purchased at a government surplus store and sat in the chair behind it.

She was definitely overdone for the utilitarian office. Although it was situated near Research Triangle

Park, it was in a warehouse that was away from the ultramodern buildings of the successful companies the area was known for. The really big bucks had just begun to trickle in—thanks to her and Keith Baker's vision. Right now the money went to more important needs than an expensive interior decorating job. The only concession toward frills was a fresh coat of paint Delilah had convinced Keith to apply a couple of months ago. She'd been at her wits' end staring at ugly gray walls for more hours than she cared to count. It stifled her creativity, she'd told him, and she was sure the drab walls were partly the reason for the employees' sour dispositions. But their attitudes hadn't changed after the paint job. The amount of money would change. Attitudes, more than likely, wouldn't.

Delilah placed some papers on her assistant Paige Lipton's desk. Paige was a recent college graduate eager to learn, willing to work long hours without complaint—and she was a fast learner. Once more money started coming in, Delilah could move Paige into an office near her own. Delilah was leaving at noon, but Paige needed to finish a project before she left for the weekend.

Even the stark surroundings couldn't dampen Delilah's spirits today. Keith was taking her to Charlotte for the weekend, and she'd blown almost an entire paycheck on a suitcase packed with new outfits to tempt him. He was going to propose. She was sure of it, and that was worth every dollar she had spent. He'd given her many hints recently, even asked for her ring size. What else would prompt him to splurge on this special weekend?

Now and again, Delilah wondered if she was

truly in love with Keith. She knew she liked him— a lot. They respected each other. Well, if it wasn't quite love yet, she was certainly on the verge, and by the time the wedding took place, well, she was sure she'd tumble over that cliff.

With fine features and a cinnamon complexion, Keith exuded an aura of charm and authority. He worked out daily, and his toned body was enough to make any woman's heart beat a staccato rhythm. Besides, she was thirty-three and her baby-making potential was quickly declining. Delilah wanted a couple of babies while she was young enough to enjoy them and while her eggs were still functioning properly.

Delilah smiled. After all these years, she'd finally found a decent man. One not unlike her cousin Cecily Anderson's husband, Ryan. *Thank you, God.* For years she'd believed there had to be someone for her too. For goodness' sake. How many times could she strike out in one lifetime? She'd had her share of duds and then some. Delilah, the temptress, a respectable married woman. She liked the sound of that.

"Pretty outfit, Delilah," Barbara Ward said, bringing Delilah out of her dream. As usual, the woman's nose was out of joint. Compliments were alien to Barbara, but Delilah knew she was looking good today. Never having been around so many catty females in her entire life, she'd looked long and hard for the sisterhood spirit. Usually she easily befriended other women. Yet, Delilah couldn't break the icy shell most of these women built around themselves.

Delilah said simply, "Thank you."

"Going somewhere special?"

"Just felt like a change." She wasn't about to divulge her business to these jealous women. Her attempts at friendship were met with stony silence and cold shoulders, which she couldn't understand because she was an asset to the company, even making it possible for them to earn higher salaries. But did that make a difference? Heck no.

"Well, well, well. Look who's coming to . . . lunch."

Delilah glanced at the window where she saw a woman, arms swinging like pistons, barreling toward the glass door. Wearing blue spandex, she looked like she'd come straight from a gym. Her hair was pulled back in a ragged ponytail that was unflattering to the sharp angles of her face. Wearing her hair down would certainly soften her appearance.

Delilah returned to her work. The woman was no concern of hers.

In an attempt to quadruple the size of his small company over the next five years, Keith had hired Delilah as proposal manager several months ago. She'd convinced him to bid for the largest contract he'd dared so far.

The government was spending billions on homeland security; and security companies were the hottest things around. Delilah's company had submitted a proposal and won the contract. Now she was laying the groundwork for the next proposal.

Delilah often worked eighty-hour weeks. Many times she worked seven days straight, hammering out strategies for staffing. She'd put her heart and soul into this fifteen-million-dollar project, and they'd won the bid.

As long as the company's work was superior, the company's reputation would spread, giving them an edge on other projects of similar size and importance.

But there were benefits for Delilah, too. Keith agreed to pay her 2 percent of the contract if they won. It was an insider's secret that when the company won a contract, male managers who developed the proposal were often paid a percentage in addition to their salary. But women seldom came in for performance bonuses. For most it was straight salary.

But Keith promised to be fair. If the company won, so would she, he'd said.

Delilah was on top of the world. With the windfall, she'd make enough to pay cash for a house. She'd be able to retire early. She'd be able to build a cushion and enjoy herself. Why shouldn't she benefit?

"You little slut!" The office door crashed against the wall, bringing in a blast of North Carolina's April wind. "I'll teach you to mess with my man."

Delilah glanced up from her papers to see who the woman was referring to, then scooted her chair back when the woman, who looked like she could easily bench-press 150 pounds—and who didn't possess an ounce of fat—charged after *her*.

Delilah was less than 125 pounds soaking wet, and when an iron arm swung at her she moved an instant before a tight beefy fist flashed past her head. The air ruffled her hair and propelled the woman forward to crash on the desk. She smashed picture frames, shattered a vase holding silk flowers, strewed file folders and papers in an arc for six feet around her. No way could Delilah fight this woman fair. She had picked up her chair to slam it across the woman's back when Keith's voice stopped her.

"What the hell's going on out here?" he demanded, running out of his office with a stack of papers in one hand. His Paul Stuart shirtsleeves were rolled up. He'd plucked his glasses off and held them out in his hand as if to punctuate his words. His voice froze everyone in place. But only for a second. When he saw Delilah darting glances between him and the woman who was picking herself up from the desk, his eyes widened.

"Laurie?" he asked. "What are you doing here?"

A huge circle of water from Paige's overturned water bottle soaked the front of her shirt. "To put an end to this little hussy who thinks she can take my man," she shouted.

"Your man!" Delilah shouted in return.

Breathing hard, the woman swiveled around to face Delilah and pointed a finger in her own chest. "Yes. My man," she said with belligerent ownership. "Who do you think helped Keith finance this place? I'm not going to give him up to a cheap whore like you."

Delilah blasted her glaze at Keith, who'd told her he didn't have a woman in his life when they met. She waited for him to set this Laurie straight. This was a mistake. Keith was the first good man to cross her path. Ever. Delilah had a knack for attracting the wrong kind of man, but for once she'd thought her luck had changed. The sour feeling sinking in the pit of her stomach told her she'd set her hopes too high—again.

"Laurie, honey, I can explain," Keith said, advancing closer. "Just wait until I get home tonight, okay, baby?"

Delilah's mouth flew open. Shock froze her in place. *Okay, baby?* What the heck?

"I'm in the middle of an important call to Tokyo," he continued.

"Not until you fire her." Laurie's long arm pointed straight at Delilah.

"Okay . . . okay." Cautiously, he grasped Laurie's arm, and while gently brushing debris from her clothes and smoothing out her lopsided ponytail, he led her to the door.

"You know I love you, baby," he continued. "Why would I date anyone else? Now, would that make sense?"

Was this guy for real? Would he know the truth if it smacked him in the face?

He tugged Laurie closer. "You've got to learn to trust me, baby." He kissed her sweetly on the lips.

Taking this all in, Delilah rounded the desk and heard a cackle at one side. She didn't spare her co-workers a glance. She'd been there only months, but they'd worked with the company for several years. Everybody else in the office must have known Keith was involved with this woman, but no one had bothered to inform her. She worked with a bunch of jealous biddies.

"If you don't straighten up, I'm going to call my brothers and take back my money," Laurie said.

"No need to do that, sweetie. You're my one and only. We're going to get married. Come on, now," he said playfully. "Would I fool around on my future wife?"

Delilah seethed at his conniving game. She almost felt sorry for Laurie. It might be over for Delilah and him, but Delilah wouldn't be the last woman he fooled around on. By now, Laurie knew Keith. If she were fool enough to marry him, she'd play this scene for years to come.

"Married?" Laurie's startled eyes held tenderness that belied her earlier fury. For a moment she looked delicate and pretty. "Really, Keith? You want to marry me?" She grasped Keith's face gently in both hands. Joy warmed her face and voice.

Delilah almost gagged.

"You knew we were," Keith continued. "Eventually."

"A Christmas wedding." Laurie kissed him with all the pent-up love she possessed for the man who wasn't worth the effort.

When their lips parted, Keith said, "I've gotta go, baby. The Tokyo call is still waiting."

"Don't work late. I'm going to have something special waiting for you."

"I can't wait to get home."

Delilah made it across the room, ending right behind Keith.

He shut the door.

Through a bank of glass windows, Delilah watched Laurie walk to the parking lot with brisk steps. Keith blew out a labored breath and turned.

Delilah's fist landed in Keith's face. He staggered into the door.

"I'll pack my things, you SOB," Delilah said. She

wished she'd crashed a chair across his thick, lying head instead, because her hand was hurting like hell. Never mind her heart. "You've got five minutes to write my severance and bonus check, because if you don't I'm going to sue for sexual harassment and give your sweet Laurie an earful about the facts of your life."

Delilah turned, walked to her office, pulled out the drawers, threw her few things into a box, and stormed out, leaving behind the mess the other woman had made. Let the others clean that up.

She enjoyed the North Carolina atmosphere and weather. She'd been there two years already, the longest she'd stayed in one place in a very long time. Perhaps it was time she moved from Raleigh.

As anger and dignity drove her out of the office, her more pressing concern was that she'd made a mess of her life once again. The same sad story. A long time ago, she'd stopped counting the times drama happened to her.

Six weeks had passed since the fateful day Delilah left her job and she still hadn't received her bonus check. She was forced to do freelance consulting on a proposal for another company to tide her over. Luckily she lived in an area where freelance work was readily available.

That job was now over and she was reluctant to take on another project. A sense of restlessness settled in and refused to budge. She needed something different, something meaningful, and the thought played in her head. She needed something more than a paycheck for food and rent.

Keith had promised her a check in a week—half of what he owed her. In two months he would pay her the remaining half.

Delilah longed to spend the weekend on the beach, smell the salty ocean water, feel the breeze caressing her skin, sink her toes into the soft sand. She sat at the table with the day's mail, tossed aside the junk, and placed bills in a pile.

Picking up the portable phone, she dialed her friend Sylvia Adams. The number was disconnected. Then she reached her on her cell phone.

They quickly caught up on the past and talked about Keith.

"Don't let him get away with not paying you. Did you get that 2 percent promise in writing?" Sylvia asked.

Delilah still got angry when she talked about that man. "I certainly did."

"Good, because as a woman, this is one of the few cases where it doesn't matter if you're white or black. Women don't get the bonuses male proposal managers get. That ticks me off because I work every bit as hard as any man."

"You don't have to tell me about the glass ceiling."

"Honey, in this case it's a brick wall. I haven't talked to you for a while, so you didn't know that I'd moved to Morehead City, did you?"

"I was wondering why your phone was disconnected. When did you move? And why didn't you tell me?"

"You were working crazy hours and I was working like a madwoman, too. But my company needed an accountant who knew how to do pricing for government proposals. I needed something different. You know me. I don't hang around in one place too long."

"Good for you," Delilah said, flipping pages in a magazine. "It just so happens that I'm going to spend the weekend on Coree Island. It's near you. You know—sand, surf, and shade under a tree. Although it's going to be crowded, the breeze will do us good. Spend the weekend with me."

"I don't know," Sylvia said slowly.

"We can rent a cabin if one is available," she continued. "Or even pitch a tent."

"Oh, please. Like Miss Glamour has ever roughed it in her life."

"I prefer a comfortable bed with a roof over my head, but the last time I was there I wondered what it would be like to sleep under the stars and let the waves lull me to sleep. Away from the campground, it's the quietest place on earth. I'm going to find a quiet stretch of beach and spend Saturday there. Not a soul in sight to bother us. Come on. I've got a cooler already packed with sodas just for you even though that sugar is hell on the figure."

Sylvia scoffed. "Why do you care? You're not human like the rest of us. You can eat like a pig and don't gain an ounce. I hate you."

Delilah laughed. "So maybe I'll steal a sip or two. I'm not a young chick anymore."

"All right," Sylvia conceded. "Pick me up on the way. How is that?"

"Perfect. See you at nine."

"A.M.?"

"Of course, silly."

"You must have country living in your genes." Sylvia waited a heartbeat before she said, "You didn't love him, you know."

Delilah knew she was speaking about Keith. "With time it could have gotten to that point."

"I never liked him."

"You pointed that out on several occasions."

"Maybe what happened is for the best."

Delilah was grateful she didn't say the words she least wanted to hear. That her man would come someday. They both knew it was a lie. Not even Delilah believed it any longer. Or she was just too hurt, too old, too jaded to believe in miracles.


"My word, this place is bustling," Sylvia said once they reached the campground. Her blue shorts and a white T-shirt matched her honey complexion to perfection. She raked her hands through her short brown hair that had been mussed by the wind.

The yard was covered with flowers bursting with color against the scrub oaks and pines.

"This place is so spread out, it doesn't feel crowded, you know?" Delilah said, following orange and blue signs to where their cabin was located. She parked her sky-blue Sebring in front and they grabbed duffel bags and made their way inside. Two children standing on the front porch of an adjacent cabin were jumping up and down calling for their father to take them swimming.

"I know exactly how they feel," Delilah said.

"Yeah. I can't wait to get to the beach." Sylvia opened the door and stopped. Delilah almost ran over her.

"Go on inside. What's the problem?"

"I didn't expect this." Sylvia moved forward. "Most cabins at campgrounds don't have creature comforts. This is like a hotel room."

"Everything plus the kitchen sink and air-conditioning."

"We need it. It's pretty warm out there."

"And you want to go lie in it," Delilah said. "Truthfully, it's only warm because the cabin is in the sun. We're getting a nice ocean breeze. If you're hot we can open the windows to cool the place."

"We're not going to be here that long."

"So let's start moving," Delilah said.

They quickly unpacked their suitcases and changed into swimsuits, pulling shorts on over them.

"I hope you brought something dressy to wear. We're going to Phases tonight. The crew from my job hangs out there sometimes," Sylvia said.

"I thought this weekend was going to be low-key."

"It is."

Grabbing beach bags and coolers, they ran to the car.

Farther down, the campground was littered with both tents and impressive RVs. Plenty of trees provided privacy, but what impressed Delilah most was how pristine the place was.

Once she and Sylvia were in the car, they passed swimming pools, a fenced-in area with swings, slides, sandboxes, and monkey bars for smaller kids. Parents lounged on benches watching them. Others pushed their children in swings.

A stream of teens and college kids flocked to the video arcade and snack shops.

At the entrance, an impressive log cabin that served as a camp store took center stage. On the other side of the main road leading into the campground was the glass and wood building housing the reservation center.

Delilah waved to the guard on their way out.

He smiled and hollered out, "Have a nice day."

Delilah wiggled her fingers and gunned the motor.

"Girl, you need to stop."

"I was just being friendly," Delilah said. "He was very helpful when we checked in."

"You'll have them all wrapped around your finger in ten seconds flat."

They left the campground behind and in ten minutes, turned down a narrow road.

"Are you sure it's okay to be here?" Sylvia asked.

Delilah saw single-family homes scattered here and there. "Sure. I don't see any no-trespassing signs." In moments they passed a huge stately house that was being renovated and traveled down a long narrow path that ended at the sound where trees grew close to the water. A couple of them had toppled over, more than likely during a storm.

With a cheer, they hopped out of the car. The gray water was a welcome sight. A brisk breeze stirred the air. The serenity of the water was breathtaking. Words of poetry began to stir in Delilah's mind.

Sylvia kicked off her shoes and dug her toes in

the sand. "I don't care if we're trespassing. This is worth a ticket."

They unloaded the car and Delilah placed her chair under the gnarled branches of a scrub oak tree that provided some shade. They placed a cooler between the two chairs.

"I hope you loaded up on some books."

"I don't go anywhere without a book to read," Delilah said. "Check my bag. I've been riding so long I need a dip." She peeled her shorts down her legs, stepped out of them, flung her knit top over her head, tossing them both on the chair, and sprinted to the water. She screeched when the shock of cold water took her breath away and wet her swimsuit, then dove under until she felt normal again and stroked out.

"It's great!" Delilah said, wiping water from her face. "Come on in!"

"I'm coming, I'm coming." Sylvia was hopping on one leg trying to keep her shorts out of the sand as she discarded them. Then she tossed them on a bag and ran to the water, splashing and laughing. They stayed in the water for half an hour, playing like children and swimming, before they dried off and Delilah sank into her chair.

Sylvia spread out her towel in the sun. She always tried to get a tan during the summer.

"One day you're going to look like a dried-up prune," Delilah said.

"I don't care. What's life without a few pleasures?" She spread sunblock on her body. "Put some on my back, please?"

"Sure." Delilah rubbed the sunblock on her back,

then she returned to her seat, selected one of the romance novels she was halfway through, and began to read. She read for an hour before she nodded off.

"Delilah?"

"Hmm?"

"Are you asleep?"

"Not now." She opened her eyes and stretched. The sun had moved, hitting her directly in her face. She moved her chair to another position.

"I've been lying here thinking about you."

Puzzled, Delilah asked, "What about me?"

"The company I work with isn't going to get this contract if they don't get a proposal manager in there who knows what she's doing."

"You've been working on it awhile, haven't you?"

"Well, they're being considered for a subcontract by a huge biochemical company. Because of the A-76 regulation, they're required to have a smaller company do a percentage of the work."

"That's a bonus for your company."

Sylvia rolled to her back. "Except the owner's brother-in-law is the proposal manager, and trust me when I say Stan Hamilton doesn't have a clue. He's never really worked on government proposals before. He doesn't know anything about staffing. Even he knows he's out of his element."

Delilah groaned. "Another one of those." She'd worked with her share of clueless managers.

"He's a whiz with computers though, which is really his forte. But because he did a little editing during college to make some extra money, our boss thought he was qualified."

Delilah shook her head. How did companies expect to grow if they were unwilling to hire qualified staff?

"It's a black company and I want it to succeed," Sylvia continued. "The owner is nice, a really hard worker. He's capable of doing the job. It's just proposal management requires a special skill. A company can't win contracts without a good one."

"That's true."

"Stan's a decent person. I like him. He could probably work with you following your directions. But he really needs to get back into computers. I can tell he's worried," Sylvia said. "The company is trying to expand. I'm sure they will give you the same benefits package Keith offered."

"Hmmm."

"You might not like this," Sylvia said with a sheepish look. "But I've already mentioned you."

Delilah scoffed. "That's exactly what I don't want. I don't want another situation like Keith."

"The owner is married, if that's what's worrying you. Not only married, he loves his wife and kids. He's not going to make a pass at you."

"That's good to know."

"You don't have another assignment right now. Just take a week and think it over."

"To tell you the truth, I was considering going in a different direction once Keith paid me my bonus."

"Oh yeah? What had you planned to do?"

"I'm not sure yet." The truth was Delilah didn't want to tell anyone, not even her best friend. She needed to curb her defeatist attitude. *If you want something badly, it isn't going to happen,* her inner voice kept telling her. *Go for the sure thing.* The proposal management position was a sure thing. Her dream wasn't.

"These people really need you, Delilah. Or someone like you." Sylvia just didn't know when to quit. "It's not like it is in Washington, with a lot of competition to choose from."

"You've made your point. Now let me consider the situation." Delilah stood to stretch the kinks out. She'd planned to take some time off. Proposal management wasn't a relaxing nine-to-five job where she could come home to the beach every evening and relax. Often she arrived home late, only to work a few more hours on the project, and that included weekends. Even if the ocean was twenty feet away, she'd rarely have time to take advantage of the view, much less a dip into the water.

Delilah inhaled the salty spray. If she could find a place to rent on Coree Island, she'd be merely a ferry ride away from Morehead City.

"I'll think about it," she finally said.

"Thanks. And you can stay in my spare bedroom until you decide what you want to do."

"Thanks." Delilah appreciated the offer, but she realized it wasn't that easy. She'd need her own place because she'd have to set up her computer, be able to spread out. She often worked from home and she wouldn't be able to work comfortably from Sylvia's place. She'd be imposing.

She glanced at her friend. Already Sylvia had fallen back asleep.

Delilah picked up her book and started to read again, but then realized she'd relaxed enough that now she needed some action. Dropping the book on the chair, she opted to walk along the beach.

She hadn't seen one person since they left the campground except for those she saw on boats cruising the sound.

At the water's edge, with cool waves lapping around her legs, Delilah debated whether she should take the position in Morehead City, even though she was tired of the consulting circus. Huge proposals paid well, but the work was draining.

Delilah had waded in the water for some time, thinking, but coming up with no decision. Finally she let the matter rest. At least the water had a calming effect. She didn't feel as stressed, as edgy as she'd been when she called Sylvia.

She was unaware of how long she had been standing there staring into nothingness when she saw a man and a boy jogging along the beach trailing a frisky black Lab. The man waved and she waved back.

Father and son, Delilah thought. They probably lived around here. She imagined his wife was home preparing dinner on an outdoor grill while the two played. She knew how sexist that sounded, but she wouldn't mind having a family to prepare dinner for. Somehow dinner alone wasn't nearly as appetizing. And Delilah loved to cook and share meals with friends. She shook her head. She'd loved preparing meals for Keith.

Delilah had always wondered why he never spent the night. He left, crying that he needed to get some work done before the next day.

He had work, all right. With Laurie.

The two dashed in and out of the waves. This was some woman's happy family. What a happy child, Delilah thought as she listened to the dog barking, running alongside the boy.

She'd almost made up her mind to move here. It was silly to wonder if something good could happen to her. Just because it happened to her cousin and it happened for the man she'd seen and his wife didn't mean it could happen for her.

She thought of Sylvia's offer. It was nice to know she had options.

Delilah hated bar scenes, but Phases was pretty neat. Sylvia seemed to know everyone. And when two smooth-looking buff guys walked in, Sylvia sat straighter in her seat.

"Who are they?" Delilah asked.

"We call the taller one Donnie. He's chief of security at my job," she said just before they stopped at their table.

"Evening, ladies."

*Have mercy,* Delilah thought. No wonder Sylvia was going crazy over there. That voice was enough to make any woman close her eyes and dream.

"Delilah, meet Donnie Jarrett and Percy Wright."

"Pleasure, ma'am," Percy said.

*Bless those southern men,* she thought. Such manners and a smooth way about him.

"Percy's the assistant chief of security at Moore's."

Percy extended a hand, which Delilah took. His swallowed hers whole and held on for longer than necessary.

"Are these seats taken?" Donnie asked.

"No. Join us," Sylvia invited.

Percy slid into the seat next to Delilah. He asked

her what she'd like and ordered drinks when the waitress arrived.

They talked and danced the night away. Percy wasn't exactly her type, but he was fun. He had a good sense of humor.

It was a pleasure dancing in the arms of a man built that well.

Damn, it was good to be out again.

# Chapter 2

After listening to Mrs. Jackson badger her daughter during her yearly physical, Dr. David Washington wished for the days when doctors treated ailments and left the reproductive talks to parents.

"You tell her, Doctor," Mrs. Jackson barked. She was a tall, thin, no-nonsense hypochondriac. She hauled her charges into the office for the tiniest sniffle. Sometimes he thought the woman made up ailments. "Tell her those boys are looking for one thing and one thing only. All they want is what they can get for free. To ruin her life. Tell her to leave them alone."

"Mommmmm . . . please." Cheeks shining with embarrassment, Trina looked at the floor as if hoping it would open up and swallow her whole.

The cheerleader-build girl was very pretty with ebony skin and raven eyes. David knew the boys would be looking and doing even more if she allowed it. But he didn't want her to feel any more embarrassed than she was already. Or to defy her mother just because she felt she was being pushed over the edge.

"Don't 'Mom, please' me," Mrs. Jackson exclaimed. "I've talked and I've talked until I'm talked out."

David thought he heard a mumbled "That'll never happen," and stifled a smile.

"I came home the other day late from work and who do I see planted on my front porch, but that no-good Marcus Duvall!"

"He's not no-good."

"That brother of his . . ."

"But he hasn't done anything bad," Trina defended. "You can't blame him for what someone else does. That's not fair. And you always said a man is what a man does, not what somebody else does."

Mrs. Jackson's chin jutted out. "Life isn't fair. You tell her, Doctor."

"Your mother said you were in the county's college prep program," David said, trying to change the subject of the conversation.

Trina glanced up from her shoes long enough to say, "Yes."

"How do you like it?"

She shrugged her narrow shoulders. "It's fine."

"And she's going to college for three weeks this summer," her mother said, pride dancing in her eyes.

"That's an exclusive program, which means you're doing very well in school."

The girl shrugged again.

"Which wouldn't mean a hill of beans if she gets mixed up with the wrong boys," Mrs. Jackson continued.

"Mommmmm . . ."

"Could you get Nurse Camp to come in here please while you see about your other daughter?" David asked. "I think she's with Dr. Peters now."

"Oh, this child has me so worried I plum forgot." The woman pinched her lips into a thin line and waved her hand, letting it flap like the wings of a seagull. "I'm not going to say another word. You talk to her, Doctor." Then she leveled an eye at her daughter. "And you listen to every blessed word." The woman tucked her purse underneath her arm and marched out of the office and down the corridor. She entered the examining room without bothering to give Nurse Camp his message. It didn't matter since the errand was to get her out of the office anyway. He could buzz her if he needed her.

Now that Trina wasn't under her mother's demanding eye, she rolled her eyes heavenward. "Mama's driving me crazy," she said, but not loud enough for the nurses, who were marching back and forth, to hear. "I can't even talk to a boy without her going ballistic." Trina looked expectantly at him as if *he* could curb her mother's actions. "I'm not stupid. I wouldn't do anything crazy."

"You'll be a senior next year?" David asked.

"Yes."

"Have you decided on a major or what you'd like to do careerwise?"

She picked a piece of lint off her blouse. "I want to be an astronaut."

"Very impressive. What colleges are you considering?"

"I'm thinking about Hampton for my under-graduate, then graduate work at MIT."

David nodded. "You'll be our next Dr. Mae Jemison." Trina seemed to have her future all mapped out. Most teens didn't have a clue of what they wanted to do.

"That's very commendable. I remember your mother saying you were in one of the NASA pro-grams in Alabama one summer."

"That was really something," she said, perking up. "I enjoyed it. I think I made my mind up then that I wanted to explore the universe. I want to travel to another planet. I don't just want to see earth from a screen or photos, I want to be there to feel the experience."

"Your mother said that you've already been of-fered scholarships at several schools."

She nodded.

She was nervously fiddling with the calendar on the desk. David reached across the desk and patted her hand. "That's impressive. I think what worries your mother is that you have a promising future ahead of you. I imagine you've talked about hor-mones and such in health class. And your mother has definitely given you the talk about the facts of life."

"Oh, God. Has she ever!"

David chuckled. "She's concerned that boys are very hormonal at this stage of their lives. But when they think of sex, they're thinking of the moment, not of the consequences. As much as they crave sex, they aren't prepared for the consequences, and you aren't either. There's so much more to ex-plore. Try not to let yourself get sidetracked into something you aren't ready for."

"I'm not. Marcus wants to go to college, too. And he wants to be a doctor. We're not going to do anything to jeopardize our future. I wish Mama trusted me more." She shook her head. "She's got everybody talking to me. It's so embarrassing. Just last week she hauled me into church to talk to the preacher. I could have died."

"I'm sure you've talked to her about it."

"But do you think she'd listen? And Daddy's no help. He just ignores her. But she drives me crazy. Sometimes I think about doing it to prove her right."

"Don't do that. I'll try to talk to her."

"Good luck."

They talked about prophylactics, abstinence, and a whole slew of things before her mother returned from the examining room. Where were the days when doctors just treated disease? These talks were very uncomfortable, but they'd become par for the course for today's teenagers.

After Trina left, David went to the reception area where Kendall Taylor was waiting for him.

He bounced out of the chair when David approached him. "Do I get to stay with you all weekend, Doc? I have my duffel bag all packed," the boy said. David knew the past had taught him not to hope for much. Even at that, Ken had come a long way in the year since his mother died.

"Until Sunday, anyway. Ready?" David didn't need to ask him that.

"Yup. I've been ready for hours." Now that the kid knew he was spending the weekend with David, some of his wariness diminished. "I guess we can't stay in the glass tower," he said.

"The cupola? There aren't any beds up there, but I think I can scrounge up a couple of sleeping bags. Do you want to stay there?"

Ken shrugged.

Seconds later, he said, "I guess we can't go to the campground."

"To play videos, and miniature golf, and swim? Maybe pig out on hot dogs and hamburgers?" David asked.

"I guess we can't, huh?"

"I'm sure we can squeeze *some* time in there."

The nurses were still in the office. "Night, everyone," David called out.

"Night. Have a good weekend, Kendall."

"Thanks," the boy mumbled. At least he replied. Months ago he wouldn't have.

They left David's office in the medical complex. David rented space across the hall from his father's set of offices, the choicest ones in the complex because his father was the primary investor. For once they left at the same time. Dr. Howard Sommars was a neurologist and his biological father. David had discovered his identity three years ago.

"Hello, Dr. Sommars," Kendall said.

Howard ruffled the boy's hair. "Hello there. Where're you on your way to?"

"I'm spending the whole weekend with Doc."

"I hope you're coming by my place for dinner tonight." He raised an eyebrow at David.

"How does that work for you, Ken?" David asked.

Ken frowned but nodded anyway. "I guess it's okay." But David knew he was eager to get to the beach.

"Not tonight, Howard. Another time, perhaps."

Ken perked up immediately. He half skipped on their way to the door. David wished Ken trusted him enough to reveal his true wishes the way self-assured children did. But Ken was in the foster care system. In addition to dealing with grief from losing his parents, he wanted someone to want him, to love him, not just take him on weekend jaunts.

Mrs. Greenwald, Ken's foster mother, was a good woman, but Ken knew the arrangement was temporary. David knew very well how Ken felt. He wasn't so old that he didn't remember the fear he'd felt as a boy in the foster care system himself. Even though the Robertses loved him, he'd always feared that one day his social worker would come and take him away to live with another family. A family he didn't know, and separate him from his foster brother, Carter. David had considered adopting Ken himself, but he worked very long hours. Ken would get far less attention with him than he did with Mrs. Greenwald.

Ken burst through the outside door with David on his heels. The dog sitter was waiting with David's black Lab.

"Midnight!" Boy and dog greeted each other. Ken let Midnight in the back of the sports car before he hopped into the passenger seat and buckled in. The dog's head hung over the armrest.

David thanked the sitter and they exchanged pleasantries before the young man drove away in his beat-up Mustang.

It was a splendid day and David stashed Ken's

duffel bag in the car trunk and put down the top
to his Porsche.

The engine purred. Ken ran his hand over the
rich leather upholstery.

"I love this car. I'm going to have one just like
this one day," the boy said.

"I love it, too," David said, steering in the direction of the ferry. It was Friday and the traffic was
thick. Some of the vehicles belonged to islanders,
but most belonged to vacationers spending a week
or so at the island's campground, so well known
throughout the country for its estuary.

David pulled up behind a mobile home. Once
he'd parked on the ferry, they left the car to stand
near the railing. He gave Ken a bag of stale bread
to feed to the seagulls that followed in their wake.

While they moved slowly across the sound, David
thought of the woman he'd seen on the beach the
weekend before. God, was she gorgeous in that bikini! Magnificent body, voluptuous breasts, shapely
hips and legs. The image of her kept returning, and
that was unusual for David. His body tightened with
the memory.

But her face looked familiar. He'd seen her
some place before. He'd wanted to stare, to see if
he could remember where, but Ken had wanted to
jog and David didn't want to be rude.

The woman had parked herself under the tree
on his property. Perhaps she would return.

Ken gave a shout. The seagulls swooped down
to take food out of the boy's hand. He laughed
with glee, a rare and precious vision these days.

Although the social worker agreed to let David
take Ken on some weekends, both of them were

concerned that Ken might bond with David and would have to be snatched away again. Ken had already closed himself off to any expectations of a normal life. The only living creature he wasn't aloof with was David's dog. David considered giving the dog to the boy, but his foster mother couldn't take care of it. Besides, if he moved, the new family wouldn't necessarily accept the animal, leaving Ken with another loss.

The boy needed a home. For months now, David had considered adopting Kendall, but he was single and worked long hours. It wasn't fair to leave Ken in the care of a housekeeper.

Less than two weeks after Delilah's last visit, she'd received half of the money Keith owed her. She'd sold what little furniture she owned, except for the bedroom set she'd given Sylvia. The rest of her things were stuffed into the tiny U-Haul trailer, the backseat, and the trunk of her car. After she turned in her apartment key, she escaped to Coree Island.

Who in her right mind would leave her apartment without a guaranteed roof over her head to move to an island where not even a cabin was for rent?

From the time she was eleven, Delilah had gone to school and completed homework between shampooing and conditioning heads of hair in her mother's beauty salon. When she graduated from college she worked long hours. She was due a rest, damn it. And without guilt.

She needed solitude to mull over her next move,

or perhaps think about nothing in particular. And the three-hundred-thousand bonus certainly gave her the means to take a week off. For one solid week, she wasn't going to think of a new career, a new job, or even where she wanted to live next.

The breeze was warm and refreshing, just sufficient to rival the June heat and wash away her troubles. She parked on the same stretch of beach where Sylvia and she had spent the day. Somehow, it seemed much longer than one week.

Unpacking a cooler filled to the brim with sandwich meat, bread, milk, and juice, she spread out a sleeping bag on the ground. Next to it she placed her flashlight, just in case. The place was isolated, after all, except for a huge house and a much smaller guest cottage a ways up the beach.

Delilah thought of the isolation again and dug through her kitchen gear for a cleaver and butcher knife. Stashing them under her pillow with a container of pepper spray eased her fear a little.

She was absolutely crazy for even thinking of spending a night on the beach alone. But ever since she had visited Virginia Beach and seen a family spending the night on the packed sand under the stars, and hearing the rushing of tides against the shore, she'd wanted to try it.

The sun began to sink. She turned on her CD player and put in Luther Vandross. Smooth, soft music filled the air. She tossed her shoes beside the sleeping bag, walked out to the water's edge, and began to sway to the beat of the music. Slowly as the ebb and flow of the tide washed against her legs she began to relax.

*  *  *

She was back.

The Lab was romping in the sea grass somewhere. David leaned against a tree trunk and watched the vision dance to a slow, graceful, and sensual rhythm. Her body swayed and the curves outlined by her sheer wrap enchanted him.

He watched as if mesmerized by a siren of the sea.

He felt the stirrings of an old tale. She would have inspired a boatload of pirates into hacking their way through treacherous sandbars and rock-studded coastlines to kidnap her. Like the men on ships hearing the mermaid's song, he was equally mesmerized—equally lured into danger.

Slowly she brought both hands up, brushed her hair up, revealing the delicate column of her neck. The hair fell back into place, but her arms danced skyward until fully extended as if they were paying tribute to the sun. Slowly, her hips moving from side to side, those beautiful graceful arms danced their way back down until they were in line with her body.

He was in love. Oh, he surely was. And he was as hard as the proverbial rock. David hadn't been attracted to a woman like this in a very, very long time. If ever.

Suddenly a black Lab that resembled the one Delilah had seen before approached her with a stick in its mouth.

Delilah glanced around, hoping the owner was nearby. The beach was deserted.

The dog padded closer to her, insisting she take the stick.

"Nice doggie," Delilah said, inching away and hoping the dog wouldn't drop the stick and bite her leg.

The dog dropped the stick, barked, then picked it up again and eased closer to Delilah as if she were handing over a trophy.

Gingerly, Delilah reached for the twig. Thoughts of rabies crossed her mind, but she saw a tag attached to the collar. Hopefully the owner kept the shots current. The dog looked at her expectantly.

"Here goes." Delilah threw the stick as far as she could down the beach. With a short bark, the dog sprinted after it.

Suddenly a man appeared. The same one who was with the dog and boy before.

"Are you bothering the lady, Midnight?"

The dog yelped, then lumbered with the stick to the man who had tossed it. Muscles rippled in the man's strong arms. He was very attractive, Delilah thought. He wore khaki shorts. His café au lait complexion looked as if he'd spent time in the sun. He was six-one or two and fit without being overdeveloped like Donnie and Percy. His curly hair was combed back.

"She's got energy to spare," he said. He moved across the sand, stopping beside Delilah. Extending a hand, he said, "I'm David Washington." Up close, she was reminded of how tall he was and how handsome.

"Delilah Benton." He wasn't wearing a wedding band. She assumed he was one of those divorced weekend fathers, unless he was married but didn't wear the band. If she were married to him she wouldn't let him leave the house without the ring.

Delilah decided to immediately get the 411.

"Where's your son?"

He frowned. "Son?"

"The little boy you were with before?"

"Oh, he isn't my son. I just keep him some weekends."

Delilah gave him that *oh sure* look. *Tell me anything. I'll believe it.*

"He's a foster child and he loves the beach," he continued. "I have family here. There are lots of kids for him to play with. But mostly he likes to play with Midnight."

The dog barked and jumped up on David for a pat. David scratched behind her ears. Satisfied, Midnight went dashing into the surf.

"Her name's appropriate," Delilah said.

He smiled. Then he looked at her bedding. "Looks like you're settling in for the night. Are we disturbing you?"

"No. It's just there's nothing like the ocean breeze on a warm night."

David sat on a fallen log and stretched out his long legs. Delilah sank on the sleeping bag, crossing her legs Indian style. The sun sank lower in the sky and David didn't show any inclination of being ready to leave.

Midnight lumbered over and dropped to her haunches beside Delilah. She rubbed the dog behind her ear and Midnight flipped over to give Delilah access to her stomach. "You're a spoiled beast, you know that?" Midnight kicked a leg and closed her eyes in doggy bliss.

"Are you from around here?" David asked.

"Unfortunately, no."

He tilted his head to the side. "You look familiar."

"You may have seen me before. My cousin runs the tea shop here."

"Cecily is your cousin?"

Delilah nodded.

"Well then, we're related in a way, by family anyway. My brother is married to Ryan's sister."

"Carter Matthews is your brother?"

He nodded.

"Then you're the doctor."

"A pediatrician."

He'd looked comfortable with the boy on the beach. He was probably an excellent physician.

"Why aren't you staying in the spare apartment at the tea shop?" he asked.

"Cecily doesn't know I'm here. I'm kind of in transition. I needed some space to think about things. Tonight I'm enjoying the stars and ocean. Tomorrow I'll think about where I'll stay for the week."

He leaned back on his elbows. "Do you mind company for a while?"

"No."

They talked for a couple of hours until David's stomach growled.

"Guess I skipped dinner. May I take you to the tea shop or Wanda's place for dinner?"

"I'm not moving from this beach. I can't offer you a four-star meal, but I'll share sandwiches and fruit with you."

"Sounds perfect."

He should offer to take her to the guest cottage, but he was comfortable here. He needed a break from the ordinary. No one would dream that the straight-and-narrow Dr. Washington would spend a night under the stars with a siren like Delilah.

The light from the lighthouse on the other side of the island blinked a reflection into the night. At one time it had kept many ships from running to ground. Now it merely served as a beacon of history.

David gathered driftwood for a fire while Delilah prepared the food.

So this was the man-eater, Delilah, who sent women scurrying to hide their menfolk.

Carter and Ryan often mentioned her, and not by any means favorably. But she seemed harmless enough right now. The wind blew through her hair. Instead of the hot mama, she looked refreshing and cute.

Was she destitute and too proud to admit it? Cecily had always said she was a hard worker. In fact she'd worked from the time she was a young girl. So what brought her to Coree Island with her car packed to the gills and a U-Haul trailer hitched behind it? It looked as if she'd towed everything she owned in it, except for furniture.

When the fire was started, he watched her finish her preparations of dinner. Then she put the rest of the meat from a package on a paper plate for Midnight, who wolfed it down in two gulps while they munched on their sandwiches.

David had fed Midnight earlier, but the dog never turned down food.

Delilah seemed troubled. He got the same feeling he had with Kendall the other week, that she was holding things inside. That she might need someone to talk to. From Carter's and Ryan's conversations he gathered she'd feel uncomfortable confiding in Cecily.

When they finished eating, David asked, "Was it job burnout or is this a vacation?"

She hesitated. He was waiting for an answer and Delilah certainly wasn't going to say she messed up one more time. "A little burnout, a little . . ."

"A little what?"

She sighed. "Just another story of an unfaithful boyfriend."

"He must have been a fool."

Delilah had remained strong through the ordeal. There were a million tasks to keep her too busy to reflect. First she needed a job to tide her over. Then she'd packed up her things and moved.

Now she felt drained. And she was embarrassed and shocked when she felt tears trickling down her face. She hadn't cried once—not once since she walked out of Keith's company. Before she knew it, David had gathered her in his arms and she'd spilled the entire sickening story.

They spent the night squeezed together in the single-person sleeping bag. They did not make love. Nor had they kissed, but David felt a kinship with Delilah. David was the first to awaken. He lay still while Delilah slept peacefully in his arms. He'd partially covered her face to keep the bright morning light from waking her. She needed the sleep. She'd seemed drained by the time she fell asleep well after midnight.

He'd lain awake since dawn thinking about the soft woman he wasn't ready to let go.

Perhaps like him, the beacon of the lighthouse drew Delilah to seek the unattainable, or at least the key to what she was searching for. He only knew that his life wasn't what he wanted it to be either. Careerwise, it couldn't be better. On a personal level it needed work. So he understood exactly where Delilah was coming from.

Waves roared in, its music their only orchestra. It wasn't long before Delilah awakened. David wasn't ready for her to leave. Delilah moaned, opened her eyes, then covered them with her hand.

"It can't be morning already."

David stifled the impulse to brush his lips across her forehead.

"Breakfast," Delilah said.

David nodded toward the cooler. "You have breakfast in there, too?"

"Of course," she said and forced herself to get up. As she prepared milk and cereal, David thought about tactics to keep her there. He wouldn't question the urgency motivating him. It was more than her surface beauty.

"Delilah . . ." He reached out, tucked strands of hair behind her ear. "Have you considered you might need time to pull yourself together? I'm thinking more than just a week. A couple of months at least, or even six or seven or more, to think about your future. I have a guest cottage down the beach. It's completely renovated."

"It's kind of you to offer, but I couldn't. My friend

offered me a position at a company in Morehead
City. I think I'm going to accept. Although I think
living here would be like heaven."

"I live in Morehead City," David said quietly. "This
place is rarely used. I have workers coming in for
repairs and I would like someone to be here just to
look in on things occasionally." He squinted in the
direction of the small guest cottage. "It's not the
Ritz but it's comfortable."

"You make it so hard to say no. What would you
have done if I wasn't here?"

"Probably continue to ask Carter to check on it,
but he works at the campground, and summer is
their busiest season," David said. "He has too
much to do as it is. An exchange of services so to
speak." He groaned at his own inept analogy. "I
didn't quite mean it that way, but you know what I
mean."

"You like to bring Kendall here on the weekend."

"The cupola is finished. Last weekend we slept
there in sleeping bags. It gives a 360-degree view.
To him, sleeping there is almost like camping outside."

Delilah thought of his offer. She could ask Cecily
if she could rent space at the tea shop, but the shop
was busy and she didn't really want to stay there.

"I'll pay you the month's rent ahead of time," she
told him. "I'll be glad for some time to be around
people who don't know me."

David was shaking his head before she finished.
"You're house-sitting for me. I can't charge you."

"And I won't stay for free."

Reluctantly, David acquiesced. Then they haggled over what she'd pay, which was more than he was willing to accept. Finally he forced her to bring the rent down, since she was helping him, too.

"I have always paid my own way, David. Contrary to what some people believe, I've never mooched off anyone."

"I don't think you're a user." David sighed. "All right. I'll accept half of what you offered."

Delilah's lips were crimped so that David finally gathered her hand in his and stroked the back of it. "Have you ever taken time off from work? I mean real time. You told me you started working in your mother's beauty shop while most kids were playing with their friends. Don't you think it's time for you to take some time for Delilah?"

"Bills have to be paid, so I work to pay them. A lot of people would like to jump off the wagon and take a breather, but can't. I've been lucky that I've always had a job."

"Now you've been given a chance for a break. Give yourself a chance to think of one thing you'd really love to work at for the rest of your life. The one thing you'd rise eagerly to do every morning. Your passion. Don't think about money or the future or worries or incidentals. Just think about your passion."

He extended a hand and reluctantly Delilah reached out to shake on the agreement. "You make it sound so simple," she said. "I have to contribute."

"Life's never simple until you step back and get off the roller coaster."

"Okay. You've convinced me."

Afterward, David drove to Cecily's tea shop for breakfast while Delilah acclimated herself to the guest cottage. By the time David returned, she'd cleaned the bathroom, bedroom, and kitchen, and had brought in a suitcase.

She opened the two sacks David placed on the counter. Scones with cream and jam, and two tall cups of tea. A carton of eggs was already in the fridge. She prepared bacon and eggs to go with the offering, and they sat together to eat.

Bookcases in the living room would hold Delilah's many books, but the table and chairs in the dining area were terribly scarred.

"These came with the house. I'll have them hauled off and buy a new set. You'll just need to pick it out."

"It's a sturdy set," Delilah said, testing for wobbly legs on the table and the six ladder-back chairs. They all held firm. These were very old chairs and held much better than the new. In the scars she imagined many stories. Delilah read *John* scribbled in a scraggly scroll. Probably scratched his name when he got bored with homework. Delilah could picture four children seated around the table each evening, the older ones helping the younger ones, the mother preparing dinner. This table held too much love, too many memories to be destroyed.

"I'd like to try my hand at refinishing them. I can't spend every day walking the beach." Delilah studied the furniture, the raw wood beneath, already picturing it in vivid colors.

She thought David was cute, but more the guyfriend type, not someone she would date. It would be pleasant to have a male friend without the pressure of going to bed with him. It surprised her that he'd spent the entire night under the covers with her and without making one pass. Was she losing her touch? Oh well. He was nice, though, and that counted for something.

He helped her move all her things from the U-Haul into the cottage. Then they swam and Delilah prepared an early dinner.

In the midst of her platonic feelings for David, they were washing dishes. As David placed a plate in the cabinet, they bumped into each other, and both whispered, "Excuse me." Suddenly her body was pressed against David's body. Her hands splayed against his chest, but she didn't push him away. This wasn't in the program. She'd just fooled herself into believing that they were going to be just friends.

"I don't want to think of you as this incredibly sexy man," she whispered in an unfamiliar voice.

"But you do anyway?"

Delilah closed her eyes. "Yes."

"I think you're an exceptional woman." His lips closed over hers. It wasn't a demanding kiss, but a slow get-to-meet-you kiss, made more sensual by its sweetness.

"I'm going to leave Midnight with you. I'll feel better about you being so isolated with her to protect you."

Delilah didn't meet his eyes as she walked him to the door.

"Will she want to stay with a stranger? What does she eat?" she asked.

"You won her over the moment she saw you, just as much as you've captivated me. Her food is in the cabinet under the sink."

Then he was gone.

Midnight lay on the rug in front of the door as if

protecting it from strangers. Delilah had done many crazy things in her thirty-three years but she'd never made a move this quickly.

Delilah called her mama later that afternoon. All she needed was for Holly Benton to call the old office and be told she no longer worked there. She could never remember Delilah's cell phone number.

Her mother was out of breath when she answered the phone on the fifth ring.

"Well, how are you, sweetie?" she asked.

"I'm fine, Mama. Just getting back from church?"

"Yeah, baby. Rev laid something on that sermon today. Did you make it to church?"

*Here we go again,* Delilah thought. "I didn't make it today."

"Well, that's too bad. It lightens our hearts to hear the Lord's word. Been a while since I heard from you."

Now Delilah was sure her mother was going to launch into the preacher's sermon. She cut in before her mama started going.

"I just called to give you my cell number again. I'm not in Raleigh any longer."

"You didn't quit your job, did you? I thought it was a good job with good benefits. That it was going to take you places. You're a single woman. Benefits are essential," she warned.

"It was good. But I'm going to try something new."

"Like what?"

"I'm giving myself a chance to think things

through. In all these years, I've never taken the time to think about what I really want to do."

"Thinking don't pay the bills." Her mother's reply was stern.

"I have enough set aside to pay my bills until I return to work," Delilah assured her.

"It's going to be hard to find some place that pays you as well as the last job. What did you do to mess it up?"

"Why did I have to do something? It just didn't work out, that's all."

"Something always happens. You didn't go flirting with your boss, did you? You're a beautiful woman and men are always chasing you. Using sex is the last way to go about getting a raise."

Delilah sighed. Keith had approached her even before he talked her into working for him.

"I didn't use sex. Why can't you believe I'm good at what I do?"

"I know you're good, but you were so pretty your daddy spoiled you rotten."

"You always blame everything on him. He's got nothing to do with this."

"Oh, yes, he does. He always played on your looks instead of your brains. That's why you don't keep jobs long, because you're using your looks instead of the sense the good Lord gave you."

"The thing that holds me back most is being a woman, not my looks. Look, I didn't call you to argue. I just wanted you to know how to reach me."

"Where are you?" her mother finally thought to ask.

"On Coree Island."

"Hmm. Isn't that where Cecily's staying?"

"Yes."

"At least you won't starve. She'll give you a meal if it comes to that."

Delilah's patience snapped. "Mama, I'm not destitute. I've always taken care of myself. Why can't you give me credit for that? Have I ever come home asking for money or a roof over my head?"

"Well, no . . ."

"Have I ever asked to move back home?"

"No, but—"

"I could have done a lot worse," Delilah said, incensed.

"A lot better, too."

"Here's my number," Delilah snapped. "Do you have a pen handy?"

"Yeah, yeah. Hold on." A minute later, she was back. Delilah rattled off the number.

"So what're you doing while you're there?"

Delilah didn't want rain destroying her rainbow, but maybe for once her mother could encourage her. At least she'd know Delilah wasn't sitting around doing nothing. She had a plan.

"Remember how I've always wanted to be a writer?"

"I thought you do a lot of writing."

"I do, but it's not the same. I want to write novels. I've already finished the first draft. I'm thinking about getting the proposal together to send to editors."

"It sounds awfully iffy to me, giving up your job and benefits for something like that."

Not the response Delilah had hoped for. *Have faith,* she thought.

"Anything's possible," Delilah reminded her.

"I guess it is. It's not going to have sex in it, is it? Inspirational books are becoming more popular now."

"We'll see."

"You can always help me out in the beauty salon."

"Thanks, but I'm not living on the streets yet," Delilah said with a dry tone, and they disconnected.

Maybe it took another writer to understand what she wanted to accomplish. Maybe what she was doing sounded crazy to someone who never had the passion or desire to write. For someone who never looked at the sunset and saw a story. Or a man rocking on the front porch of an old broken-down house. Or an old lady wearing spectacles with knitting needles clacking because she didn't know the meaning of an idle moment.

But everyone had dreams. Her mother was young once and must have had dreams of her own. Delilah wondered what had killed the hope and vision of her youth.

# Chapter 3

Mondays were always considered the worst day of the week because the entire workweek lay ahead. However, for Delilah one day was like the other. Early that morning she towed the U-Haul to Raleigh, then ate a late lunch with Sylvia in a small bistro near the ferry, dining on half sandwiches and soup.

"Did you get the rest of your money from Keith while you were there?" Sylvia asked.

"Not yet. I should get the next check in a few weeks. He says *he's* waiting for a check."

"He's stalling."

"I know."

"Your chances of getting any more money are really slim. Lots of companies refuse to pay once you leave unless you take them to court."

"Not this time. I'm getting my money. Because you know what? He didn't have to lie to get me to work for his company. I would have worked for the bonus alone. He didn't have to court me." Delilah twisted the glass on the table. "He convinced me he really cared."

"What a jackass."

After lunch, Delilah stopped in Morehead City at a grocery store that offered more items than the smaller one on the island. Her refrigerator was practically bare and she purchased enough food to last her a couple of weeks. Two weeks was enough time to at least decide how long she'd stay on the island.

Delilah had left Midnight with the dog sitter before she drove to Raleigh. She picked the dog up from David's house before she left the mainland. She had qualms about whether the dog would remember her. But she did.

Delilah put the navy roof down on her convertible and Midnight rode with her head hanging over the side.

"It's just you and me, kid," Delilah said later as she fed the dog.

While she performed the chores that would soon become routine, she thought of David. She thought of the night she had spent in his arms pressed against his warmth in the cramped sleeping bag. The slightly woodsy, citrus cologne he wore. Her back pressed against his chest. He was a stranger in a sense, yet she'd wanted to kiss him, to run her hands over his strong chest and biceps.

She'd done none of those things, however, but she'd lain awake thinking about him, about his tenderness, and about the changes occurring in her life.

She was still left with a question mark concerning her future. According to David, that was okay. Time healed everything.


On Tuesday, Delilah's first chore was to buy supplies to strip and paint the table.

The hardware store was located on the outskirts of downtown Coree, but first Delilah drove down the sleepy street past well-maintained buildings that catered to tourists until she reached the wharf. Small fishing boats unloaded their catch and locals haggled.

Leaving her car, Delilah called out to a man on one of the boats. "What's good today?" she asked.

"Depends on what you like. Got some nice butterfish, then there's flounder, snapper, and crabs."

"Definitely butterfish." She was going to fry it with the skin on, the way her mom used to.

"Good choice. These are some pretty babies. Not too big. How many?" he asked, displaying the impressive array.

"Four please." This was silly. She couldn't eat that many. *But maybe if David . . . That's ridiculous.* David wouldn't return until the weekend. And why was she eager to see him? They'd spent one night under the stars, after all. Well, not to forget they had shared one unforgettable kiss. The temperature suddenly spiked, but had nothing to do with the weather.

She'd eat the leftovers for lunch tomorrow. That's exactly what she'd do.

"Do you want them packed in ice?" the man asked.

"Please do." She remembered how quickly the temperature rose and she had shopping to do.

"Going to be visiting on the island long?"

"How do you know I'm not a local?"

The man chuckled. "Two things. Your accent, and I'd know you."

"I'll be here for the summer."

"Come back, now. I pull in here every other morning. Best catch around." He handed the package to Delilah.

"I'll remember that," she said, turning away. Now, on to choosing paints.

In the hardware store, she looked for paint chips, varnishes, and brushes. She took her time, studying different hues of reds, yellows, greens, and blues until she found the colors that suited her. She wandered through aisles looking at blinds and shades. The ones hanging at her windows now wouldn't do. David had said she could change all that. She wanted the cottage to have that breezy tropical feel without the stark white.

She pushed her cart around, lost in the prospects of decorating before she glanced at her watch. *Oh my gosh*, she thought. Two hours had passed. Poor Midnight was cooped up. By now she'd be ready for a walk.

Delilah rented a sander, quickly made her purchases, and hurried home.

Having a dog was like having a child. You couldn't leave it unattended for too long.

It was another windy day, and once Delilah returned home she threw the windows open. The brisk breeze kept it from being stifling. She let the dog out and watched her lope off into the bushes before she disappeared. Then Delilah changed into shorts and a T-shirt and prepared her supplies for stripping.

In a sense, Delilah liked the isolation, but when she looked around and saw no other buildings or humans, she wondered if it wasn't a little too isolated.

David closed himself in his office at one, bit into a sandwich, and stared at the phone. He craved the sound of Delilah's voice. Well, he could use the excuse of calling about Midnight. Although Delilah was a stranger, Midnight was a friendly dog and was familiar with the beach surroundings. Midnight was fine. He dialed Delilah anyway. Any excuse would do.

She answered on the third ring, sounding winded.

He chuckled, picturing her in a bikini wading in the surf. "Were you outside lounging on the beach?"

"I was stripping the table."

"I thought you'd rest today." He was irked because she was working already. "I offered to buy a new table."

"I like this one," she said, chuckling. "I thought doctors were busy from the time they got to the office until quitting time."

"Every other day they let me take a bread-and-water break."

Delilah's sexy voice warmed his heart. David tightened his hand around the phone. "How is Midnight?"

"She's fine. She had a stroll after I returned from the hardware store. I'll break soon and run along the beach with her."

"She's okay on her own. She won't run off, you know."

"What's the use of having a dog when you don't use it as an excuse to take a break?"

"If it will keep you from working . . . Did the construction crew come today?"

"No. It's very quiet."

"They come in fits and spells, it seems."

"Why is that?" she asked.

"They need specialists to work on certain projects. They have to schedule it. Some of it is related to weather and other jobs they have."

"At this rate it will take years to move in."

David chuckled. "Sometimes it feels like it."

Margaret, the office manager, knocked on his door, then opened it. "Call on line two," she said.

"I have to take a call. I'll see you Friday." David pressed the button for line two.

"Hi, Doc. It's Ken."

He relaxed. "Out of school for the summer?"

"In a few days, and I start summer camp soon after."

"I bet you're looking forward to swimming lessons."

"I've been swimming since I was a kid. My mom paid for lessons."

"Then you'll be in more advanced classes."

"I guess."

David almost pictured his shrug. "You're going to Disney World this weekend, I hear."

"Yeah."

David wished the boy showed more excitement. "Wish I could go."

"Can you?"

"Not this time, but I'll pick you up the weekend after you return."

"Okay. I'll call you before I go."

Ken's social worker feared that he would have difficulty bonding to anyone at all, but David could tell the boy was already getting attached to him. And he didn't know if that was a good thing.

He realized Ken had really called to make sure he'd see him upon his return from Florida. And that was sad, because most kids would be hopping around as if they had ants in their pants at the thrill of going to Disney World.

When Mrs. Greenwald had told him her sister was taking her brood to Disney World and how she wished she could take the foster children in her care, he'd offered her the money to take them. At first she'd refused, but he'd stressed that the trip would be good for Kendall and the other children. When they returned to school in the fall, they'd have their own treasured experiences to dwell on like the other kids. So now Mrs. Greenwald and her sister had reserved a van to carry the brood.

But Ken was more concerned about seeing David upon his return than going to Disney World. And that wasn't a good sign.

David threw the paper from his sandwich into the trash and went through his other appointments for the day.

Dr. Wayne Peters was making his hospital rounds. On a spur-of-the-moment decision, David drove to the island to spend the night. This was crazy. He never spent evenings on the island during the week.

He parked his car and walked to the guest cottage. Before he knocked on the door, Midnight barked and tried to climb through the screen to get to him.

"What in the world? Midnight?" Delilah turned from the stove and rushed to the door. "What are you doing here?" she asked, disengaging the lock. She wore tiny shorts and a skimpy tank top. He forced himself not to touch her.

"Decided to spend the night here," David said.

"I hope you're hungry?"

"Starved." He sniffed the air. "Got enough for me?"

"Butterfish fresh from the water."

He moved closer, tilted her chin, and pressed his lips to hers.

"It was only one night, but I feel as if I've known you for months," David said. "I missed you."

"I'm glad to see you," Delilah said, and looped her arms around his neck. That was all the encouragement David needed to deepen the kiss and hold her small body tightly against him.

"This is absolutely crazy," he whispered moments later. "I don't understand my emotions. I don't even know you," he said, setting her back from him, "and yet I'm feeling like some lust-filled teenager instead of a forty-year-old man."

"Well, whatever it is, it's catching. Come on, food's almost ready."

Cautiously, David followed her deeper into the house. Midnight begged for a pat and absently David brushed his hand over her coat.

"Sit down and tell me about your day while I cook."

The last thing David wanted to talk about was his day. He wanted to unwind.

Suddenly, he didn't understand himself around Delilah. By nature, he was a cautious man. He usually contemplated situations before acting. He wasn't a spur-of-the-moment kind of guy. If he wasn't careful, he'd find himself in over his head.

But he sat and began to talk about some of the more amusing moments in his day. He actually enjoyed listening to her voice more.

A wet tongue rolled over Delilah's face. She batted the head away. What felt like a thousand-pound weight settled on her and licked her face again. Then Midnight had the nerve to bark, nearly splitting Delilah's eardrum.

"Get off of me, you crazy mutt."

The idiot dog barked again.

"All right, all right." Delilah dragged herself out of bed to let the dog out.

She'd sanded until past two in the morning and now toothpicks couldn't keep her eyes open. But she was finally finished with sanding.

Delilah fell out on the couch and caught a quick snooze until Midnight barked and scratched at the door.

"I may as well feed you," Delilah said, heading to the cabinet. She dished out some food and water and placed them on the kitchen floor with the intention of sleeping for another hour, then getting up for the day. But the phone rang.

"Delilah?" Paige asked cautiously and quietly.

"Paige? What's wrong? You sound troubled."

"Things haven't been the same since you left.

The new proposal manager is really giving me a hard time."

"I'm so sorry I had to leave you in a bind like that."

"I just had to talk to someone. I'm having a really bad day."

"What happened?"

"She doesn't like my work. I tried to follow what you taught me."

Paige had a lot to learn, but she was coming along very well, Delilah knew. "I think she wants to bring her friend in here to take my place."

"I'm so sorry, Paige."

"So far, Keith hasn't let me go, but I don't know how long I'll last. If I need a reference will you give me one?"

"Of course I will. I'd be happy to give you one."

"I'm looking for another job. I wish you were still here."

"You'll find something."

"Barbara really loves this new woman, but she isn't nearly as good as you are."

"Thanks for the loyalty."

"I've got to go."

"Just call me if you need anything. Again, I'd be happy to give you a reference. As a matter of fact I'm going to start writing a letter of recommendation."

"Thanks."

The only thing Delilah really hated about leaving Keith's company was leaving Paige in the lurch. She was such a hard worker. She needed better. Instead of returning to bed, Delilah began to make calls to friends to scout out job opportunities. She was on the phone for half an hour before she got up.

By the time she dressed and called the dog to go walking with her, Midnight had finished her food and was lying on the rug next to the door.

To wake up to tides, crisp cool air, and nothing to disturb her but the seagulls and sandy beach was as close to heaven as Delilah could possibly hope for. Even with the mutt waking her up far too early.

Midnight splashed through water chasing birds, then returned to her with a stick clamped in her mouth.

"We're jogging, you silly mutt. I can't throw sticks to you up and down the beach." But she threw the stick nonetheless. Midnight sprinted after it, picked it up, and brought it to Delilah to throw again.

Delilah patted her head. Midnight sat up on her hind legs and leaned against Delilah. She was a huge dog. Delilah ruffled her fur. "You're so easy to love, you know that? Now, down."

After they'd jogged a couple of miles, Delilah sat on a log. The lighthouse had come into view, but it was still a good distance away. Although she was getting tired of her own company, she wasn't ready to let the world impose on her peace. She'd have to visit the tea shop before long, but not yet.

When she and Midnight returned to the cottage, trucks were in the yard; she heard hammering and a man was walking around the house.

"Hello." Delilah waved a hand.

The man regarded her with a frown, then he smiled and walked toward her, his hand extended. A fine-looking man, he was. A rich dark brown, broad shoulders, and a winning smile. Too bad her heartbeat remained normal, unlike the way it danced a staccato beat with David around.

Delilah smoothed her hair back, but there was nothing she could do about her clothing and the sweat stains. Now, if Delilah was looking, and she wasn't, he was exactly the type to turn her head, except this time he didn't.

He wore khaki pants with a light blue polo shirt. The clean-cut type. And now that she was closer and he'd plucked off his Ray-Bans, laughing brown eyes revealed themselves.

"Haven't seen you around before," he said.

"I'm renting the guest cottage," Delilah said. A gentle breeze plastered his shirt against his chest.

"We renovated that first. How do you like it?"

"Perfect."

"Excuse my manners. I'm Ray Chandler, the architect."

"You did a wonderful job on the cottage. David said the design ideas were yours."

Ray snorted in disgust. "David didn't have a clue of what he wanted. And he stays so busy he didn't have the time to commit to anything. I just showed him what I thought would work with the environment. Gave him a few choices. The property is spectacular."

Delilah looked around at the tall sea grass to the sides, the ocean to the back, and the wide steps leading to the main house. Not another house in sight. "I have to agree with you. It's breathtaking."

"I'm thinking about moving to the island."

"Really?"

"Problem is there's no land to buy. You have to be an insider to purchase."

"You've tried?"

He nodded. "Sure have. The islanders are afraid some corporation is going to disturb their peaceful haven."

"Many islands have become too commercial. More vacationers own land than natives."

"I just want one small piece for my little house. No disturbing house parties. Just lonely old me." They shared a chuckle. "Since you aren't a native, how did you end up here?"

"My cousin married a native. I'm considered distant family."

"Lucky you."

The workmen were banging inside the house.

"How long before this is all finished?" Delilah asked, sweeping her hands broadly to encompass the building.

"Sometime in August hopefully. David decided he wants an outdoor kitchen for entertaining. May extend the time but not by much."

"Who can blame him?"

"You can entertain outside three seasons here. But I don't know when he'll have the time. He works nearly twenty-four-seven."

"I thought he had a partner."

"Not a partner exactly, guy just out of residency, but he's considering taking on a partner. David still does the bulk of the work."

"Hmm. Doesn't leave him time to have any kind of life."

"That's for sure."

He stepped closer and Delilah fretted about not

having on makeup. She was sweaty and certainly smelly from her jog. She backed up a couple of steps and noted the pad he was now neglecting.

"Well, I don't want to keep you from your work. When you finish here, drop by for a cup of tea," she offered.

"I'll do that."

"Come along, Midnight."

Midnight had been chasing something in the bushes. She came loping toward Delilah, almost knocking her down when she reached her.

"Get down, will you?"

She was smelly from whatever she'd waddled in.

"You're going to have to get hosed off before you come in my house."

Inside, Delilah showered and donned old shorts and a shirt. Although she was going to be painting furniture, she applied her makeup carefully. The fact that she wasn't looking for a man right now didn't prohibit her from looking her best.

She pulled out the materials she needed and resumed her work. Midnight kept getting in the way until Delilah let her out to chase after a squirrel.

By Thursday, Delilah had sanded until her hands were raw and she'd painted, stained, and distressed the table and chairs. Not so distressed that the pieces looked as if they'd been dragged across the country on a wagon train. Just enough for a lighter shade to show through. The table was now a mixture of yellow and gold. The ladder-back chairs wore various hues of yellow, aqua blue, and rust.

What grabbed her attention now wasn't the furniture, but her writing. David had asked her to think about her passions. She pulled out a box that contained her writing materials.

David had set up her computer desk and single file cabinet in the tiny spare bedroom. Her computer was still packed in boxes.

Never in a million years had she thought to actually take time to pursue a writing career. Could this really happen? Could she afford a few months for her dream? She almost pinched her arm to assure herself that it was all real and not an illusion.

Even if she didn't complete her novel, she had plenty of time on her hands until January when she planned to send out feelers for jobs and return to work full-time.

She collected her notes, the outline, and the completed first draft. It was a very rough first draft and needed lots of work. Setting the notes and manuscript on the bed, she went into the tiny second bedroom and got busy setting up her computer and printer.

Tucking her hands on her hips, she scanned the room. One of her first purchases had been a box of paper. Not too much, because she was sure it wouldn't last well in this humid climate.

Her book was a historical romance about a black pirate who raided the North Carolina coast and captured the heroine. Delilah chuckled, letting the plot roll around in her mind.

She took her manuscript to the living room and set it on the coffee table. She continued to think about the plot as she fixed herself a cup of spice tea.

With a pot of tea, she sank into the comfortable

couch where she spent the next few hours reading through the story, refreshing her memory, and making notes. Other than to let Midnight out for a run, it was four that afternoon before she took a break.

Her stomach rumbled. She hadn't eaten since breakfast. It felt wonderful to be writing again, playing with plots, characters, and emotions. And she wanted nothing more than to live in that story for months.

Midnight barked. Delilah let her out again and began to prepare a salad for dinner. Later, she walked along the beach with the dog.

Gazing at ships in the distance and small boats closer to shore, she let her mind wander. David had encouraged her to stay there at least until the end of the year. Even with the money already deposited in her bank account, she could afford it with enough left over for her new start if she decided to go back to proposal management. Even if she worked on proposals part-time, she would still have time to write.

She still received calls for jobs, but rejected them. She let them know when she would be open to new projects.

Could she dare to take this chance? She was nearly thirty-four. At the crossroads of her life. For once she had the funds to realize her dreams. The real question was, did she have the nerve?

Yes. She'd use this time for her writing, even if she were the only one who believed she could do it.

It was late, but knowing Keith was still in the office, she called him as soon as she returned to the cottage.

"Keith, I haven't received my check," Delilah said without preamble.

"You left me in a crunch. I had to hire another proposal manager when you left," he whined. "She's not as good as you were."

"That has nothing to do with the work I did. The company won the bid for my project," she reminded him. "And you're getting paid for it. I want my money."

"Delilah, I've been more than fair so far."

"No, you haven't, and you know it." The weasel was trying to back out of a commitment, even though she had a signed contract. He knew very well that if he declined to pay, the only option left for her was to go to court. Never let a person know your weakness. She had another option.

"I have Laurie's number. I know where each of her fitness studios is located. I made it my business to find out before I left Raleigh," she said with a pause. "Send me my money, Keith, or I'll go to her and give her the lowdown on her fiancé."

"All right, all right."

"I want that check in my hands in one week. You have exactly seven days." She gave him her new PO box number and disconnected.

The problem was, even if she sold her book, it would take time for the money to start trickling in. She'd need something to live off in the meantime. The money Keith sent her would keep her from having to find another job if—not if, *when*—she sold it.

It would happen. She had to believe it would happen.

\* \* \*

David's instinct was to play it safe with Delilah, but he'd played it safe since his breakup with Louise three years ago. There was wildness, an intensity with Delilah that enticed a man to forget about safety, to take his own wild plunge into uncertainty.

When he saw her vivaciousness and energy he realized how stagnant he'd become. It made him feel older than he was.

He wanted more than to take her to bed and stay there enjoying her body until he found release—although he wanted that too.

"What're you smiling at?" Wayne asked. "You must have spent some time in the sun last weekend. Got a tan."

David shook his head. Daydreaming again.

"I did," he said and recorded notes on the patient's chart.

"About time," Margaret said.

David knew what was going through Margaret's mind. She'd worked in his first practice, the one he had shared with Louise and her now-husband, and had come with him when he set up the new office. Wayne was considering moving back to his hometown in Pennsylvania. David definitely needed to bring in a partner. If he did, he would have more time for Ken—maybe even adopt him.

David's last patient was gone. His nurses had shoved paperwork at him to sign. He stopped by his father's office down the hall on his way out. The old man's secretary had called asking him to stop in.

"Is he available?" he asked.

"He was about to leave." His father, an older version of David, had discarded his lab coat. He was pulling on his suit jacket as he came into the reception area. One of the major differences between the two men was the way they dressed.

His father was a neurologist. As a pediatrician David dressed more informally. He didn't advertise the fact that they were father and son. But then, he didn't have to.

David didn't call him "Dad." He used that title for the man who had raised him. His family was complicated. A long story, and David didn't even want to think of it.

"You wanted to see me?" David asked.

"Yes." They left the office and started down the corridor toward the elevator. "Sasha is sponsoring a children's benefit. She's roped me into getting friends to buy tickets." Sasha was David's half sister, and the child Howard had raised.

"I'll buy a ticket," David said.

"She left me in charge of the program and she wants you as keynote speaker since it's a children's benefit. She's out of town right now. Otherwise she would have contacted you. At this late date, it's almost a fait accompli," he said. "You're very popular with parents and you'll draw the crowd. Besides, yours is the best pediatric practice in the area."

The elevator stopped. They moved aside as everyone piled off.

"I'll do it. Have your secretary call mine for the particulars," David said as they walked to the front door. "She's lucky I don't have anything else scheduled." Everyone knew his schedule was limited. He didn't like the fact that people could predict him so easily.

Pushing the door open, David went to his Porsche and Howard a Lincoln Town Car.

David arrived at the ferry minutes before it left for the island, the only way there except by boat. The ferry usually left on the hour, except in the mornings when it ran on a half-hour schedule.

David rarely visited the island during the week unless Dr. Grant, the only physician on the island, asked him to see a patient. His brother had tried to get him to date her but the vibes weren't there for either of them. She was a very capable physician. He was surprised that he'd really wanted to spend every night on the island, not to see the house or visit a patient, but to be with Delilah. She'd been eating at him all week. He called her every day, although he didn't need to. He was only her landlord and the cottage was in perfect repair.

When he pulled into the yard, he noticed Ray's car. *He must be checking up on the work,* David thought. He went around the house, then inside. But Ray wasn't there.

Puzzled, David made his way to the cottage. Delilah stood in the kitchen laughing. Ray was also chuckling as he lounged at the bar watching Delilah work. David couldn't understand the sudden anger that overtook him. He pounded on the door.

They both stopped laughing and looked at him. Delilah smiled and walked toward the door, unlocked it.

"Hi," she said, looking delighted to see him. That pleased him somewhat. He stepped over the threshold.

"Ray's joining us for dinner."

He spoke to Ray, then gathered Delilah into his arms.

"What smells so good?"

"Fresh, just-off-the-boat shrimp, corn bread, potato salad, and broccoli with garlic and Asiago."

"Hmm." He dipped his head and kissed her. "Garlic won't stop me from kissing you."

She giggled. "Didn't think so," she said and smoothly came out of his arms.

She wore a pretty green sundress that displayed her generous breasts and long legs to an advantage. Her brown shoulders were bare. Her shapely hips were outlined against the skirt. They were enough to tempt any red-blooded man. And Ray was watching her like a hawk as she stirred something in the pot or bent over the open oven.

All week he'd thought about how he'd like to spend another night under the covers on the beach with her—or better, in a bed with her naked curves lying next to him, instead of fully dressed as they'd been Saturday night.

Then she turned and looked at him expectantly. "Well?"

"Well what?" he asked, shrugging his shoulders. He glanced at Ray for a clue. He just shook his head.

"The table, silly."

"Oh." He hadn't even looked around. She'd arrested his attention. But now as he scanned the room, it looked homey—more lived in. And the table.

"I can't believe it," he said, walking over to it,

touching the surface. "I can't believe you did all this in one week. The whole room's incredible."

The pictures hanging on the walls, the pillows stacked gracefully on the sofas, the flat cushions on the painted dining room chairs made the utilitarian room a home. A cozy little retreat.

"Can I help with something?" he asked Delilah.

"I have everything under control."

Feeling like a guest, David joined Ray at the bar. "So tell me, Ray, how much is the outdoor kitchen going to extend my move date?"

"The contractor said not more than a week, if that." They talked about the problem the contractor was having getting specialty workers in the current housing boom, and before he knew it he was helping Delilah set platters on the table. They kept up a running dialogue through dinner, but soon after, Ray left.

"Okay, you've been tense all evening," Delilah said, massaging his shoulders.

"I don't think so."

"The tension was so thick I could cut it with a knife. I think you scared poor Ray away."

"Good," he said, pulling her onto his lap. "I missed you."

"This is crazy. We're moving too fast. And the funny thing is I like you."

"There's nothing wrong with that." He tilted her head closer. "Because I feel the same way about you."

But instead of moving closer, she turned away and walked toward the door calling after the dog. "We're moving too fast, David. I'm going to walk Midnight."

David watched her a moment before he caught up and fell in step beside her. She was running from her feelings. It was true. Everything was happening too fast, but he wasn't going to let her escape what was happening with them, any more than he could escape the feelings himself.

The weekend passed too quickly. It was Sunday afternoon and David prepared to leave soon for rounds at the hospital. He and Delilah were on the beach. If she left, he didn't know how he'd be able to enjoy this beach again. She was one with the water. Already the beach seemed to belong more to her than to him.

"You seem to be settling in well," he said.

"Better than I thought."

"Are you lonely out here?"

"Not lonely really. I have enough to do to keep me occupied and I . . ." Suddenly she stopped.

"And what?" he asked.

"Nothing."

But he waited.

She picked up a seashell and brushed the sand off. "You're going to think I'm crazy," she said.

"No, I won't."

"Sometimes it takes another artist to understand . . ." She stopped. "I've always had this dream."

David waited patiently, giving her time to gather her thoughts.

She tightened her lips. Tipped her chin as if she expected him to laugh at her.

"I've always wanted to write romance novels."

"What's stopping you?"

She seemed to relax. "Nothing now. After I finished the table and chairs, I pulled out a manuscript I've been developing for a couple of years—off and on, you know. I'd get this spurt and write a couple of weeks, then I'd get another proposal requiring all my time and I'd put it aside. You kind of lose the momentum of the story."

David nodded.

"Well, Thursday I pulled out my manuscript and read through it, took notes, jotted down ideas." She closed her eyes. "I think I'm going to finish this novel while I'm here."

"Good for you," David said.

She looked at him expectantly. "You think so?"

"Of course. I can see how much you want to do this. How much you love it. It shows in your eyes." He tapped her nose. "You've found your passion."

She laughed. "This is absolutely crazy. I almost feel giddy. I know it's silly."

"It's not silly. Not for a moment." He gathered her hands in his. "If there's anything I can do to help you—anything at all—let me know."

"Oh, David. Thank you." She linked her arm around his neck, brushed her lips lightly across his, and came up laughing when he wouldn't let her go.

"Thank you for believing in me."

"I'll do one better. There was an article in the paper about a romance writers' group that meets in Morehead City. I'll get some information for you."

"Oh, that's—that's wonderful."

"I have to go. Happy writing, Delilah. I expect

you to be here for at least a year. And when you sell, we'll celebrate."

Ten minutes later, Delilah watched his car drive down the narrow path out of sight. He hadn't said *if* she sold, he'd said *when*.

# Chapter 4

"Delilah, they offered us the proposal, but Stan's still missing." Sylvia sounded anxious and harassed over the phone. "We need you. Could you possibly meet with Stuart Moore tomorrow morning? We have four weeks to get this proposal done."

Delilah sighed. This new job was going to be harder than she bargained for. She saved the file she was working on in her computer. "Do you realize how many hours we'll have to work without Stan to get that proposal out the door in four weeks?" Stan was the brother-in-law of her prospective new boss.

"Some of the prelim work has been done. It's just . . . I don't know what's going on, but Stan has disappeared. Everyone thinks he's gone off because it's more than he can handle. This isn't the first time he's disappeared like that. Stuart is really mad. This is the second time Stan has left us in a bind, and Stuart's not going to let his wife talk him into rehiring her brother."

"That's too bad."

Sylvia sighed. "I'm sorry because I think it's just a matter of him being in the wrong job, but that's beside the point. This company needs a good contract. It's crucial they get something within the next few months just to stay afloat. Say you'll come in."

Delilah studied the manuscript she was working on. Another session of eighty-hour weeks was in the making. But how could she turn down her best friend?

"I promised David I'd work in his office tomorrow. The receptionist will be out and they're understaffed anyway."

"Hold on a moment."

"Syl—" She'd put Delilah on hold. Delilah thought about her book. She thought about Paige, who showed great potential but still needed to work under a skilled supervisor.

"Stuart's clearing up his schedule for this afternoon," Sylvia said. "Can you come in today?"

"I'm not promising I'll take this project, but give me the address and directions. I'll at least meet with the owner."

Delilah glanced at the time. She needed to shower and dress immediately if she planned to make the ferry at one.


Stuart Moore was a creative and enterprising man. So much so that Delilah found herself accepting the position on the spot. Now it was late Friday, and she found herself in a daze after a day spent in David's office.

Children were hell on the uninformed, Delilah thought. Since most of her friends were single, and with her being an only child, an entire day around little ones was definitely an eye opener. It had started early that morning, far too early for someone who wrote until the wee hours of the morning. Delilah was dragging when it approached quitting time. But just as she was about to send up a shout of gratitude because quitting time was near, a woman towed in a bunch of kids. Delilah's hand was itching to lock the door. If she were to ever write about children, that one day spent in David's office offered a mountain of information.

"Sit on that couch and don't move," the woman told a boy who looked to be eight or nine.

"But I told you the man—"

"I don't want to hear another word about that man. You've been going on about that for two hours. You had no business over there in the first place."

"But—"

"Not another word, you hear me? Not another word. Sit over there in that chair while I go to the desk and don't you move. I better not have another second's worth of trouble out of you today. You have tried my last thread of patience."

The kid fell into the seat and crossed his arms. His glare showed all the outrage of the disgruntled.

The woman and three younger kids, twin girls no more than seven and one in her arms screaming a high note, approached the receptionist.

"Sorry I'm late. I was late getting off work."

After signing in and making small talk with the

nurses, the woman and her brood were quickly ushered into one of the examination rooms.

Delilah remained focused on the only person left in the reception room. Her heart went out to the kid, but what did she know about them except that she had been one a lifetime ago? She never spent much time around them. She only knew that her biological clock had been ticking little instant messages about motherhood since she turned thirty. The clock was running down and she'd yet to find Mr. Right, the baby maker.

"That Flossie Greenwald is a good woman," one of the nurses said.

"Yeah?" Delilah was surprised that such a good woman would treat a child the way she had the boy slouching on the couch.

"Has a heart of gold. All those kids are in the foster system. She's got a handful."

Delilah revised her opinion. Maybe the woman had the heart of an angel. Wiping all those noses and having her eardrums split with yelling day in and out was enough to try the patience of a saint. Personally, Delilah wanted just one or two children spaced a few years apart, but the spacing wasn't an option any longer. Yet having an only child like she had been wasn't an option, either. One could always talk to a sister or brother, if only as a sounding board. Having another person in the world that you know cares whether you live or die makes a difference.

The room was cluttered, toys lying on every surface except in the toy box. In the reception area she started stacking magazines and books that were scattered about. She had read somewhere that kids liked to be read to, even older ones. She picked up a pirate book that might interest a boy.

"Would you like me to read you a story?" she asked.

"I can read," the boy said. His face was scrubbed clean and he wore a sport shirt tucked into shorts that reached almost to his knees. His hair was combed neatly. Obviously he was well cared for.

"Well, could you read it to me?"

"Don't want to. That's a kid's book."

"Oh." A good conversation stopper.

"I've already read that one, anyway," he said. "A long time ago."

"Did you enjoy the story?"

He shrugged. "It was okay."

"I'm Delilah. What's your name?"

"Kendall."

She sat beside him. "Do you see one you might like in that stack of books over there?"

"I'm not supposed to move."

Convenient memory, Delilah thought. "I'll bring them to you."

"Suit yourself."

She picked up a stack of books and handed them over. He took them and leafed through them.

"What were you talking about a man before?" Delilah asked. "Did he bother you?"

He paused. "Not really."

"So what happened?"

"I saw two men dumping a really big garbage bag in the river. You're not supposed to dump stuff in the water."

"Causes pollution for sure." Delilah thought of

how much she liked to swim and tried not to think of the things floating in that water with her.

"Yeah, that's what the teacher said." He lapsed into silence again, then said, "You smell nice." He seemed to relax. It was too bad Flossie's patience was worn out between a full-time job and juggling those children. One person could only do so much, after all. All Kendall really needed was someone to listen to him.

"Well, thank you."

"What do you like to read?" Delilah finally asked.

"Action stories."

"What's your favorite?"

"*Harry Potter—Lemony Snickett.*"

"Do you play sports?"

He shrugged. "I play baseball. Doc gave me a bat and mitt."

One of the things Delilah noticed was that parents and children both truly loved David. He greeted children by their names, remembered sports and other activities they participated in, and commented on competitions and games.

When he came out of the examining room, he was carrying the little boy who had been crying earlier. Now the child was smiling and holding a soft toy in one of his chubby little hands.

Delilah was still with Kendall and they were sitting side by side on the couch talking about books when David approached them with the baby.

Kendall's features lit up when he saw David. The change was very measured, but Delilah could see that he was thrilled at seeing the doctor.

"Hey, Doc?"

"How was Disney World?" David asked.

"Great. You're not going to spend the weekend on the island, are you?"

"I have appointments early tomorrow morning. May I pick him up after that, Flossie?" David asked.

"Sure," the woman said with a smile. She was still at the desk checking out. "If anyone can lift his spirits, you can. But mind you, Ken has to be back in time for church. The Junior Missionary Circle is visiting the local senior citizens' home after church. He's singing in the choir."

"I'll have him back in time."

"He's a sweetie pie," Delilah said of the baby.

David handed him to her, giving her no choice. Delilah reached for him. It had been years since she held a child. Probably the last time was when she was working in her mother's beauty shop.

Gingerly, Delilah tucked him on her lap. The kid looked up at her and puckered up. Worried, Delilah started bouncing her knee slowly up and down, hoping the motion would keep him quiet. Then he looked at David and back to her and screamed the room down. Did he have strong vocal cords!

"Take him, take him," Delilah said.

David gathered him back in his arms and the boy clung like a tick.

"Babies are something else, aren't they?" Kendall said to Delilah.

Her heart was still jumping from the scream, never mind her ringing ears. "Yes, they certainly are."

"I see you've finally settled down, Kendall," Mrs. Greenwald said. She looked at Delilah. "The kids were at my sister's place over on Old River Road, and Ken and some boys went romping through the woods and on the riverbank. I asked my husband to pick those kids up and have them take baths and get dressed before I got home." Her look was pure disgust. "Do you think he did it? They were scattered to kingdom come. The first time I sat for more than ten minutes today was in this office."

"You've had quite a day," Delilah said, her heart going out to the overworked woman.

She scoffed. "And then some. Come along, children," Mrs. Greenwald said, taking the baby from David's arms. "We don't want to keep the doctor waiting."

"See you, Ms. Delilah. Thanks for reading with me," Kendall said.

"You're very welcome."

"So are you going to take the job?" David asked when the group left.

Delilah crossed her arms. "Do I have a choice? So many people are involved."

"It will put your writing on the back burner."

"I'm only going to do the one project—hopefully. Shouldn't take more than a month. I'll help them find a good proposal manager. I know a lot of qualified ones. They're occupied with their own projects right now," she said. "And there's Paige. I feel like I left her in the lurch at Keith's company. She called me the other day. The new proposal manager doesn't like her. Neither do the other workers. Mostly because of me."

"When do you start?"

Delilah picked up a magazine, her eyes roaming to the staff at the reception desk. They were surreptitiously watching the two of them. David didn't seem to notice or care. "Monday morning," she said.

"People really don't know what a soft touch you are."

Delilah chuckled. "Who, me? I'm hard as steel."

He moved closer, invading her space. "You're a powder puff," he said, lowering his voice, and ran his tongue over his lips. "The baby looked as if he belonged in your arms."

Oh, damn. He had a sexy way of lowering his voice that gave her goose pimples, but Delilah struggled to keep the tone light.

"Do you have cotton in your ears?" They were the only ones in the far corner of the room.

He was watching her, making love to her with his eyes. She wanted to take him straight home to bed.

"Stop it," she snapped. "Not here."

"I wasn't thinking of him," he said softly, looking at her mouth, then lifting his gaze to her eyes and holding her spellbound. "I was thinking of your own."


David had planned to leave soon after Delilah, but that was before he received a call from Dr. Grant about seeing one of her patients. Soon after he hung up from that conversation his cell phone rang.

"Hey, bro." Carter Matthews, David's foster brother, sounded impatient on the other end. "Heard you were on the island last night. Why didn't you stop by?"

"Had some things to take care of. I knew you were busy with the summer season."

"Never too busy for family," Carter assured him.

"Sounds pretty busy in the background to me."

"You know how it is. Campground's full. Kids running wild breaking stuff. College kids drinking too much. Otherwise couldn't be better."

"How are Delcia and the kids?"

"Great. They miss seeing their uncle. Ranetta asked about you."

"Tell her I'll try to get by this weekend," David said.

"I heard you have a renter at your cottage."

The real reason for the call, David thought. He wondered how he'd heard about that. Ray, more than likely. He rented a cabin at the campground sometimes. So much for the secrecy Delilah craved.

"Delilah's staying on the island for a while."

Carter smothered an oath. "This wouldn't be Cecily's Delilah, would it?"

"Her cousin."

"Do you know what you've gotten yourself into?"

David frowned. "She's renting the cottage. Don't make a big deal out of it."

"The woman's a barracuda."

"Carter, this subject is closed. No discussion."

He heard Carter's loud sigh over the wire. "Delcia invited both of you to dinner tomorrow night. Think you can make it?"

"Kendall's spending the day with me."

"Bring him with you. There'll be plenty of kids, and enough food to feed the island."

"I'll let you know about Delilah."

"I suppose you heard that Louise and her husband split."

"I heard a while ago," David said in resignation. Louise was his ex-fiancée.

"So I guess she's going to be tracking you down."

"What for?"

Carter muttered an oath. "For the same reason Delilah's staying there."

"They're completely different, Carter. Delilah isn't Louise. I've put Louise behind me," he said. "It's time you did, too."

"Yeah, well, just make sure she doesn't weasel her way back into your life."

"She's not as bad as you think she is."

"Much worse, if you ask me."

David had had enough. "Look, I have to go. I'll see you tomorrow."

That was so unfair, that statement about the baby, Delilah thought when she left the office. As badly as she wanted one, kids were a handful. She revised her two prospective children down to one. But the statement about the baby stayed with her as she drove to the ferry. Although the kid was loud, he was a real cutie.

She reached the ferry and purchased a cup of coffee, then stood at the railing.

People often said the water was relaxing, but it was more than that for her.

It was one thing to know David worked with kids, but quite another seeing him with those kids—noticing how well he fit. She admired the

way he worked with them and their parents. She
didn't understand her attraction to a man she
barely knew. Holding a child and looking at her in
that sexy way, well, her throat dropped to her
stomach. Why hadn't some woman snatched him
up by now?

She sipped on coffee that wasn't nearly as good
as the blends sold in Cecily's tea shop. She'd have
to go there soon. They hadn't spoken in months.

She realized she was as eager as an islander to
get back home. The island had crawled its way into
her blood already.

Her mind wandered to her pirate hero, knowing he sailed to various islands, not on the sturdy
ferry she rode. She gathered the pad and pen she
was never without these days and began to write.
The ferry was pulling into port long before she
was through with her ideas.

Not in the mood to cook, Delilah decided to
pick up dinner from Cecily's tea shop. It had been
a great two weeks living in anonymity. No pres-
sures. No censure. As she drove closer to the ocean
side of the island, she glimpsed the tip of the tall
lighthouse long before she actually saw the Victorian
tea shop. The building was impressive. It had been
in her cousin's family since the late eighteen hun-
dreds. Tourists roamed the yard, some were stretched
out on towels on the beach. The parking lot to the
shop was full of cars.

Inside, the tea shop was a beehive of activity.
Not an empty seat in sight. The owner, her cousin
Cecily Anderson, was hostess. She wore a pretty
pink maternity dress and she looked wonderful.
Everybody was having babies, Delilah thought, as

she hugged her cousin. She tried very hard to squelch the wistfulness.

"Carter just told me you've been here for two whole weeks and you haven't said a word. Shame on you," Cecily said.

"I was chilling out. Pregnancy suits you, by the way," Delilah said, holding Cecily at arm's length, then she rubbed her tummy which had just begun to protrude.

Cecily's frown disappeared and she smiled as she rubbed her own tummy. "I couldn't be happier," she said. "Is this a long summer vacation?"

"I'll be here a little longer than the summer."

"Your mother said you were managing some wonderful project in Raleigh when I spoke to her a few months ago."

Delilah shrugged. "The company got the contract. And I'm on to something new and different."

"I see, but that doesn't excuse you from at least calling to let me know you were here."

"I was taking a break."

Cecily frowned. "You didn't think we were still on the outs, did you?"

"No, no."

"Because as much as you drive me crazy sometimes, I still love you. You've got a heart of gold as long as you aren't scheming."

"Me? Scheming? Never."

Cecily chuckled. "Girl, you forget I know you."

Another group of people came in and she grabbed menus. "You're going to stay to dinner, aren't you?"

Delilah had thought to pick up something and

eat at home, but she changed her mind. "Yes. I wish you could sit with me, but I see you're too busy."

"I might be able to chat for a few minutes. I try not to spend too much time on my feet. Ryan's orders." Ryan was Cecily's very protective, very handsome husband.

"Someone will be right with you," Cecily said to the waiting customers, then called someone over before she led Delilah to the sunroom where a few tables were vacant.

"When is the little one due?"

"Early November."

Delilah smiled. "I'm happy for you."

"Thank you." Cecily patted her hand. "I'll try to chat later. Your waitress will be right with you."

Cecily had given her a table with an ocean view. Delilah picked up the menu. It had been expanded since she was last there, but the seafood salad looked wonderful. She ordered peach iced tea with her salad.

She was sipping on her tea when Cecily seated Ray at a table across the room. He was with a statuesque woman, around five-eight or nine who looked very professional in her black suit and pumps. Her hair was worn in ringlets in deference to the humidity. She gazed at him with lively and intelligent black eyes. He saw Delilah before they sat and steered the woman toward her.

"Good to see you," he said.

"You too."

"I was at the house today, but didn't see your car."

"I was on the mainland. Just getting back."

"Delilah this is Dr. Ellen Grant, the island's only physician. Is David joining you?"

"No, he's still on the mainland. I don't think he's coming until tomorrow."

"Actually I have a meeting with him tonight after he makes his rounds," Dr. Grant said. "I have a patient I wanted him to see. Which means we have to eat quickly, Ray."

"It's nice seeing you, Delilah."

"Enjoy your dinner."

Ray and Ellen went to their table but Delilah wasn't alone long. In a few minutes, Cecily sat across from her. By then the sunroom was half filled with customers.

"How did you get away?"

"A couple of extra workers came in, so I can take a break. My feet need it." She rotated her foot.

"How have you been?

"Just great. Now that morning sickness has gone away," Cecily said.

"And Glenda?"

"My aunt's happy as a clam."

"If she's working I'll stop by to say hi before I leave."

"Do that. Delilah, why are you here? Carter thinks you're trying to make a move on David."

"I'm just here to rest, not cause trouble, if that's what you're worried about."

"Yeah, but you don't ever seem to do anything as simple as resting."

Delilah held up a hand. "No critique, please."

"I won't give any. It's just . . ." She hesitated. "David's been hurt once. Are you serious about him?"

Dinner arrived. The waiter carried two plates. "The food looks delicious."

"You're evading."

"I'm only renting his cottage. David and I don't know each other that well, yet, Cecily. But David's a grown man. He can take care of himself."

"I know, but . . ."

"Have you really ever known me to treat a man bad? Whatever you think of me, I've never been a man-stealer. Take a look at some of the guys you used to date. They weren't exactly the pick of the litter."

Cecily held up her hands. "All right. I'll let it go. But I don't think Carter will. He's very protective."

"Of a grown man?"

Cecily shrugged. "Go figure."

From that, they quickly launched into a safe topic. Delilah was tired of fielding people's impressions of her, but she wasn't going to defend the way she acted. She didn't hurt anyone. She couldn't stop people from looking or thinking whatever they wanted to. And she certainly wasn't going to change to suit whatever image people thought she should portray. She didn't ask anyone to change for her, did she?

"Somebody told me the troublemaker was here."

Delilah looked up and groaned. "Not you too, Glenda."

The older woman bent and hugged Delilah, then sat in an empty chair. She wore her hair in long braids gathered in a red elastic band. "You going to stick around for a while, girly?"

"For the rest of the year, anyway. Who knows after that?"

"You're always traipsing from one place to another. Time you settled down. At least you have family here."

"You've developed a southern accent, Glenda. This place has really worn on you."

"I'm sounding more and more like Emery every day."

"How is he, by the way?" Emery Cleveland was Glenda's husband, who owned a fleet of fishing boats. Most were used to take tourists on day excursions.

"As ornery as ever."

"Good. Keeps you young. Speak of the devil." Delilah couldn't help smiling when Emery grabbed her in a bear hug, lifting her right out of her chair. She hugged him right back, laughing.

"How's my baby girl doing?" he said.

"Wonderful."

He pulled up another chair and sat. Glenda rolled her eyes.

"When Glenda told me you were here, I had to come right over to see you. I ought to whip you. Been here all that time and haven't been by once to see old Emery. Not once."

Emery treated her like the daughter he never had. And she was grateful to Glenda and him for their kindness.

"They worked me like a horse at my last job. I wasn't fit for decent company."

"Well, you've got to come out to the boat with me so I can show you around. Take you out on the ocean."

"I'll do that."

"I've got to get back to the shop. Place is running over with tourists." He stood but hugged her again. "You come by and visit me and Glenda, you hear?"

"I will." Glenda left shortly after to return to the kitchen. For the first time, Delilah felt wanted and loved on the island. Staying away seemed silly now.

Later, Carter picked up dinner from the tea shop. Cecily had left for the day and he dropped by Ryan and Cecily's on his way home. He hadn't been able to rest once he heard Delilah was in town and staying at David's place. He and his brother-in-law, Ryan, stood in the yard.

"This is no reflection on your wife, but David's like a homing device for the wrong kind of women. Tell me, how can someone so intelligent be so dumb when it comes to women?"

Ryan commiserated, but shook his head.

"Louise was bad enough," Carter continued. "But Delilah. She lives up to the biblical character. Just reel him in like a frigging defenseless fish."

"It can't be that bad. Delilah is all flash. He should be able to see through her," Ryan offered.

Carter shook his head. "You'd think so. But she appears to be like one of those little sick puppies he used to bring home when he was a kid. And I tell you, he was real defensive when I mentioned her name earlier. Real defensive. I thought he was going to hang up on me, his own brother, if I said another word about her. Turning brother against brother already. She's got her hook in him all right."

Carter paced back and forth across the grass.

"Jeez. Why did he have to end up with the man-eating woman? He can sure pick them."

Ryan howled.

"It's not funny, man. It's a sad situation I've got on my hands."

"Looks to me like it's David who . . ."

Ryan's dad and mom, Clay and Pauline Anderson, came onto the porch. "Your brother seems to have a mess of trouble on his hands," Clay said and pulled out a lawn chair for his wife.

"Let's not be too hasty," Pauline said. "Delilah didn't seem so bad when I met her."

"She's a wolf in sheep's clothing," Carter assured her.

Pauline tried to reason. "Well, the quickest way to estrange David is to malign the woman he likes. You have to treat her with respect or he'll start avoiding you."

"Jesus Christ. I can't stand by and let her ruin his life. I should have stepped in when Louise latched on to him."

"He's forty. What do you think you can do about a grown man?" Pauline asked.

"Maybe I can convince Delilah to leave."

"Oh, please. What are you suggesting? That you run her out of town? And cause a huge fight with your brother. There are some things family can't get involved in, and his woman is one of them," Pauline assured him.

"You may be assuming too much," Delcia, Carter's wife, said. "Did he actually say he was dating her? I thought she was only renting the cottage."

"He was living in the cottage. He told me he

wasn't going to rent it out. He fixed it up so he could spend weekends there while they're fixing his place, and after that he was going to let Mom and Dad stay there when they visit. You know how they like their own space."

"She knows a good thing when she sees it, trust me," Ryan said.

"We'll all get a better perspective at dinner tomorrow," Pauline said. "Let's let the topic rest until then, okay?"

Carter grumbled, but before he acquiesced he said, "As sure as God made nor'easters, Delilah is going to bring David down just like her namesake in the Bible brought Sampson to his knees. You just watch and see." He stopped pacing and glared at them all. "The only thing that will solve this dilemma is to get Delilah off this island and away from David as quickly as possible."

"Amen to that," Ryan agreed, to his mother's utter disgust.

"Well, Delilah must be very powerful indeed to have all you strapping men running for cover," she told them, her voice dripping with sarcasm.

David was dying to take things slowly with Delilah, but he couldn't afford to allow her to ponder their relationship too long before he made his move. His conversations with Carter worried him. He knew his brother. Carter would try to intimidate Delilah, perhaps even try to convince her to move away.

He had a feeling that Delilah was strong, that she was a fighter. He was counting on that. Just in case, he'd better plan to spend most of his nights on the island. Besides, any number of men would like to cut in on him. He was sure Ray liked her, but Delilah didn't seem to have romantic designs on him.

Perhaps he could take her to dinner before his appointment with Dr. Grant and one of her patients. But by the time he arrived at the beach house, Delilah's car was gone.

He toured the new construction. This was the third extension so far. They'd been repairing the house for close to two years already. No telling when he'd be able to move in.

When he went around the back, he saw Delilah's car hidden by bushes. He looked toward the water. She was swimming, looking like a mermaid who was one with the sea.

As he walked toward her, she swam to shore and picked up the towel there.

"Want to join me on the beach?" she asked, dropping the towel.

"Wish I could, but . . ."

"Oh, that's right, you're meeting Dr. Grant."

Seeing all Delilah's generous curves in the revealing two-piece swimwear created another problem.

"Have you eaten?" she asked.

He shook his head.

"There's a seafood salad in the fridge. When Dr. Grant told me you were meeting with her, I knew you wouldn't have time to eat after your hospital rounds."

"You're so thoughtful. Thanks. But what I'd like

to do is kiss you." Actually he wanted to kiss every curve of her delectable body.

He drew her near. Her skin was cold from the water. He kissed her softly, wove his hand through her hair, and held her head still so she would look at him. "It was hell working with you all day, wanting to kiss you but having to keep our relationship all business."

"I was thinking the same thing."

"You're going to have me moving to this island full-time, woman."

"That's not a bad thing." She smiled up at him. Her hair was wet and slick. He raked his fingers through the mussed strands, lowered his head, and touched his lips to hers again, her lips still cool and salty from the ocean. Yet they were soft. Very soft. He lifted his head to look down at her.

"I hate to leave."

"Just don't be away too long."

She wrapped her arms around him, rubbed against his chest. The friction caused them both to moan. It was pure torture having her body pressed closely to his. He deepened the kiss, swirling his tongue with hers and sucking gently. He slid his hands down her shoulders to the indentation in her back.

Finally their lips separated. "Come on. I'll go to the house with you."

The towel slipped to the ground. He picked it up, looped it over his arm. It was warm enough that she didn't need to wrap it around her. More importantly, he didn't want her generous curves hidden.

"You've got a big wet spot on you," Delilah said, rubbing his chest lightly.

"It'll dry before I leave," he said. "Carter invited us to dinner tomorrow night."

Delilah pursed her lips. "Us or you?"

"You were invited, too."

"Carter hates my guts," she said. "He's not pleased that we're . . ."

"Who the hell cares? *I'm* dating you. I'm the only one who counts." He wrapped an arm around her shoulder. They began to walk slowly to the cottage. "He doesn't even know you. Trust me. He'll be on his best behavior."

"Are you sure a relationship with me is what you want? You're the saint. I'm the hussy."

Looking down at her, he lowered his head and kissed her deeply, swirling his tongue in her hot mouth. In no time, the heat soared to a fever pitch, and so did his heartbeat.

"You keep doing that and you'll never make it out of here."

"There's something to be said for hussies. Besides, you can't hide forever."

"I'm not hiding from anything," she said indignantly. "I was using the peace to make headway on my book. And it's going very well, thank you very much."

"I'm glad."

Delilah had hoped to spend Saturday working on her book, but she said, "All right. I'll be ready."

# Chapter 5

David met Dr. Grant in her office a few minutes early to discuss her patient and review the tests he'd taken. The little boy and his parents arrived ten minutes later. After David examined the boy he sent him to the reception area to play with toys while he spoke to his parents.

"I want to begin a new treatment for him," he said. "If that doesn't work we'll take it a step further. Sometimes it's a matter of getting the correct medication that will respond for him."

David scribbled out the prescription. "The druggist here can order it. It's not something he would keep on hand. He should be able to get it in a few days," he said. "I'll be going to the mainland tomorrow. I have a small supply in my office I'll bring back for you. This should keep him going until more arrive."

"We really appreciate that, Doctor. Dr. Grant's a wonderful doctor, but we do need a pediatrician

on the island. Could you see yourself working here
at least on a part-time basis?"

"I could consider that," he said. Now it was a
more attractive idea.

David chatted with Dr. Grant a few minutes before he left for the house. Delilah was asleep on
the sofa when he arrived. David showered, then
slipped onto the couch beside her.

She awakened when she felt the press of a kiss
on her neck.

On the dregs of sleep as she was, her look held
a question. But there was no question about what
he wanted, or what had been on his mind as he
watched her in those tight clothes most of the
day.

He drew her close. She smelled sweet and entic-
ing. He wanted to devour her.

"I wanted you the moment I saw you on the
beach. Are you ready for us?" he asked, unwilling
to direct the relationship onto a course she wasn't
ready for.

"Definitely," she whispered and ran her tongue
over his bottom lip. He nipped her gently and
closed his lips over hers delving his tongue in her
mouth.

He caressed the curves of her body and felt her
soft hands on him. "Your skin feels like silk," he
said, reveling in how curvy her small form was.

Delilah smoothed her hands over his chest, felt
springy hair against her palms, touched hard muscles through velvet skin, thinking he must work
out because the solidity of his shoulders and arms
and back was not that of a pampered man who examined children and pushed a pen across paper.

But the feel of his hands roaming her body took her breath away. She moaned her pleasure.

"Like that?" he asked.

"Yes, yes . . ." she whispered, gliding her hands over his back and pressing him tightly against her.

"What do you want? Hard and fast, or slow and easy?"

"I can't take slow and easy. Hard and fast, then slow and easy."

"Your wish is my command. We have all night, sweetheart." She nearly ripped off his clothes and he tore into hers until they were naked. He plucked her up and carried her into the bedroom, dropping her on the bed.

He dropped the package on her stomach and returned to kissing her. She ripped into it. With one knee on the bed, he sat up. Slowly she slid the prophylactic on, sliding her hands around him, gently stroking him.

He groaned. "You're driving me crazy."

He captured her nipple in his mouth, flicked his tongue over the rigid bud. He pressed her legs open, caressing her inner thighs, driving her insane with wanting him. Her breath was hitching by the time he lowered to her and she felt the heaviness of his body. And then he was sliding into her, stretching her until he was completely sheathed.

"Oh, baby, baby. I've died and gone to heaven," he whispered and then he was moving and her hips reached to gather him more fully.

She was too spellbound for words as they rocked to a beat as old as time. She tightened her legs around him, and he placed his hands beneath her hips to sink more deeply.

And then together they were soaring to a place so special it rivaled their love of the island.

Early the next morning, Delilah prepared breakfast while David showered. They ate together before he drove to the mainland for early morning appointments and rounds at the hospital.

Delilah washed the few dishes she and David used and wiped down the countertop.

The only sane solution for a hot and sticky day was settling under the beach umbrella with a cooler and a good novel. The ceiling fan wasn't enough. She'd have to turn the air conditioner on. The little-known secret was that there was often a soft breeze, just enough to make the heat tolerable, but so far a breeze wasn't stirring.

Delilah first made a banana pudding for the evening's cookout, then did the weekly cleaning, applying orange oil to the wood cabinets in the kitchen, and scrubbing the tile floor within an inch of its life. Thoughts of David and their night together made the work seem less like drudgery. From there, she attacked the living room, dusting, polishing, and vacuuming. Then she scrubbed the bathroom. After all the outer rooms were completed, she attacked her bedroom. When the work was finished, she stretched out on the bed. A lovely light orange scent permeated the rooms.

Delilah sighed and debated taking a shower, but since she was going for a swim, she might as well wait until after.

Within minutes, she fell asleep.

\* \* \*

"I thought you'd never get there," Kendall said.

"I had some appointments," David said. "They lasted longer than I thought they would."

"I'm going to be a doctor when I grow up."

"Why is that?"

"You make kids happy. I want to make people happy, too."

"Well, there's a lot more to being a doctor than making people happy. It takes years of school. Then you have to do an internship where they work you sixteen- and seventeen-hour days. Sometimes you're on call twenty-four-seven for a couple of days before you get time off. You can't just leave if there is no one to replace you."

"Hmm."

"And you have to love what you do. Don't forget the studying and good grades."

"Yeah, I know. You remind me all the time."

David chuckled. "Are you hungry?"

"Mrs. Flossie made me eat before I left."

"Then I guess it's straight to the beach."

"Yeah."

"Let's pick up your friend Reggie first. I called his mom earlier. She said it was okay."

"Oh, great. Did Midnight miss me?"

"She always misses you."


Delilah felt something tickling her nose and swatted it away.

"Not now, Midnight. I'm sleeping."

But the persistent dog landed on her arm. Half

asleep, she swatted again. "Go away. I just walked you."

But the damn thing kept nagging at her until she finally brushed her arms and opened her eyes.

She stifled a screech. Pressing a hand to her heart, she said, "You scared the daylights out of me."

"It wasn't fair, you sleeping so peacefully," David said.

She linked her arms around his neck. "Where's Kendall?"

"Romping around outside with Reggie and Midnight," he said, taking little nipping bites of her breast. "Think we can steal a quickie?"

"When the kids can burst in any minute? I don't think so."

"We can't lock them out?"

"Nooooo . . ." He suckled on her breast.

"You sure?"

"Yesssss." He kissed his way down her abdomen.

"Positive?"

"My mind's gone blank."

"You're a siren," he said, his voice husky. "A siren who'd tempt any red-blooded man."

"Am I tempting you?"

He lowered his head, his lips an inch above her. She felt the whisper of his breath when he said, "Oh yes." And then he kissed her.


Kendall was dressed neatly in shorts and a T-shirt. He and Reggie climbed into the backseat of Delilah's Sebring when they were ready to leave. The four of them couldn't fit into the Porsche.

Although Delilah was apprehensive about entertaining with David's family, she was sure no one could tell. When they arrived, she lifted her chin and climbed out of the car. The kids had rocketed out as soon as the car came to a stop. Obviously Kendall had been there before.

There was another little boy Kendall's and Reggie's age. They immediately ran to the beach under the watchful eye of Ryan and Carter, who also watched Ranetta and the other kids. Delilah's tight white pants and vivid blue top were very flattering to her figure.

Everyone was hanging outside and Delcia greeted them as they approached the patio. The smell of grilled food wafting in the air reminded Delilah that she'd skipped lunch.

David bent and kissed Delcia on the cheek. "Any woman who can keep my brother in check deserves a medal," he said.

"I've earned it, you can be sure," she said.

"Have you met Delilah?" David asked.

Warm brown eyes greeted Delilah. "It's been a while. I'm so glad you could join us."

"Thank you," Delilah said, handing over the bowl of banana pudding.

Delcia lifted the cover, then closed her eyes briefly. "Banana pudding, my absolute favorite. Thank you. This is going to be the hit of the dinner."

"Where's Ranetta and the little one?" David asked. "Tearing up the place?"

"The men are supervising them on the beach. Go on and join them. Delilah's in good hands."

As David walked away, Delcia said, "Cecily should be coming soon. Let me introduce you to my parents and the other guests."

She was sure that they all had it in for her, so she was surprised when the group engaged her in a cordial and friendly conversation.

"What can I help with?" Delilah asked Delcia.

"Everything is under control."

"David says you're a writer," Delcia's mother, Pauline Anderson, said. "He says you're spending the next few months on a book. What do you write?"

"I'm writing a romance novel," Delilah said, waiting for noses to shoot up in the air.

"I love good romance," Pauline said.

"Partners in crime," Ryan said as he snatched some chips from the table.

"Just because you never appreciated good books," Delcia said.

"I was always working," Ryan said.

"Since when is sticking a fishing pole in the water, a hat over your eyes, and nodding off considered work, little brother?"

"Man's work," he said, dancing out of the way of the kitchen towel she swatted at him. He headed off before the other women ganged up on him.

"Men," Delcia said with the correct amount of disdain.

"Well, Lordy, you've got a crowd," Willow Mae said, toddling along with her husband, Harry. The poor man was loaded up with several containers of food that looked as though they might topple any moment.

"Woman cooked up a storm for two days," he said. "There's more in the car."

"Aunt Willow Mae, I told you not to do all that cooking," Delcia said, taking the food from Uncle Harry. "Go on and join the men by the beach,

Uncle Harry, and you have a seat, Aunt Willow Mae."

"I think I will. My feet and legs are swollen. Stood on them all day. Had to cook Ryan my potato salad and deviled eggs. You know how he likes Aunt Willow Mae's deviled eggs."

"You need to stop spoiling him."

"You know I can't disappoint my baby. He's always coming by to check on me."

"And now you have aching legs."

"They gonna ache no matter what I do."

Delilah went to the car to help unload. There was enough food to feed four times the number of people present.

"I don't care what we have, that woman always cooks too much. I should have brought her over here this morning so she couldn't have cooked."

"It smells wonderful."

"She's a fabulous cook. I guess Uncle Harry doesn't eat enough for her. And Cecily's been complaining that Ryan's gained a few pounds. She's always got a willing mouth in my brother."

They set the food on the table.

"Aunt Willow Mae, meet Delilah, David's friend," Delcia said.

"Well, bless my soul, he's finally dating again. I was beginning to wonder if he'd ever find somebody. He's getting up in age, you know. It's not good for a man to stay single too long. It's gonna be hard to train him now, girl. Best to catch them when they're young." She frowned at Delilah. "Shoulda brought my glasses with me. Come on over here and let me get a better look at you."

Embarrassed, Delilah moved closer.

Mrs. Anderson leaned back in her chair. "Aren't you a pretty little thing?"

Delilah didn't know what to say. "Thank you" would have to suffice.

"As pretty as you are, you aren't going to have a minute's worth of trouble out of him."

Delilah couldn't keep the blush from her cheeks.

"She writes books, Willow Mae," Pauline said, to detract from the beauty comments.

"Oh yeah? What kind? I hope they're interesting stories I'd want to read."

"Romance novels."

"Is that right? Just the kind of story I need to get this ole ticker racing. Hope the reverend's not around when I sneak to the bookstore and buy one. You let me know when it comes out, you hear? I hope it's nice and spicy."

"You going to try some new tricks on Uncle Harry?" Delcia teased.

"Old man don't want to hear about no new tricks. But I can read those books and think about the younger days." She patted her curls. "Don't let this hair fool you, now. There might be snow on the roof, but there's still plenty of fire in this old heart."

"Go on, Willow Mae," Pauline said. "You tell them."

Everybody cracked up. And Delilah began to relax.


Although Delilah hadn't expected to enjoy herself, she did. It was a family picnic where everyone was low-key and ate the best food on the island. It was the warm familiar setting she often wished for in her own family. Her mother always worked extremely long hours in the beauty shop. She didn't believe in a lot of socializing. She believed that idle hands were the devil's playground.

But Delilah would have appreciated a few hours of idle chatter when she and her mother talked one on one while just relaxing. Perhaps half an hour sipping tea on the spotless back porch that never held porch furniture because no one ever had the time to sit there. Maybe that was the reason she'd worked so hard for so many years, barely taking time for a break. Perhaps that was the reason men like Keith could take advantage of her. They didn't mind her working long hours because they were only using her.

Thankfully there weren't any conversations, within her hearing anyway, about the wicked Delilah trying to trap Saint David. But later David dragged her away to the beach. The older kids were still playing on the beach, while the younger ones were at the house.

"Have they staked the wicked Delilah yet?" he asked.

"That isn't nice."

"I know, but you seem to be enjoying yourself."

"I didn't expect to, but I am. Very much."

He pulled her close, lowered his lips, and kissed her.

Fury snapped in Carter's voice. "Will you look at that?"

"Don't you dare start, Carter Matthews. Everyone has had a wonderful time, including Delilah, and especially David," Delcia said. "He needs to be able to unwind with family without you spoiling for a fight."

"I just can't stand by and let him throw his life away."

"It's not your decision."

Carter prowled like an angry tiger. "You expect me to do nothing while she ruins his life?"

"Who says she's going to ruin his life? You don't know her."

"Oh, I know her, all right. Women like her are a dime a dozen. The only thing they're looking for is a good man to take care of them while they do God knows what."

"Stay out of it, Carter. If you interfere, you'll alienate him. Not many men would let a brother or anyone else come between him and the woman he loves."

"Loves!" He looked at her as if she had two heads. "Are you out of your mind?"

Delcia put a hand on his tight shoulders, and rubbed to soothe him. "There are some needs that only the right woman can fulfill. You might as well get used to having Delilah around."

"I'm not crazy. I know he needs a good woman. And I repeat, a *good* woman." He jerked his head toward the beach. "Delilah's not it."

"How do you know? You can't choose who he loves."

"He's infatuated. He doesn't love her," Carter bit out between gritted teeth.

"Oh, yes, he does. You can see it in the way he watches her. And she feels something for him, too, because she watches him the same way."

"Watching for his paycheck. Not for him."

"Hey, hey." Ryan came closer, looped an arm around their shoulders. "Everybody's watching you, wondering which one is going to throw the first punch."

"It's going to be me if Carter doesn't straighten up," Delcia said, crossing her arms and glaring at her husband.

"What's going on over here?"

Delcia pointed a finger toward the water. "Look at the beach. Do you need to ask Mr. Paranoid here?"

"I'm getting ideas. Good thing I'm about to take Cecily home and tuck her under the covers."

Carter cursed and stalked off.

Delcia shook her head. "He's driving himself crazy over David and Delilah."

"I know, but David loves her. And as much as Carter wants to, there isn't a thing he can do about it."

Sunday, Delilah attended the local church with David. After the service they ate brunch at Cecily's tea shop.

Since it was an island tea shop and there were fewer eateries than on the mainland, Cecily had turned it into a place where one could dine as well as experience an English tea.

David reached for her hand. "What will you do while I make rounds?"

"Actually I'm meeting with my critique group."

"On the mainland?"

"At the cottage. Once they discovered I actually

lived on the island, the consensus was to meet here." Delilah signaled the waitress. "I'd like ten scones with a container of clotted cream and lemon curd to go, please."

When the waitress left, David said, "I'm glad to see you're progressing on your novel."

"I'm determined to finish."

David smiled.

"Spend next weekend with me, Delilah," he asked her.

Delilah hesitated. Were they moving too fast? She knew now that what she felt for Keith would never have turned into love. What she felt with David was so much more powerful and building too quickly.

Her mother had taught her caution, which she seldom used. Her father had taught her to be free.

She wanted to use caution, but she also wanted to experience what was happening with them. She couldn't second-guess every action she made. Everything in the past was calculated. For once she was going with gut feelings.

"Yes. Anything special planned?"

He tapped the end of her nose. "It's a surprise."

The critique group comprised four women, including Delilah. One was a published author, the other three aspiring. Two of the women had already sent in proposals for their work.

They had met at a local romance writers' meeting, and had hit it off immediately.

Of course Delilah jumped at the opportunity to join them. It was always nice to get another person's perspective on her work. They could also be a mutual support group.

Delilah took the blackberry tea she'd blended out of the fridge and set out some of the scones from Cecily's tea shop.

A car door slammed, but when she didn't hear the doorbell, Delilah went to investigate.

The three women had taken off their shoes and were wading in the shallow water.

Delilah went out to join them.

"We were coming, promise, but this was so heavenly."

"This place is a writer's paradise."

The third voice said, "How do you get any work done? I'd spend my days on the beach."

Delilah started to say, "You get used to it," but she really hadn't.

"It's tough."

"I'd never get any writing done here unless I could do it on the beach."

"Believe me, I often sit out here with my pad and pen."

The first woman said, "Come on, ladies. We didn't come here to sunbathe."

"Speak for yourself."

But finally they deserted the beach and made their way to the house.

"Is that beautiful place yours?" one asked, pointing toward David's house on the hill.

"No. I'm renting the cottage from the owner."

"If you ever leave this place, let me know. I'm next in line."

Delilah chuckled and poured tea for everyone.

"Clotted cream. Lemon curd. When have I last had these?"

"While we're stuffing ourselves, we can work."

This was their first official meeting, and they each discussed their respective projects.

"I've completed my proposal," Delilah said. "Now I'm ready to send it off."

"Who are you pitching it to?"

Delilah mentioned the two publishing houses she planned to query.

Someone named other houses that were accepting. "I don't have that information on me, but I'll e-mail it to you tonight."

"Since we didn't bring anything to critique, would you like us to take a look at your proposal?"

"Certainly."

Delilah made three copies and handed them out. For the next couple of hours they sat quietly around the room and critiqued her work.

After that, chapter by chapter, they discussed their opinions. They made some suggestions that Delilah hadn't seen from a reader's point of view. She needed to elaborate one scene in more detail. She didn't agree with or plan to use all of the suggestions, but some of them would enhance her work.

It helped to have another point of view.


Monday morning, Delilah made the trek to the mainland to Moore's, Inc., where she would work on their proposal. Stuart had had her sign the nondisclosure agreement on Thursday. She immediately dived into Stan's files and made notes. She sat through meetings with other managers, and afterward she read through the regs, preparing herself for the big meeting two days away.

There was a lot of conversation about the missing Stan before they began to discuss the work. She didn't look up until lunchtime when Sylvia knocked on her door.

"Come on. Let's get a real lunch. No snacking at your desk allowed."

Delilah plucked her reading glasses off, and squinted at her watch. "Time is really flying. Where are you going to lunch?"

"Next door. We don't have a cafeteria here," Sylvia said. "Marcia is joining us. She's a little down because she and her fiancé are having problems."

A young and energetic Marcia Scott was waiting for them at the door. Sylvia introduced the women and everyone piled into her car for the five-minute trip to Phases. They were quickly seated in a booth near a window and in record time they had ordered their meals.

"Are you following Stan's notes all right?" Sylvia asked.

"They were surprisingly neat. He kept everything together, so I easily picked up from where he left off. It wasn't as bad as I thought it would be."

"He was really trying," Marcia said. "He was trying to be more responsible. Ran into a little trouble a while back, but everybody's keeping it hush-hush. It shocked me when he left."

"Shocked a lot of people," Sylvia said.

"I'll tell you one thing. He really hated working with Redcliff. He hates that company," Marcia said.

"Tried to get Stuart to reject the proposal, but Stuart wouldn't. Said we need the business."

"We do," Sylvia said, "if we want to stay solvent. That's something for Stuart to deal with. So what's up with the fiancé?"

"Oh," Marcia said, waving a hand. "He wants us to get married."

Sylvia snorted. "And you find that a problem? Most men are running in the opposite direction."

"I'm only twenty-five. I want to live a little before I settle down. I don't want to go straight from college to Mrs."

"You've been out of college for how long?"

"Only a year. I got my master's. But Mark has been on his own for years."

"Well, I'm sure he'll be patient," Delilah said.

"Anderson men aren't known for their patience. Ryan rushed Cecily to the altar. Carter and Delcia barely knew each other when they got married. But I'm renting my own little cottage. I love it."

"She lives near you, Delilah," Sylvia said.

"Oh yeah?"

"A mile down the road. My nephew plays with Kendall sometimes."

"We'll have to invite you over when Kendall visits," Delilah said. "Although you don't need that excuse. I'm surprised you weren't at the cookout."

"We were invited, but Mark and I were fighting as usual. He got mad and left."

"Men," they said in unison and laughed, but Sylvia stopped abruptly when Donnie stopped at their table.

"Afternoon, ladies."

Delilah noticed that Sylvia didn't speak.

"They actually let you out of the office, Donnie?" Marcia said.

"Now and then." Donnie's name didn't fit his character at all. It was a childlike name, and there was nothing juvenile about this man.

"Welcome to Moore's," Donnie said to Delilah.

"Thank you. Where's your sidekick?"

"We don't always hang together. You ladies enjoy the rest of your lunch," he said.

"Check you later, Donnie," Marcia said playfully.

*Well, well, well,* Delilah thought. *Wonder if Mr. Steroids and Sylvia have ever dated.*


When David called Wednesday night, Delilah asked him where they were going.

He had just finished answering phone messages from patients.

"I don't want to waste half the weekend traveling some place. All the beach places are pretty busy. But I still want to get away from work. Any suggestions?"

"I say we stay right here. I'll stock up on groceries. You can hide your car in the garage and camp out at my place."

"You deserve a real trip."

"I love it right here. Working on the mainland helps me appreciate this place more."

When David disconnected, Wayne came into his office.

"David, I need to talk with you." The tense expression on Wayne's face forewarned David he wasn't going to like the conversation.

"Okay. Have a seat."

"I hate to tell you this, but I've decided to join my uncle's practice in Philadelphia."

David had a sinking feeling in his heart. He'd hoped so much that Wayne would decide to stay on.

"Well, we knew that he might offer."

"Yeah, my cousin and I will eventually take over. I hate to leave you in the lurch this way."

"I'll be fine." David waved away his concern. "It shouldn't be too difficult to find a partner." As he said it, he only hoped it would be true.

# Chapter 6

David's last appointment was at five on Friday. He immediately left for the island, and just as Delilah had said, parked his car behind her cottage out of sight of the road.

Delilah opened the door wearing a long dress of wispy mauve.

He wrapped his arms around her. "This week goes on my calendar as the longest in my life," he said huskily.

"Mine, too."

As he looked around the room, he saw that the table was lit with two candles. Something smelled delicious. Delilah must have estimated his arrival just right.

"What's happening with Kendall? He seems to spend a lot of time with you."

"He's having trouble adjusting to losing both his parents just a year apart. His father had cancer, then his mother died unexpectedly in an accident."

"Losing one parent is a blow, losing both of them is devastating, especially for a child. I'm surprised he isn't acting out more." Delilah left his side to pour two glasses of wine.

"At least with me, both my parents died together. But to have it happen so close together . . ."

"He's bonded with you."

"Somewhat. Not that it's a good thing."

"I think it is. He needs something solid to cling to, and until another family adopts him . . ."

"You mean if."

"I would hate to think that no one would want him."

"It's not always a matter of want. Sometimes it's whether a person can give him what he needs," David said. He accepted the glass she handed to him. Then she sat beside him.

"You want to adopt him, I can tell."

His expression was grave. "I've thought about it."

"What's stopping you?"

"He'd rarely see me. Wayne's leaving soon. That means my patient schedule will increase. It also means I have to make all the rounds at the hospitals. Many nights I won't get home until ten. That's no life for a child."

"What about a partner?"

"The ideal solution if I can find one."

"I'm sure someone out of residency would leap at the chance to become part of a thriving practice."

"Sure, but that can bring its share of problems, too. It will take a while for us to begin to work as a team. I have to train him or her. Someone out of residency won't come on as a full partner, which is what I would prefer."

Delilah massaged the tense muscles in his shoulders. "I'm sure something will turn up. Have faith."

David clasped her hand, kissed the back of it, then quickly pulled her onto his lap.

Delilah's surprised laughter rippled through the air.

"Do we have to talk business on our mini-vacation?" David asked.

Delilah ran her tongue along the seam of his lips. "Not if you don't want to." She caressed his cheek with gentle strokes. "I think I can come up with something to occupy our time."


The next morning, David pulled Delilah out of bed at seven.

"Why so early?" she asked, rubbing the sleep out of her eyes.

"We've got big plans today."

"I'm game," Delilah said, pushing the covers back. "How shall I dress?"

"Very casual, and comfortable shoes, but bring a warm jacket and sunblock."

"It's going to be ninety degrees," she said, straightening the covers.

David plopped his pillow in place. "I know."

Delilah shrugged. "I'm easy to please." She dashed into the bathroom for a shower. By the time she finished, David was dressed and quickly ushered her out the door to the dock—where a boat was waiting for them.

"Where is Midnight?"

"With the sitter. We'll be away most of the day."

"Do you know your way around these waters?"

"I've been here for years. Of course I do. Don't worry, this isn't my first time out alone."

Delilah was awed at the sleek-looking boat. "Shouldn't I fix breakfast and pack food to take with us? How long are we going to be out?"

"It's all taken care of. I might not be the best cook, but I won't starve you." He winked at her. "Trust me." With the devilish look on his face, he was the last man she should trust.

"I submit to your capable hands."

"That's a loaded statement. No telling what I might do with you."

"Use your imagination, sugar."

The smile tilted a moment, and his green eyes sparkled. "Now, that might frighten you."

What on earth did he mean by that? Delilah wondered. "Are you telling me I don't want to know?"

"No. Just that you don't want to know right now."

"I'm really perplexed."

"Let's not worry about it," he said when they reached the boat. "Let's climb aboard."

A man wearing a golf shirt with *Cleveland Tours* stenciled on it appeared on deck. "Good morning, Dr. Washington, Ms. Benton. I'll be your guide today."

Delilah rolled her eyes at David. "I thought you were our captain."

"In my line of work when a doctor needs a specialist, what does he do? Sit back and enjoy the executive treatment."

"I will, I will. I get the impression that you know as much about boats as I do. And that's absolutely nothing."

"We have to do something about that."

As they sailed out to the open water, David pulled out a picnic basket with *Cecily's Tea Shop* emblazed on the side. Delilah peeped inside. There were containers labeled *breakfast* and *lunch*. She pulled the breakfast items out. After smoothing cream and jam on a scone, she fed it to David.

He ate it and kissed her.

*I could get too used to this very quickly indeed,* Delilah thought.

Instead of preparing separate plates, she piled food on one and they both ate off it.

The captain was in another area of the boat, giving them privacy. None of the men she'd dated before had gone out of his way to give her special treatment. They always took more than they gave.

But David, a man she'd known for only a few weeks, treated her better than even those who professed to love her. She'd tried. Lord knows she'd tried. But she couldn't keep the glassiness from her eyes. She felt so full of emotion she could absolutely explode. The food she swallowed made a lump in her throat. David wiped the single stupid tear that made a track down one cheek.

"None of this," he said. "I'm trying to make you happy, not sad.

"I am happy. Very happy," she said. "You keep this up you're going to make me . . ." Suddenly she stopped, shocked at what she was about to say.

"Make you what?" he asked, but Delilah couldn't, or wouldn't, answer.

"This is a wonderful surprise, David," she said instead, fighting against overwhelming tears.

He gave up trying to convince her to talk. Instead, he took the plate from her before it toppled onto the deck and gathered her close in his strong arms, held her against his steady heartbeat.

She closed her eyes, loving the feel of his arms around her, loving his unique scent she'd become so familiar with. She inhaled a deep breath to steady herself. As she often heard islanders say, she had to find her sea legs. But around him she didn't have to pretend. She didn't have to be strong. She could be just Delilah, weak sometimes, more often strong. The elements that were a part of both men and women whether they admitted it or not.

"I have to agree with you," she finally said. "You do know how to get the job done. Thank you."

Delilah was enjoying the sights of the port with its huge container ships docked and the many pleasure boats about, and the seaside buildings. David even pointed out the campground. They passed the lighthouse, nearly two hundred feet tall.

But the most puzzling part was when they reached the port in Beauford and a cab was waiting for them. It took them to the Maritime Museum.

"I can't believe it," Delilah said when the cab pulled up in front.

"You said you wanted to learn maritime history and get more information about the pirates."

"And you knew I planned to go."

"At the rate you were going, you might make it

there and you might not. This way I was sure you'd get there."

Her heart filled like a helium balloon. "You believe in my work that much?"

"Of course I do. I would do anything to help you."

By then they were climbing out of the cab and made their way into the museum. Delilah immediately headed for information on pirate ships. David had arranged for someone to talk to her.

There was an exhibit on "The Revenge of the Sea," a ship believed to have been stolen by Blackbeard, which had been exhumed from the waters of the area.

Delilah studied the ship, even took notes in the notebook David conveniently provided. She stayed there for a couple of hours gathering information to use in her book.

Meanwhile, David patiently studied other exhibits and Delilah didn't feel rushed as she began to move from one exhibit to another looking for things that would help in her writing.

Before she knew it, she had several pages of notes.

When she went to where David was absorbed in another exhibit, she said, "I bet Kendall would love it here."

"He probably would. I guess I should bring him one weekend."

"You'd make a wonderful father. When I watched you with those children, I knew you were in the perfect profession. You are truly blessed for that. Because most people work because they have to. You work because you love to."

"I know you understand, because you feel the same about your writing. I'm just surprised that it took you so long to recognize it."

"Creative people don't always get the support or respect other professionals get. Then you put 'romance' in the mix and it's even worse. Look at all the grins and elbow jokes you get when people talk about romance novels. When you read interviews and reviews of literary fiction, it's taken much more seriously. Yet, readers truly enjoy romance novels. Most people crave it in their lives. They want that one someone who thinks they are the most special person."

"Don't we just?"

"But romance has always been considered a woman's thing, and just like everything else women have done, it isn't considered serious."

"I bet the money publishers make from it is taken seriously."

"You bet it is."

From the museum, they strolled back to the boat and explored the port. They went through several shops, even a shop featuring pirate gear.

When they were on the boat again and sailing for home, David asked, "So what do you think is the key to a productive relationship? What do you think is the key to a lasting marriage?"

"There's a difference between a good and happy marriage and a lasting one. Couples have had lasting marriages through the centuries whether they were good or not. They were forced to tough it out. But I'll be the first to say that I've never been married, so I'm no expert." She paused in thought before she continued. "I think the most important thing is to continue nurturing each other," she said, gazing into the sound. "Just think about friendships. They last because friends nurture them. If they didn't, the friendships would die. I think just because two people sleep together, eat together, and pool their money, they take each other for granted. Being good to one another is a choice. Most people are good to their friends. Why not their spouses? At least that's the kind of marriage I want."

"So the man who marries you has to make it his life's work to throw roses at your feet?"

"I want him to feel that I'm worth—that *we're* worth taking some time for. That's all I'm saying. I know life interferes, children come and they take time, but I don't want 'us' to be put on the back burner and forgotten about until he retires. Because then it's almost too late. Too many good years have been wasted," she said. "Now aren't you sorry you asked?"

"Never. I'm getting to know the real Delilah," he said, looping a finger around a curl. "So tell me, from where do those views come? Do your parents have that kind of marriage?"

Delilah thought before she spoke. "My parents are complete opposites. My dad is a fun-loving, happy-go-lucky man. He likes golf. He tries to get my mother to do things with him sometimes, but he can't. My mother works, and that's practically all she does, besides going to church. Don't get me wrong. Daddy works, too, but he leaves work at the job. His time at home is his own."

"At least I know where you got your work ethic from."

"Yes. But since I've been renting your cottage,

I've begun to see that I want a meaningful life, too. I don't mind working and working hard. I want a happy medium. There are many other things to enjoy. And I don't want to forget that."

David squeezed her hand. He'd begun to do that quite often lately. "You won't forget it. I think you've learned the best from both parents." They enjoyed the quiet for moments.

"You know, the Robertses, my mom and dad, they have that kind of marriage. I think it's the reason it was so easy to love them. They loved each other and I could see they had love to spare for Carter and me, although Carter had been in so many foster homes that he didn't trust their love. He was grown and had moved out long before he trusted anyone. Other than me, that is. We formed a bond right from the start. Two lost souls, we were. But the Robertses loved us. They made a place in their home and hearts for us."

"They must have been exceptional people."

"They are. I want you to meet them."

Delilah tripped. David caught her before she fell flat on her face. She stood still a moment absorbing his words before her legs were stable enough to walk again.

When a man tells a woman he wants her to meet his parents, then he's usually ready to take the relationship to another level. Delilah contemplated how she felt about that. Was she ready for that? In a sense they had already elevated their relationship.

*He wants me to meet his parents.*

It was one thing having fantastic sex between the sheets. Making love was private. Going home to meet Mom and Dad was entirely different.

\* \* \*

They were exhausted by the time they returned from their boat trip. They showered and fell asleep. When they awakened, they made love, tender, wonderful lovemaking that brought tears to Delilah's eyes.

The next day they viewed underwater wreckage and the waterfowl museum.

Late that afternoon, they picked up Midnight from the sitter. She was so happy to see them she was jumping and slobbering all over them.

"Get down, you mangy creature," Delilah said, but rubbed her fur anyway. Midnight might belong to David, but she felt the dog was hers, too. They loaded up in David's Porsche and headed home.

After only a few weeks, this place felt more like home than any place she'd lived since she left her parents. They arrived home, ate dinner, and tried to savor the last vestiges of the weekend.

David said, "You thought I was going to keep you cooped up in the cottage, didn't you?"

"If you did, I'm sure we would have found something interesting to occupy our time, but I'm not complaining," she said, walking her fingers up his chest. David was lying on the sofa and Delilah was on top of him.

Midnight barked, then put her front paws on Delilah's back.

David laughed. "She's happy to be home."

Delilah groaned, dropped her head to David's chest.

"I may as well let her out. It's back to the grind tomorrow and I haven't done laundry."

She rolled off the couch and let Midnight out. Then she gathered and sorted laundry. She wondered how she'd sleep that night, she felt so invigorated. She wasn't ready for the weekend to end.

By the time the first wash load was started, she went to join David, but he was fast asleep.

Delilah went outside and Midnight charged to her.

"Come on, girl. Let's take a walk," she said. While they walked, Delilah let her mind wander. She thought about her book and began to organize in her mind the things she could use that she'd seen the last two days.


David was roused from his sleep by the doorbell. He expected to see Delilah beside him, but quickly realized that both she and Midnight were gone.

He answered the door to Louise. She wore a sleeveless beige pantsuit. Although it was still warm outside, she still managed to look cool. He wasn't surprised that she knew he owned a cottage here. The medical community was small and people talked.

"It's been a while," he said.

"Oh, David, we were once friends. You don't have to be so formal with me." When he didn't move to open the door, she said, "Aren't you going to ask me in?"

"Sure." He pushed the screen door open.

"Have a seat," he said, and poured her a glass of Delilah's lemonade. "So what brings you here?"

Taking her time, she sipped the lemonade. "Delicious. Don't tell me you learned to cook. Not too sweet, not too tart. A mixture of lemon and lime, isn't it?"

"Like you said, I'm not much at cooking. Delilah made it. She's a fabulous cook."

Her eyelid flickered. "I see. Well, it's delicious."

David leaned back in the single chair. "I know you didn't come here for lemon-limeaid."

"Are you trying to get rid of me before . . . Delilah, was it . . . returns?"

David remained silent.

"I'm sure you've heard that Spiedel and I have parted ways."

David shrugged. "I'm no longer involved with you or your practice. I don't keep up with the news."

"Well, he's moving to California and joining a practice with some college friends. I don't want to work in a one-physician office. It's a lot to handle. It would give me virtually no downtime. With a partner, even if the practice was busy, at least each of us could get every other weekend off."

That arrangement sounded too normal and too convenient on the heels of Wayne's resignation. But David didn't know if he even wanted to work with Louise again.

"I'm not asking for a personal relationship, only a professional one. I know that too much has happened for us to consider going in that direction. Although if I had it to do all over again . . . I thought you were dead, David," she said softly. "Please don't hold what I did against me professionally. I was really in a terrible situation. I had no choice."

David wasn't going to broach the issue that Louise had never loved him. She was only using him, the way she used Spiedel, who eventually got stuck with her. But that was personal. It had nothing to do with any professional relationship.

"I don't have a grudge against you. As you can see, I've moved on."

"I know that. And I'm sure your Delilah is a big part of that."

"Yes, she is."

"Please think about it. Margaret says you were on a short vacation. I don't want to intrude on your time. This isn't something I felt could wait. As part of our separation, I'm getting most of the equipment. Duplicate equipment can be sold off to generate cash for the partnership. I'm willing to invest my share."

Louise stood and David walked her outside, where he saw Delilah approaching the door with Midnight, who barked upon seeing Louise. Before either of them could stop her, Midnight had her paws on Louise's pristine suit. As Delilah pulled her back, wet paw prints from her mad dash into the ocean left a discernable stain.

Louise screeched.

"Bad dog," Delilah said, rubbing Midnight's side.

"Sorry about that, Louise," David said. "I'm sure we have something that will remove it."

Louise was brushing furiously at the stain. "Don't worry about it. I'll just put it in the cleaner's. You always loved animals."

Delilah hated the familiar way the woman behaved with David, but she was sure her jealousy was unfounded.

"Delilah, meet Louise Spiedel."

"David, you know I never used my married name.

And now there really isn't any reason to." Louise extended a hand to clasp Delilah's.

"It's a pleasure to meet you," she said.

With a questionable eyebrow raised to David, Delilah said, "Same here."

*So this is the infamous Louise who broke David's heart,* Delilah thought. And what on earth was she doing here? This woman was on the make, she was sure.

"Well, think about my proposition, David. It was a pleasure meeting you, Delilah."

Delilah gave her a smile that she hoped revealed that she knew what this woman was about.

"I know what you're thinking," David said as Louise drove down the path. He opened the door for Delilah. "But it's totally wrong."

"How do you know what I'm thinking?"

"By the look on your face."

Delilah dug some food for Midnight out of the bag. The dog hopped around as if she hadn't eaten in weeks.

"Just wait, girl. I'm trying to feed you." She set the bowl on the floor, then filled her water dish with cool water.

"Now, since you've taken care of that chore, perhaps we can discuss this like civilized adults without you getting angry."

"I'm all ears." Anxiety churned in her stomach. She didn't trust Louise.

"I didn't mention this to you because I didn't want work to intrude on our vacation. Wayne told me Friday that he's leaving for Philadelphia. His uncle has a general practice there that he wants to turn over to his son in a few years. He wants to add pediatric services in his office. And Wayne has accepted."

"I'm sorry. I know you were hoping he'd stay on."

"The office needs a second pediatrician."

Suspicious, Delilah asked, "What does this have to do with Louise?"

"Louise has recently separated from her husband."

Delilah crossed her arms. "The husband she jilted you for."

"She thought I was dead."

"So you're making excuses for her already? You were barely missing a month when she got married. Did you forget that?"

"No."

He was so defensive he didn't have a clue, Delilah thought. Like a fool, she'd gone and fallen for somebody else's man. Even though he was sleeping with her, clearly a portion of his heart still belonged to Louise.

"I know what's going on in your misinformed head. I'm not in love with Louise. I've known that for a very long time."

David hadn't made her any promises. The assumptions had been in her head. "Hmm. Truly, David, your business has nothing to do with me."

"I care for you. What we've shared for the last few weeks entitles you to a lot. I'm too old to go to bed with a woman to satisfy an itch. If this weren't leading somewhere, I wouldn't have spent so much time with you." He paced. "Damn it, Delilah, I care about you more than I thought I would. This isn't a cheap fling. Your opinion matters. Ever since I've met you, I've unconsciously included you in my plans."

Delilah wanted him to tell Louise *hell no,* but she couldn't do that.

"What do you want to do, David?"

"I don't know. She just sprang it on me. I haven't had time to think about it, much less make a decision."

"Well, you think about it and do what suits you best."

"And you're going to leave it like that?"

Delilah sighed, tried to be reasonable. "How did you like working with her before?"

He watched her carefully. "She's a wonderful physician. If I were to find another partner, I'd want someone with her capabilities."

"Then I guess you have your answer."

"It's not that simple, though. It's . . ." He swiped a hand across his face. "I just don't know. Suddenly I was facing seven-day workweeks. Now . . . I don't know." He raked his hands through his hair. "I'll still interview physicians who might be interested."

"I don't want the rug pulled from under me when I least suspect it or to find myself on my butt and clueless," Delilah warned.

"That's not going to happen."

With someone else, Delilah would have bailed before she got hurt. She realized it was already too late for that. David was about to take a step back into his past and she didn't know if he'd dealt with it completely.

"You can't decide on the spur of the moment. Just give yourself time to think about it."

But Delilah could tell that he really wanted to work with Louise. The question was, was it professional or was it personal?

# Chapter 7

"You need to kick that hussy to the curb, you hear me?" Glenda said. "Just tell him, hell no. Find another partner, a male preferably."

Delcia was in the tea shop trying to get some comfort from sister friends.

"I can't do that. Choosing a partner is a professional decision," Delilah said, sipping on tea to soothe her rattled nerves.

"You know David loves you, don't you?" Cecily said.

"He has never said that. Not once."

"Have you told him that you love him?"

Delilah shook her head and ran her hand around the cup rim.

"Honey, I saw the way he was watching you at the cookout."

"Since when didn't men love my body? But I want to be more than breasts, butt, and hips."

"You are, honey. You've got a heart of gold when you aren't scheming," Glenda said.

"I can't tell you how much I appreciate that," Delilah said with veiled sarcasm.

"It's the truth."

"I don't scheme. I might have to plot to get things done, but it's all in good faith. Besides, we can't solve one thing sitting around this table."

"But you feel better after getting it off your chest," Glenda said.

"I don't know. But I know that I brought work home that I have to complete before tomorrow. Thanks for listening."

"That's what friends are for."

Glenda had called Delilah a schemer. Perhaps she was.

Delilah thought of her parents as she drove home. At times she'd felt like a pawn between them. If she wanted to see a movie her mother didn't want her to see, her father would take her and say, "Don't tell your mother." Or when her parents fought, he'd take her places and she could tell when he was hurting.

And then as a teenager, she never knew how to deal with men who approached her when her body started filling out. Mama told her to ignore the boys and pray. So she learned to be cunning. She learned to maneuver men without putting out.

Sometimes it was tough playing it straight, but she was trying to be real with David.

Every morning that David stayed with Delilah, she prepared breakfast for him before he left for the office. That morning she didn't even turn over when the alarm woke him. He grabbed a bagel on his way out. He knew he was in the doghouse.

Got treated worse than the dog. She fed Midnight. Women.

He'd planned to propose to her the night before, but after Louise interrupted their vacation, and with Delilah being so out of sorts, she'd probably have thrown the ring in his face. He was damned if he did and damned if he didn't. Had he asked her, she would have said he'd proposed to convince her that he wasn't in love with Louise, or something equally ridiculous.

After Delilah had given him the chilly shoulder last night and after he'd simmered down enough to think logically, he came to the conclusion that joining their practices would produce a workable situation for him and Louise. His practice was larger than Louise's. But she was a capable, and even more, a caring physician. If Louise was true to nothing else, she was true to her patients.

The other benefit was that if they worked together, he'd have time for an outside life to spend with Delilah and children, even Kendall if Delilah agreed to adopt him.

And he wasn't in love with Louise. Hadn't been for a very long time. There was no mistake about that.

It even surprised him that he felt nothing more than curiosity when she came to the cottage. He knew he wasn't in love with her, but he'd expected to feel . . . well, something. But there wasn't anything.

And if that was the case, how did one trust love if the person you *thought* you were in love with couldn't even conjure up a flutter of the heart three years later?

Was the answer as simple as that it wasn't love in the first place? And if it wasn't, how the hell did you tell when it was real? Because he certainly felt as if he was in love with Delilah. He tried to think of what his feelings for Louise had been three years ago. The sad thing was he couldn't really remember.

Louise and he had met in college. They'd been in the same study group, and for some reason they began to hang out together. Louise wanted to open a practice once she graduated, and so did he. He respected her skill and dedication. Their feelings were a natural progression of working so close together and working so hard once they graduated. Lots of medical couples met that way.

With Delilah it came unbidden, hot and piercing from the very beginning. Immediately, he was thrust into a state of confusion because it was so different from what he'd known before. There was no getting to know her before he felt his heart beating like a drum when he was around her. The attraction was just . . . there. . . . He could travel to the far corners of the earth and yet he couldn't hide from what he felt or reason it away, nor did he want to. And what he felt wasn't all sex. As she had explained her definition of marriage he'd wanted so much more than the meeting of bodies and souls.

If he could distinguish his feelings that clearly, then there was no question that he was in love. He only knew that he wanted to spend the rest of his life with Delilah.

Whether she believed he hid ulterior motives or not, he would not delay proposing to her.

Delilah met Sylvia for happy hour after work.

"I can tell when something's bothering you. What is it?" Sylvia asked.

"We're working on part of this homeland security proposal."

"Of course I know. I brought you on."

"We've hired book bosses, proposal managers, technical writers. And you know management is paranoid about everything, especially the people at Redcliff."

Redcliff was another company in Morehead City working on the proposal in a collaborative effort. Moore's Inc. and Redcliff would each share half of the proposal.

"We can only work on secure Web sites. We signed nondisclosure contracts," Delilah continued.

"We've always had to sign nondisclosure contracts. Are you going to get to the point today or in a month?" Sylvia asked impatiently.

"On this contract, we can't e-mail anything."

"And?"

"I think I tapped into a secure site at Redcliff. They're even more paranoid than Moore's."

"And?"

"I don't know, but I've worked with Redcliff's proposal manager on another contract, so she's accustomed to copying me on things. But the things in this file . . . I think . . . it's possible . . . she's sending information to a competitor."

"You think she's a mole?"

Delilah sighed. "I don't know what is going on."

"My God."

"The thing is, I'm not a hundred percent certain of it, and I wouldn't want to get anyone in trouble if it was an innocent mistake."

"But certain files are blocked. If you can get access to them . . ."

"The thing is, it isn't a file that has anything to do with this contract. It's . . . I don't know, she might be covering her bases in case we don't get this contract. She'll win either way."

"Do you trust Redcliff's proposal manager?"

"I have no reason not to."

"What if you're being paranoid simply because the managers at Redcliff are?"

Delilah thought about that, but . . . "Something doesn't feel right."

"We can both keep an eye on things and see what happens. I don't think Stuart would get involved in anything dishonest. It's his company and he cares about his employees. Now, I can't say the same thing for Redcliff. Those employees aren't nearly as satisfied. It seems a lot of people hate the CEO. But Moore's can't get the contract without working with them. We simply aren't big enough yet."

"Nothing says Moore's can't grow into a much larger company in a few years."

"If they're able to keep a proposal manager like you. The ability to get good contracts and employees doing a stellar job are the key to this business. Especially for a small company."

"Well, I'm here for now."

\* \* \*

Sometimes on Wednesday nights Carter, Ryan, and David met at Wanda's for drinks after work. Depending on his work schedule, frequently David didn't make it. Tonight he was there.

David ordered a beer and they sat at a corner table.

Somebody started the jukebox. The volume was turned up so loud that Patti LaBelle's voice nearly drowned out conversations.

Ryan's cousin Mark came over. He did the accounting at the campground.

"You know a man can't win with women now," he said as Ryan slid over to make room.

"Everybody's got women problems. What's your problem?" Ryan asked.

"Marcia still hasn't answered after I proposed." Then he hit David in the arm. "Here you got women tripping over you, and I can't even get the one to make up her mind. Go figure."

"I don't have women tripping over me."

"Not what I hear. Women are whispering all over the place. You got Louise, you got Delilah," he said with equal measure of disgust and envy. "Man, you got choices. Wish I were so lucky."

"What good would it do to have women hanging on each arm? Fifty of them aren't going to have you," David said, sipping on his beer.

"I'll tell you one thing, you know you're in trouble when the women start hovering together in their little tête-à-têtes. Home is no decent place for a man at that point. Delcia looks at me like it's all my fault," Carter said.

David put his mug on the table. "Is there anyone who hasn't heard about Louise's proposition?"

"I don't think so," Ryan said.

"You can get the pick of the litter now," Mark said.

"No wonder that girl won't marry you," Ryan said, slapping Mark on the shoulder. "Women aren't puppies."

"It's getting late. I've got to get home. Good seeing you all."

Carter walked out with David. "So do you need an ear? You know how I feel about both of them, but you know I love you, man. I'm here for you whatever you decide."

"I can count on that?"

Carter looked at him as if he wanted to hit something. "Do you even need to ask?"

David chuckled. "Doesn't take much to get you riled. I'll catch you later."

Just to ensure herself of a good night's sleep, instead of her usual walk along the beach, Delilah jogged. Midnight was in seventh heaven jogging along with her. Of course she couldn't keep up with the dog's gallop, but it was enough to tire her out. After less than a mile, she turned around and jogged back.

"Why couldn't David be like you? You didn't betray me. You put your dirty paws on Louise and growled at her. I'm going to buy you a treat tomorrow for being my champion."

Once Delilah returned to the house, she ran a tub and soaked for an hour. She needed the pampering, and she hadn't expected David to come from the mainland that evening. She'd already walked the dog and prepared for bed, although she'd planned to work an hour or two before she fell asleep.

At nine-thirty David arrived. When he came in he shoved his hands in his pockets as if something weighty was on his mind. He leaned against the doorjamb for long seconds before he advanced into the room.

"How do you really feel about me, Delilah?" he finally asked.

"Why do you ask?" His eyes were a little red. Had he been drinking?

"Because I love you and I want to know if you feel the same way about me."

"You're sober, aren't you?"

"Of course. I only had one beer. I don't drive drunk."

Delilah carried a hand to her chest. Never had a man said he loved her and really meant the words. But looking at David in the twilight, and considering the seriousness of his mood, she knew that he meant the words. They weren't lines he used to get something out of her, she hoped.

She reached a trembling hand to his cheek. "I love you."

He gathered her in his arms. Tilted her chin. "Then marry me."

Delilah thought she would faint. Everyone viewed her as a man's playmate. Never someone to marry. Never to take seriously. She wanted to shout . . . *Yes!* But life had taught her caution. She'd taken too many chances in the past.

"Marry you? Do you really mean that?"

He chuckled. "I wouldn't have said it if I didn't."

"You want to marry me? Delilah . . ." She started to say "Delilah the flirt," but she'd promised to stop the negative remarks. If she didn't take herself seriously, nobody else would.

"You're the only Delilah Benton I know. You're the only woman standing here. Yes, silly, you."

She wanted to say the hell with reason. For the first time in her life, she was standing in the arms of love and she wasn't going to reason it away.

"Does this have anything to do with Louise?"

"I had planned to ask you Sunday, but I didn't think you'd believe me once we had the fight." He tugged her close.

"Do you realize this has been our first fight?"

"We didn't really fight."

"Close enough. The best part about it is making up. I know I love you, and it has nothing to do with Louise."

"I think she still loves you or at least still wants you."

"Even if it were true, and I don't believe it is, what does that have to do with us?"

"A lot if she's going to spend her time trying to get you back."

"May I say this for the last time? I don't want her."

"Uh-huh. I love you too, but I don't want to jump into anything too quickly. You seem to still have unresolved issues there."

"Delilah, the moment she married another man, the two of us were consigned to the past. I've put her out of my heart, out of my mind."

"The two of you have a history. We can't ignore that. You and I haven't known each other that long. We need to think about it, consider if we really know what we're doing."

Disappointed, David walked across the room, unbuttoned his shirt.

"Perhaps *you* need more time."

"I know what I feel for you," she said softly.

"Then believe me when I say I'm intelligent enough to know what I want."

"Love has nothing to do with intelligence. It's a matter of . . . well, it defies logic, doesn't it? It just is. People who are in love do crazy things. Make crazy commitments. And most of them, these days, don't work out."

"And many do. Are you saying no?"

"I'm not saying anything yet. I'm asking for some time. I think we both need time to seriously consider this step. It's huge."

David yanked his shirt off and threw it on the bed. "Does my decision about choosing a pediatric partner weigh into your decision?"

"I won't interfere in that decision. It's a separate issue. And one that you have to resolve."

"I'm not so sure about that. But if it wasn't keeping you from saying yes to my proposal, your jealousy would be kind of cute."

Her chin jutted in the air. "I'm not jealous. Merely concerned."

Approaching her, David smiled and kissed that chin, then her lips.

She hit him.

Later that night while they snuggled together listening to the news, the broadcaster announced that a body had been dragged from the ocean near Atlantic Beach.

Delilah wondered if . . . but Kendall said garbage bags in the plural. And the bags were dumped into the river, not the ocean, right?

"They told me you went on a vacation," Kendall said. David heard the feeling of rejection in his voice.

"Just a very short one," David told him.

"Where did you go?" Kendall asked.

"Actually I stayed around here. I didn't go any place."

"Why would you want to do that?"

"A chance to get away from work, really. It was nice. How is summer camp?"

"It's okay," he said with a shrug.

David wished he could tell Ken that he and Delilah were getting married and that they were going to adopt him. First, Delilah had not said yes, and second, since he didn't have a commitment, it was still too early to speak to Ken's social worker. As impatient as he was waiting for Delilah's answer, it would affect Ken even more.

What the hell was there to think about? Either she loved him or she didn't.

"I haven't seen you in a while. Guess you've been busy," Ken was saying.

"Pretty much. Let me check my schedule and see what's up for this weekend. How does that sound?"

"Want me to call you back?"

"Why not? Give me a couple of days."

"Okay. I've got to go."

\* \* \*

At the end of the day, while they made rounds in the hospital, David ran into Louise. They walked to their cars together.

"I hate to rush you, David, but I really need an answer soon. It's not easy finding a good partner. We know we work well with each other. The lease to my office will soon be up. I'm losing some of my equipment. I can't function only partially stocked."

"It's a hard decision to make."

"But purely business, and an advantageous one for both of us."

"I'll try to get back with you by the end of the week," David assured her.

"That's fair enough."

*Too bad Delilah won't feel that way,* David thought as he reached the Porsche.

Louise was walking to her car, two vehicles away, when she turned. "David I'd like to invite you and Delilah to dinner tomorrow night. A friend of mine will be there also and I think it will give us a chance to get to know each other again."

"Let me get back to you on that after I speak with Delilah."

"Well," she said, digging into her purse and retrieving a business card, "here's my home number." She scribbled on the back of it.

David looked down at the number when she handed the card to him, then shoved it into his pocket. So Louise was dating again, and soon after the divorce. But he guessed it wasn't so soon since they were probably separated for at least a year. One sunny side to this was that if Louise was dating, Delilah didn't have to worry about her trying to get him. And it might be good for Delilah to see Louise with another man.

As much as David hated the fact that Louise created a problem between Delilah and him, her jealousy kind of turned him on.

He drove out of the parking lot, flipped his cell phone on, and dialed Delilah.

"Am I still in the doghouse?" he asked.

"You were never in the doghouse."

*Yeah, right.*

"Where are you?" she asked.

"Just leaving the hospital."

"Just to show you you're still in my good graces, I've fixed dinner. Something light since it's so late."

"Well, thank you, darling."

"Is that why you called, to see if I'll feed you?"

"Actually, I ran into Louise at the hospital," he broached, cautiously.

"Oh?" Even her voice stiffened. He could just imagine her face. Louise was going to be a problem, still, he thought.

"She invited us to dinner tomorrow night. I told her I'd get back with her after I spoke with you."

A pregnant pause. "Sure, why not?"

"Are you sure?" He could almost see her gritting her teeth.

"Yes."

"I'll let her know."

While David rode the ferry to the island, he confirmed the dinner with Louise.

The more he thought about it, and he'd been thinking about it a lot, having Louise for a partner would solve a lot of problems. Not that he couldn't *find* another partner, just that the adjustment period would have to be considered. And if he was to get someone straight out of medical school, then he'd have to teach. That person couldn't be a full partner and wouldn't have the responsibility of one.

He hoped the fact that Louise had a new boyfriend would convince Delilah that they could work together in a professional capacity—that Louise didn't have romantic aspirations for him.

Delilah pushed open the door and Stuart looked up from some papers on his desk.

"Got a minute?"

"Sure."

She was late leaving and quickly sat and launched into her spiel. "The young lady I worked with in Raleigh was doing a wonderful job with proposals. I want to hire her for a full-time position here. She isn't ready to manage a proposal yet, but she's quite capable."

"I've already given you cart blanche with hiring to get this job done."

"I'm not thinking of her in temporary terms. I'm thinking of a staff position for her."

"She's that good?" he asked and leaned back in his chair, forming a steeple with his fingers under his chin.

Delilah nodded.

"I'm impressed with the work you've done for us so far. I trust your judgment."

"But know that I don't plan to stay on after this project. I will stay long enough for you to hire a good replacement, even help you find one if you choose."

"I appreciate that. Hire this person."

"Great. She already has clearance. I know you have to do your own check."

"Bring her on, then. And thanks for the tremendous job you're doing."

Delilah left and drove to David's house in Morehead City to dress for Louise's dinner. She carefully selected a sleeveless pantsuit that was both flattering and dressy. Although a dinner with David's ex wasn't the highlight of her day, she couldn't evade it simply because she was insecure. She never ran from anything in her life. She wasn't going to run away from David's ex either.

Was refusing to marry him before she was sure of Louise's motives an example of running away?

She'd have to think about that. What did Louise's motives matter if David was sure of his emotions? After all, their marriage wasn't about Louise. It concerned only the two of them.

Louise answered the door in a stunning royal-blue lounging outfit. It was sleek on her trim body. Her hair was worn up in a sophisticated style, displaying her neck. Delicate ringlets softened her face.

"It is so nice of you to join us," she said, every bit the gracious hostess.

"Thank you for inviting us, Louise," Delilah said, and handed over the flowers and a tall bottle of herb vinegar she'd brought.

"This is so kind of you. I love these herb vinegars on salad. Thank you," she said. "Come in and meet my friend."

The man who seemed to be around six-one stood to his full height. He was very attractive and looked to be at least three or four years younger than Louise. Delilah didn't have a problem with older women dating younger men. Men certainly did it all the time. At least he wasn't thirty years younger, and at least they were close enough in age to share common experiences.

They were halfway through dinner when the doorbell rang, seconds before a key rattled in the lock and the door opened.

"I hope you have something to eat..." The younger man came to a stop in the middle of the floor.

"Sorry. Didn't know you had company."

"This is my brother, Derrick Lester," Louise said. "Starving as usual."

"Had to work late. One of the guards was late coming in. But I don't mind. Overtime for me."

Louise stood. "We have leftovers. There's more in the kitchen. I'll fix your plate."

"I can get my own. Didn't mean to crash the party. I can eat in the kitchen."

"There's plenty of room at the table," Delilah said. "You look familiar."

"I've seen you at Moore's. I work there." He shrugged. "People don't usually notice or remember the guards."

"Obviously, I noticed you," Delilah said, but his statement was true. They seemed almost like fixtures at a place while everyone else passed through.

"Excuse me." He walked to the powder room, but by the time he returned, Louise had fixed him a plate as if he weren't old enough to fix his own.

He pulled a chair from up against the wall to the table. He seemed more approachable than Louise, more like a spoiled kid brother, while Louise played the role of mother hen. But Delilah liked his youthful veneer. *Must be nice to have siblings,* Delilah thought.

This other side of Louise was less cunning and more genuine. Delilah had wondered what David had found attractive about the woman. For the first time she saw what David had fallen in love with.

Delilah hoped with all her heart that Louise had real feelings for her date, but from the look of things he was just another man she was using.

# Chapter 8

The authorities identified the body that was dragged from the ocean as Stan Hamilton's. His death created a pall over the workers at Moore's. Everybody loved him. He was easygoing and friendly.

And he had been murdered.

"Who would want to murder him?" Delilah said, when they were in the ladies room.

"Beats me. He didn't hurt anyone. Rarely argued," Sylvia replied.

Marcia dried her hands on paper towels. "I heard the body was taken to the state coroner's office since he was murdered. I wonder what condition it was in."

"I don't even want to know," Sylvia said. "They haven't released it yet. It's really sad. And all this time everyone thought he'd run off."

"I heard someone say he was involved with drugs," Marcia said.

"I don't believe that for a moment," Sylvia replied.

"He didn't even like to take aspirin for headaches. Why would he take drugs?"

Marcia held both hands up as if it were a stick-up. "I'm only repeating what I heard."

"Can't believe everything you hear."

They separated and returned to work, but the pall of Stan's death still hung over Moore's.

By Friday, David had worn Delilah down. She finally said yes.

Shouting with laughter, he picked her up and twirled her in a circle. Delilah looped her arms around his neck and laughed aloud with him.

"This is either the smartest thing I've ever done or the dumbest. I don't know which yet. But I love you. I want to spend the rest of my life with you."

"You won't be sorry," he said. "Remember what you believe about marriage?"

"I do."

"We'll have all that and more."

Delilah smiled, believing him. "But there's something else we need to talk about."

"You mean other than a wedding date?"

She nodded. "Kendall."

"What about him?"

"I know you want to adopt him. You love him, don't you?"

David nodded. "I do. But it's a decision both of us would have to agree on. I won't force you into it," he said. He nudged her chin. "We haven't discussed children, whether you want them. Or even how many?"

"I've always had this dream of two. I'm an only

child. I think it's good for children to have siblings, somebody to talk to, someone to share with, someone who'll be there. I'd like for our children to have at least a sister or brother."

"We'll still have our two children. They'll have an older brother."

"They would like that."

"The Robertses were really good to me. They loved me and made me feel welcome for the first time. Kendall was in a loving home before his parents died. I'd like him to have that kind of stability again."

"He will."

"We'll wait until we talk to social services before we mention it to him," David said. "I hate to spring this on you immediately. I know you expected to have time to adjust to the two of us first. Marriage in itself is a big step. Taking on a child in the beginning can be pretty traumatic and intrusive."

"No matter what, we'll have to make adjustments. You have your idiosyncrasies and I have mine. In today's world, it's commonplace to start marriages with ready-made families."

"I know, but this is a first marriage for you. I want it to be special."

"It's your first marriage, too. It will be special."

"I'm pretty old to be getting married for the first time." He chuckled. "Hope you don't find me too set in my ways."

"I'm no spring chicken."

David nodded. "Kendall will be in school soon, and you can write all day once you finish this job."

"Writing isn't going to be a problem with him. David, you're trying to solve every problem even

before we're married. Marriage is one of those situations where we'll have to make up the rules as
we go. We can't plan for everything. Even if we
could, we might not like the outcome."

"You're a wise woman. You're so beautiful, so
damn beautiful that everyone underestimates you.
They look at that gorgeous body and face and for-
get there's a brain underneath that beautiful hair.
I'll be sure to never make that mistake," he said.
"I'm the luckiest man in the world."

Tongue in cheek, Delilah said, "Yes, you are."


"You what!" Carter said in disbelief.

"You heard me. I want you to be my best man,"
David repeated.

"David, David . . ."

"Don't start that. Delilah and I love each other.
Can't you be happy for me?"

"She's not the kind of woman you marry.
She's . . ."

The muscles in David's arms stiffened. "Don't
make me hit you."

"You're letting her come between us?" Carter
said in outrage. "Your brother? Your closest friend
in the world?"

"What if I said something inappropriate about
Delcia?"

Carter snickered. "Delcia is not Delilah. You remember Sampson?"

"It's only a name. Don't get caught up in a name."

"I wouldn't if her personality didn't fit so perfectly. Her mama aptly named her." Carter tried
reason. "David, Delilah isn't one of those women

who's going to wait meekly when you work long hours. You'll have to dance in attendance to her. She's not solid—"

David interrupted. "I'm not going to spend the next six weeks defending her to you. I'm marrying her, not you. Are you going to be my best man or not?"

Carter let out a whoosh of breath. "Yeah. I'll be your best man."

"Thank you. Well, I have to get back to the mainland."

"Where is it going to be held?"

"I'm thinking the church on the island."

"Where Delilah has barely stepped foot in since she's been here."

David chose to ignore the sarcasm. "It's not going to be a huge affair, but there are some colleagues I have to invite."

"And Delilah's family as well."

"Carter?"

"Yeah?"

"I know how your mind works. You feel threatened. You were a SEAL. You're used to strategic tactics. Don't approach Delilah. If she changes her mind, and I don't think you can make her, I'll be very unhappy."

"I wasn't thinking anything of the kind."

David glared at his brother. He knew better.


Early Saturday morning Delilah ran with David along the beach. Afterward, while he showered, she prepared breakfast.

"What are you going to do today?" he asked.

"Outlining plans for the wedding. Probably contact the church to see if it's available for our date."

"Delcia is a member. She might be able to help you."

"I don't really know her, but I'll get Cecily involved. She's a member, too. We have to pick out invitations right away. When would be a good time for you?"

"Choose whatever you like." Looking harassed, he started to the door.

"Don't you want—"

"You'll be better at that. I'm out of my element."

"At least let me know how many people you want to invite. And you need to start getting a list together. Is it just going to be friends of the families, or do you want to include business associates, too?"

"Both."

"David, it's your wedding, too. You can't leave it all to me."

"I'll have a list by the end of the week. Promise. Margaret has most of the addresses. She'll get something together for you."

Exasperated, Delilah said. "What would you do without Margaret?"

"I'd be lost."

"Coward."

At the door, he kissed her. "It's going to be hell leaving you in the mornings."

Delilah smiled. "Give you a reason to return early every evening."

As soon as David left, Delilah woke Sylvia with the news.

"Wait a minute. I was up partying until two this

morning. I'm not totally with it yet." The mattress squeaked in the background, sounding as if she was sitting up. "Now, repeat what you just said."

"I'm getting married, silly."

"To who?"

"I see you're going to drag this out. To David, who else?"

"You're kidding."

"No, I'm not."

"That was fast. You just met this guy. Are you sure? Do you know what you're doing?"

"Girl, you're shooting out questions like bullets." Delilah laughed, then sobered. "It's never felt this right before."

Delilah heard a rustle of covers in the background.

"How are you going to plan a wedding now?"

"I have no idea, but the wedding's in six weeks. Will you be my maid of honor?"

"Wild horses couldn't stop me."

"We've gone through a lot together, you and I. It wouldn't be right without you there. Plus, I'm dying for you to meet this great man I'm marrying."

"Delilah, you love him, don't you? You're not acting on your biological clock, are you? Because you've got to live with him after the babies come."

"As much as that clock has been ticking—and it has since the day I turned thirty—I'm not crazy enough to marry a man I don't stand a chance in hell of making it with, or don't love, just to appease it."

"You love him then?"

"I'm madly in love with him. I've never felt this

way before, never." She jumped up to pace because she wanted to do a wild dance around the
room.

"I'm jealous."

"I used to hate people who told me mine was
coming one day, so I won't say it although I fer-
vently believe it. Sylvia, who would have thought
I'd find a man I love this quickly? And a good man
who loves me. Not just someone who wants me for
decoration."

"You were never just decoration," Sylvia said quietly.

"I was always treated like icing. Forget the cake,
thank you."

"It's the idiots who don't look beyond the surface. And they deserve exactly what they get."

"Men are impressed with the outer package before they begin to look at what's inside."

"It's not an equal playing field."

When they disconnected, Delilah started a to-do
list.

Did she really want a huge wedding, or a small
intimate affair with close friends and family? David
wanted to invite business associates, so forget intimate.

She'd enlist Cecily's and Glenda's help in planning the reception. They'd lived here long enough
to know the ins and outs of the island. But then
she remembered she hadn't called her mother. For
some reason she hated to make that call. Her mother
had never been happy about any decision she'd
made, much less any of the boys she brought home.
None were good enough.

Her mother would be up early, probably putting

together dinner in the Crock-Pot before she left for the beauty salon.

"Hi, Mama," Delilah said when her mother answered.

"It's good to hear from you."

"Yes. I have two reasons for calling. First, I'm getting married in six weeks."

"I didn't know you were dating. How long have you known this man?" Holly Benton's voice was full of suspicion.

"Long enough to know we love each other."

"That's not saying much," she said. "Who is he?"

"His name is David Washington. He's the local pediatrician."

"You got a doctor this time. But is he a good man? A decent man? The profession doesn't make the man."

"You'll approve. He's a good man."

"Maybe your dad and I can get down there in a couple of weeks to meet him."

"I'd like that. Tell Daddy hi."

"If you had called yesterday, you would have caught him home. He left for an early golf game."

"I'll call one evening this week."

"You do that. He's been complaining that he hasn't talked to you lately."

"Tell him hi for me."

"Wait a minute. I need some details. Have you set a date yet?"

Delilah told her.

"I'll see what we can do about getting there to help you," her mother said, but Delilah knew her mother didn't miss days from work.

She said, "All right, Mama," anyway.

"You love this man, Delilah?"

Delilah closed her eyes briefly. "Yes, Mama."

"Well, good."

They disconnected, and when Delilah thought the morning rush had ebbed, she drove to Cecily's. There were several cars still in the yard. Young college-aged groups and families were carrying backpacks. Some held paper cups with the tea shop's logo on the side. Some sat on the porch and steps.

"You don't believe in long engagements, or taking six months to plan a wedding, do you?" Glenda asked, flipping through brochures.

"When the man makes up his mind, who am I to argue?" Delilah said.

Glenda tucked the package under her arm. "Come here and give me a hug with your sassy self. I'm happy for you."

"Carter is going to have a fit," Cecily said, "but I'm happy for you."

"Who cares what Carter thinks?" Glenda asked. "He's got his woman. I think Delilah's just what David needs. He needs a little spice in his life. For Christ's sake, the man only works and goes home. Comes to the cookouts alone. That's no kind of life for a healthy buck," she said. "You're going to have to chase the women off with a stick. Everybody thought he was still suffering over that Louise. I guess you showed them."

"Louise is one woman I'm not worried about." But in the back of her mind, she wondered sometimes. "Well, getting to business, we'd like to have the reception here."

"I have banquet rooms upstairs that you might like. Once we decide on how many people you're inviting I'll show you a menu. I have a package you can take home, and discuss it with David," Cecily said.

"We love customers like you where money is no object," Glenda said.

"I'm a relative. Don't I get a break?"

"Absolutely not."


David and Delilah met with Kendall's social worker during lunch on Monday.

"You have been spending time with Kendall on a regular basis for the last year, Dr. Washington, but adoption is a commitment that shouldn't be taken lightly."

"My fiancée and I are aware of that," David said.

"Have you spent much time with Kendall, Ms. Benton?"

"Some, but not as much as Dr. Washington."

"What was Kendall's reaction to you?"

"We get along very well."

"On weekend excursions, you can take him back to his foster parents when things get tense. But once you adopt, he'll be there every day. It will take some time to win his trust. How do you feel about bringing a new child into a new marriage?"

David clasped Delilah's hand in his. "We've discussed it and we're prepared to grow to know each other together. We don't expect it to be easy. But we already love Kendall. That has to count for something."

"I'd like you to take some classes. It would help you with what to expect from children who are dealing with grief. It will also help with bonding and examining some of the problems adopted children experience. There's an adjustment period that isn't always easy. Do you plan to adopt other children?"

The meeting took off from there and lasted over an hour. Delilah felt as if she'd been put through the wringer when they left.

After work, they drove to Dr. Sommar's house for dinner.

"If this keeps up, I won't have to cook very often," Delilah said.

"I thought it was time you met my father."

David drove up the long driveway to an imposing Georgian house. When he parked, two Pomeranians ran around the corner to greet them. He rubbed them both behind the ears before they dashed over to Delilah, barking at a high pitch. David grabbed them by the collar before they reached her.

"They're friendly, more likely to lick you to death," an imposing older man, the same height as David, said. "I'm Howard Sommars. And you must be Delilah."

They enjoyed a pleasant dinner and later Delilah and Sasha, David's half sister, walked together around the house. "I'm glad David met someone nice," she said. Her complexion was the same as David's, but she was Delilah's height.

Delilah smiled. "David tells me you're a psychiatrist."

"Yes, I delve into the problems of others." Sasha sounded troubled.

"You sound as if you have problems of your own."

"Who doesn't?" Sasha asked.

"Well, you're the shrink. Who do you go to when you need an ear?"

Sasha smiled. "Another psychiatrist, of course. I believe the friendly ear part is what most people need. A matter of having someone to listen. A sounding board. After that, many people can arrive at their own conclusions."

"Unfortunately, everyone doesn't have that convenient sounding board."

"That's what keeps people like me in business."

"And then there are the ones who really need help."

"Too true. I really have to go. Please have David bring you by my place sometime."

"I will. And I hope you can get out to the island. It's paradise on earth."

"Well, you have like minds. David described it just that way as well, which is why he wants to move there permanently. I hope he'll find a pediatric partner who will let him spend more time at home."

Delilah just nodded.

"Did I say something wrong?"

"No. It's just . . . I'm sure he's mentioned Louise."

Puzzled, Sasha said, "No, he hasn't."

"She wants them to join their practices."

Sasha nodded. "And how do you feel about that?"

"She's single, he's single." Delilah shrugged.

"How does he feel about it?"

"They worked well together before. He really wants a partner. And I think he really wants to work with Louise."

"But you're afraid that they'll restart their personal relationship?"

Delilah sighed, and looked off into the forest. "They didn't just date. They were engaged."

"But she's married. That shouldn't be an issue."

"She's divorced."

"Ah, I see. Do you trust David?"

"Of course. But I don't like the idea of temptation working with him every day."

"Temptation is always there whether it's an ex-fiancée or another beautiful woman. Can't get around that. But the issue isn't really temptation. It's the two of you. Do you love him? Does he love you? Do you trust him?"

"So it boils down to the two of us."

"Always."

"If only it were that simple."

"That's the funny thing. Life rarely is."


While Sasha and Delilah took their walk, Howard culled plants in the greenhouse, with David watching him.

"I understand you and Louise are considering joining practices," Howard said.

"Nothing's been decided."

Howard regarded his son, wishing there was some way of bringing their relationship closer. David had built an impenetrable brick wall against Howard. On the surface everything looked fine. Very sociable. Trouble was, their relationship never broke the surface barrier. He'd like to have more with his only son. He'd hoped to have more children, but his wife could only have Sasha. He longed to share the closeness with David he shared with his daughter. Howard kept telling himself David needed more time, eventually he'd come around.

The Robertses were his parents of the heart. And he was grateful that they loved him when he needed it most. He was envious. He knew he couldn't recapture those young years, but he wanted to create something special in the adult years.

"Do you think it's a wise decision going into practice with her again?" Howard continued. "How does Delilah feel about this?"

"She's leaving the decision up to me. Louise and I worked well together before. I'm sure we can work on a professional basis again."

"When you joined practices before you shared a personal relationship."

"I love Delilah. I don't love Louise. End of problem," David snapped.

"Does Delilah see it that way?"

David shrugged again.

Seemed he'd hit a nerve with the Delilah-Louise debacle, Howard thought.

"If you're searching for a partner, there are other alternatives. Did you choose Louise because you've worked well with her in the past and you don't want to consider another partner? Have you even spoken with other pediatricians?"

"Not yet. My schedule's been pretty hectic. Now the wedding . . ." David shrugged. "And we're trying to adopt Kendall."

"Pretty heavy load all at once."

"He needs a family. School starts soon and we don't want to switch him in the middle of the year."

Howard was sure that David saw himself in

Kendall. That was one hot topic that he couldn't broach, that David wouldn't allow him to interfere in.

Maybe this was something he should run by Sasha. She kept urging him to try to bring their relationship closer. He was a little hurt because David had been dating Delilah and had only now brought her by. Maybe he should be grateful that he visited with her at all.

Howard glanced at his son. He'd grown to love this man, his son, who resembled him in a younger form. He wished he could offer advice without David taking it the wrong way or throwing it back in his face. Patience, Howard thought. Perhaps, in time, things would work out.

"Raymond assured me the house will be finished at least a week before the wedding. So we need to select furniture," David said to Delilah.

"I'm sure you want to keep some of the furniture you already own."

"Maybe, not much. My place is much smaller. I'll give you carte blanche on that. Decorating isn't my strong suit and I can see that you have excellent taste."

"I'd prefer if we chose together. After all, you'll have to live with what we choose."

"Delilah, I'd just be a pole walking around the place with you."

"You're not that bad. You decorated your office and it's wonderful."

"Margaret decorated the office. She wouldn't let me choose anything."

"All right." Delilah pulled out the memo pad she was never without these days, and jotted down *furniture*.

"I'll probably spend a couple of days in High Point. We'll get it quicker if I order it from there. It can take three months for some things to arrive. And then there's the curtains. I have to go through your place to see what we can use."

"Probably not much. I decorated my place."

Delilah was beginning to feel pressured. "Maybe we should move this wedding back and give ourselves more time to take care of things."

"Absolutely not. Everything doesn't have to be done by our wedding date."

David pulled into a parking slot on the ferry.

"Six weeks is really rushed. I don't even have a gown yet. And all the preparations. I'm overwhelmed."

"You can take care of it. We could always elope."

"Our families will—"

David's lips pressing to hers stopped the barrage of words spilling from her mouth, the cloud of doubt filling her mind. For a moment, she forgot that she was in way over her head. She remembered that they were marrying because they loved each other. Everything else was just incidentals.

"David, I'm still going to write."

"I expect you to. I don't want you to get lost in my career or give up things that are important to you."

Not feel lost? *Please*. With the mountain of duties piling up, she already felt lost. She could forget trying to get any writing done before the wedding. But she'd at least attend the critique meetings, she promised herself. Her career was very important to her.

"Delilah, there's no reason for you to continue your job at Moore's, especially if it's more than you can handle. You're not going to work there after the wedding."

Delilah didn't like him assuming things. "Are you asking if I'll continue working there?"

"With the extra responsibility of Kendall, why would you want to?"

"I don't, but I'm committed to this project, and to helping them find a replacement for me. Jobs are on the line here. It's not just me. I do important work."

"I wasn't making light of what you do. I know your work is important." He massaged her shoulders. "I don't like it that you're so stressed. You're riddled with stress."

"If you had a schedule like mine, you'd be, too."

"I'm sorry, darling. Hire all the help you need. I'll help out where I can."

Delilah looked at him and knew he was totally clueless. What the hell was she getting herself into?


"Mom? Dad?" Delilah stared at them unbelieving. This was a mirage. The Bentons weren't at her front door.

"Hey, baby." Her daddy grabbed her in a big bear hug and swung her around.

"James Benton, if you don't put her down, you're going to be singing the hurting-back blues tonight," Holly Benton said.

"I'm still strong enough to lift her. She's as light as a feather."

When her dad set her on her feet, she kissed and hugged her mother.

"What are you doing here?" Delilah asked.

"Staying a few days to help with the wedding plans," her mother said.

Her father looped an arm around her shoulder. "I can't believe I'm losing my baby to some knucklehead."

"What did you think, she was going to stay single forever?" her mother chastised.

"No, but . . . it's a tough pill for a father to swallow."

"Are we going to stand outside all morning?" her mother asked.

"No, no. I'll help with the luggage," Delilah said.

"I can get it, sweetheart. Were you going some place?" her father asked.

"Shopping for a gown with Cecily and Delcia."

Delilah helped her father unload the car, changed the linens on the bed, and got cool drinks for her parents before Cecily and Delcia arrived. The sofa in the living room was a Hide-A-Way. She'd sleep there.

# Chapter 9

Delcia took Delilah's father to her parents' home before the women left for the mainland with Holly in tow. Clay Anderson pulled out the golf clubs before the women left.

"I knew there was something I was missing. Where's the mutt?" Cecily asked. "He didn't try to take a bite out of me."

"Midnight wouldn't bite you. David took her to his house on the mainland so the dog sitter could exercise her. He doesn't leave her alone all day."

"He treats that dog like a toddler," Delcia said. "Who ever heard of such in the country? We let them run wild."

Delilah scoffed. "This is David. He loves his pet."

"When do we meet David?" Holly asked.

"Tonight. He's in his office today."

"You're going to have to do something about his hours," Cecily warned.

"I've got enough on my plate," Delilah said. "I have to leave something for him to do."

"Where to first?" Delcia pulled behind other cars leaving the ferry.

Delilah rattled off the names of shops she'd visited so far. "Nothing suited me there."

They drove to several bridal stores and Delilah was quickly losing patience.

"I can't find a thing. Not anything close to what I'm looking for," Delilah said, disgusted.

"We'll find something," her mother said. "Be patient."

"It's early days yet and we will help you until you find that perfect dress," Delcia said. "They have plenty of dresses here. If not, they can order something or we can shop elsewhere, even if we have to go to Wilmington or Charlotte. I don't think it will come to that."

Delilah sifted through the dresses on a rack, her face turned down because nothing she saw was unique. At least the saleslady in this store was very helpful. Even now the woman was frantically looking for something to appeal to her.

"Thanks for taking the time off," Delilah said. "I know how busy you all are and I'm sounding unappreciative. This is your busy season. I shouldn't bother you with shopping."

"Are you kidding?" Cecily asked. "Marriage is special. We wouldn't dream of sending you out on your own. Besides, it's fun."

"This one just came in. We only have one," the saleslady said. "I hope it fits you. Let me see." She pulled the dress out of the plastic bag.

"That's absolutely beautiful," Cecily said.

"It looks like you," Delcia said.

Delilah agreed and prayed it was in her size and

that it would look as lovely on her as it did on the rack.

"Let's try it, shall we?" The woman whisked the ladies back to the changing room and hung the dress on the door. "While you try this on, I'll look for others," she said. "I'll be back in just a moment."

"You take a seat," Holly said to Cecily. "You've been on your feet a lot."

Cecily sank into a chair and Delcia and Holly helped Delilah into the dress.

"Oh. Oh. This is it. Don't you think so, Mrs. Benton?" Delcia stood back with her hands on her hips.

"She's a beauty all right."

"Look at yourself," Delcia said. "But not here. Let's put you on the platform for the main effect."

Delilah trooped out of the room with Delcia holding the train. It was a very long train, which Delilah adored.

"Ever since I saw *The Sound of Music* I've loved long trains," she said.

"It's grand."

Cecily stood. "You're going to take David's breath away. He'll be a babbling idiot through the ceremony," she said.

Delcia stood back and Delilah finally looked at the dress. It was gorgeous. Absolutely perfect. Bare shoulders and sleeveless, but it was also elegant.

The saleswoman pinched a little extra material at Delilah's waist. "We'll only have to take this in a little. And heels would set this dress off wonderfully," she said.

"David is tall enough that you can wear heels and still look petite."

"I'll bring accessories," the woman said, knowing she'd finally made a sale. "Gloves, purse, we'll try on veils."

When the woman walked off, Delilah said, "This woman deserves her commission."

"She would have made this sale if she had to pull out a sewing machine and sew that dress herself," Cecily said.

The pressure that was stressing Delilah began to lift. Finally, something was working. She had only a million things left to do instead of a million and one.

Delilah had chosen the shoes, purse, and other accessories before they left the bridal shop.

Cecily was eating a salad in the backseat as Delcia drove to the printing shop to select invitations.

"Did David give you a guest list yet?" Delcia asked.

"Margaret, bless her heart, faxed it to me on Friday. I have never seen anyone as clueless as David."

"It's time that you knew men were deficient that way."

"And then some. I've cut pictures of furniture out of magazines to show David. He tells me if it's okay with me it's okay with him. He hasn't a clue."

"A good thing with David. You have seen the furniture in his house, haven't you?" Delcia said. "He finally broke down and got somebody to pick out something for the living room."

"Unfortunately."

"He's a brilliant doctor, but when he says he doesn't have decorating sense, the man is right on target. It's best he stays out of that," Delcia said. "If you want a decent-looking home, that is. The architect made many of the decisions on the beach house. You need to thank Ray because your fiancé has no talent for space or color or arrangement."

"So what are you going to do, and when are you going to find the time to search for furniture?" Cecily said.

"The gown, the reception, and the invitations are the big things. Now that they're taken care of—"

"Except for the invitations."

"Yes, but she's already written out what she wants," Delcia said.

"It's just a matter of choosing among the three I like and then I can order them. And I'll be able to breathe again."

"You needed six months to prepare for this wedding," her mother said.

"We didn't have that much time," Delcia said. "And we managed to pull it together."

"Well, as soon as the invitations arrive, Delcia, Glenda, and I will help you address them," Cecily said.

"I'll help, too," her mother said.

"You can take that much time from the beauty salon?"

"I've rescheduled to take two weeks off."

Delilah was shocked. First her mother had insisted on paying for the wedding. Had even said she and her father had saved up to pay for it. And as much as Delilah argued that she could afford it, her mother told her it would insult her father. This wasn't just her day, it was their day as well. Let them do their part.

Delilah wouldn't think of them paying for the entire thing. They had their retirement to consider and she could afford it.

And now, her mother was taking two weeks off from work to help her plan. Her mother never took time from work.

"How many hours is this going to take us?" David asked when Delilah ordered him to hold the tape measure.

"Stop complaining. We're just beginning." She was determined that he contribute. They were in the new house measuring the rooms for furniture and curtains.

David had charmed her mother and father instantly. They'd already fallen in love with him. That charming personality was the key. With some men, you knew it was fake, but David's charm was real.

"Why don't you just hire a decorator and let her do the work?"

"Because we have to live here. And I have an idea of what I want. I am going to have someone make the curtains."

"Graph paper. Exact measurements. Why can't you just buy a set and have it hauled in? The room is big enough that just about anything you buy will fit."

Delilah shook her head, ready to bop him upside the head. And then he smiled innocently and she couldn't help but love him. "Just take the tape measure and do as I say. You're not getting out of this, no matter how much you complain."

"I'm not complaining, but it looks like you need a week to do these measurements."

"We have tonight. I'm going to High Point tomorrow. And you're taking Midnight with you tomorrow, remember?"

Before he could answer, Sasha came in rattling paper. "Is he still complaining?"

"I'm almost at the point of knocking him on the head."

"At least that's something he and Dad have in common," Sasha said.

"There are no chairs around this place?" Dr. Sommars asked.

"You're not supposed to sit down, Dad. We're measuring. Which room do you want us to tackle next, Delilah?"

"Kendall's bedroom, please." Delilah shuffled through her pages in the notebook until she found the proper sheet. Then she handed it to Sasha.

"Come on, Dad. We aren't half through with you."

With a look of defeat and an eyebrow raised to his son, Dr. Sommars followed his daughter out of the room.

With three couples working, Delilah with David, Holly with James, and Sasha with Howard, they worked two more hours before they completed all of the measurements. Afterward, David, Howard, and James went to the cottage to eat while Sasha, Holly, and Delilah walked through the rooms. Delilah talked about how she planned to decorate each room. Sasha and her mother added suggestions.

"I wish I could go with you to help out, but I can't get out of my appointments," Sasha said.

"I'll be fine. These measurements help a lot. At least I know what I'm working with and what I need. I don't expect to find everything there. Some of it will have to be done after the wedding. But at least we'll have beds to sleep in and a couple of couches to sit on."

"I'm going with her. Your dad wanted to go too, but we don't need him along to sit in the car sleeping. He loses patience with shopping quickly," Holly said.

The ladies went to the cottage and ate.

Later David pulled her outside, leaving the guests in the cottage. They walked to the beach and he held her in his arms and kissed her.

"I miss you. I like your parents, but how long did you say they would be here?"

"One more week," she said.

David groaned. "They're cramping my style."

Her smile was mischievous when she said, "If you do without for a while, you'll feel more like a newlywed when we marry."

"It isn't safe having a horny doctor running around the place."

Delilah laughed and ran her hands over his shoulders and arms.

"I miss you, but I kind of like this courting, and seeing you frustrated."

He dipped his head, nuzzling her neck. "You're going to pay for that."

Delilah moaned. "I can't wait."

\* \* \*

Sasha, Howard, and David left for the mainland.

Delilah showered and gathered her clothing for the next day, then she grabbed papers to complete an hour's work that had to be done before tomorrow. It was midnight, but David called before she could get into the project.

They'd attended an adoption preparation class the previous night and were given overwhelming information. Delilah was trying not to think about all the possible problems they could encounter.

"More is involved than we thought," Delilah said.

"After we left, you looked as if you were stunned. Are you sure you don't want to wait a few months? Ken doesn't know yet and it isn't too late."

"I still want to. The two of you are already attached. He really is a wonderful boy."

"There will still be adjustments."

"It's something we'll have to work on. Even with our natural children, problems will crop up. Life isn't perfect," Delilah said. "I've been thinking about Louise a lot. After taking this class I know you're going to need to spend more time at home. If you really want her as a partner and if it will give us more family time together, then I don't want to stand in the way of her becoming your partner."

"Do you really mean that?"

"I wouldn't have said it otherwise. Kendall has a lot of grief and adjusting to deal with. It will help having you around more."

"You won't regret it," David promised. "Louise and I worked well together before. Our schedules will be so busy that when we're there we're working. It's going to be even busier with the practices combining, but at least I'll have every other weekend, and every other night, off. Actually it should be better than now because Wayne came here directly from residency. I had to train him in many areas."

"Good. It helps that she's dating. I better not catch her eye on you."

David moaned. "Delilah, you have to trust me. There's nothing outside of business between us."

"I trust you."

He chuckled. "Why don't I believe that?"

"I have no idea."

"I'm going to miss you the next two days."

"I really love shopping, so I hope looking through acres of storeroom samples is going to be like a trip to a candy store."

"I'm glad your mom's going with you."

"Me too. It surprises me that we're getting along better than we ever have," Delilah mused.

"You're both adults. She can deal with you on another level now. Try to stop by before you leave town tomorrow."

"I'll try."

"Love you, darling."

Delilah pushed the off button and placed the phone on the hook. She gathered her papers and went to the office to start work.


When Delilah arrived at work at six-thirty Friday morning, Derrick waved at her.

"This is early for you, isn't it?" he asked.

"Need to leave early."

"For a change. You're known for working late."

"I didn't know I was the talk of Moore's."

"Of course you are. You're beautiful and you're kind of running things. You're not snooty like some people," he said. "You have a lot of power, so people talk."

"I see. Well, good seeing you. I have loads of work to do before my meeting."


With magazine pictures, graphs, and notes on the rooms in a notebook, Delilah left very early for High Point with its showrooms with acres of furniture.

Delilah had spent hours on the Internet and made plans ahead of time listing the order in which she would visit each store. Rooms were listed with the items she needed to purchase for each.

"You aren't going to be able to continue at this pace," Holly said, when Delilah picked her up from Howard's house. Her father was spending the weekend with him.

"Things will get better after the wedding," Delilah said and maneuvered onto the highway. They were arriving late and she'd already made hotel reservations.

"You're adopting, and that isn't going to make things easier."

"We'll adjust."

"I'm just saying you're doing everything. David is a wonderful man, but you're setting a precedent by doing everything yourself. You may have roped him into measuring for furniture, but I don't see that anything will change in the future. You'll raise Kendall. David might spend a little time with the boy now and then, but I don't see him taking on the bulk of the responsibility."

"I know things seem hectic now, Mama. Everything is happening at once. The house, the wedding, and Kendall. I'm not going to be working this job for long after we marry. I'll have more time at home."

"I thought you wanted to write books," Holly said. "That's a job and it takes time to create stories. It's a full-time job. I know you haven't been writing on a regular basis. Not enough time."

"I didn't think you noticed I wanted to write or that it was important to me."

Holly shifted in her seat to gaze more closely at Delilah. "Girl, I notice everything about you. Always have. Where do you get such notions?"

Delilah shrugged. "I don't know. It's just . . . you've always worked so hard."

"I always had you with me. Why do you think I kept you in the shop after school? It was more to spend time around you and teach you values. It was more than the work."

Holly reached over the console, tucked a strand of Delilah's hair behind her ear. "You're beautiful, always were. You heard stories of women's lives in that shop, their pain, their pleasure, their hardships. You learned to work for what you want, not to stand on looks. You're brilliant," her mother said. "I didn't want you to grow up settling to be satisfied as some man's decoration. I could wash heads, girl. Always have."

"I didn't know that," Delilah said quietly.

Holly looked forward. "You weren't supposed to. And there was just too much trouble in the streets. Boys always wanting to chase you. The shop was your haven. You were safe there."

Delilah had never viewed her upbringing with her mother's perspective.

"I'm worried about you, Delilah. You should have taken more time for this wedding. Give yourself time to get things done. The invitations haven't gone out yet."

"Everything will be okay, Mama. You'll see."

"For your sake, I hope so."


Delilah and her mother arrived at the first store when it opened. Most of the people were roaming around alone. In the third one, once the salesperson discovered how much furniture Delilah planned to purchase, she offered suggestions and was generally very helpful. Delilah showed her pictures and she steered Delilah to furniture that was in line with what she wanted.

Delilah and her mother spent the rest of the afternoon selecting various pieces. She was glad her mother was with her. Late that evening when they stopped by a restaurant for dinner, she hadn't furnished the entire house, but she'd made a dent in the items she needed to get started.

Originally, she'd planned to spend two days in High Point, but since she'd found the necessary pieces, she and her mother would leave in the morning.

She loved this area of North Carolina and would always want to visit the Raleigh area again. But there was something about the island that was home. She'd always loved the beach, but it was more than that. It was a feeling of truly belonging for the first time in a very long time. It was being loved and completely accepted for who she was. She didn't have to pretend with David.

Gazing at her mother across the table, Delilah was very glad that her parents had come. She gained a new perspective her mother had never revealed before.

David was on his way out of the office when Louise called.

"I've decided to take you on as a partner," he said.

"I'm so glad. You won't regret it."

"Now that I'm getting married, I want to spend more time at home," David said. "I'm still thinking of bringing on one more person. With the practices combined, we're still short at least one person."

"You're right."

"I guess at this point, we can get together with our respective lawyers and accountants and see what we can come up with."

"Sounds good to me. We could talk about it ahead of time. Are you free tonight?"

"As a matter of fact I am. Delilah's out of town."

"Perfect."

Delilah accomplished a lot in the next week. One evening, she sat around a table in the back room of the tea shop with her mother, Cecily, Glenda, Pauline, and Delcia, and with lists of names for the wedding, they addressed envelopes.

"Glenda, do you remember Marva and Otis's wedding?" Holly asked. Otis was Glenda's brother and Marva was Cecily's mother.

"Like it was yesterday."

"If that man wasn't a lovesick fool. He was so nervous. Wasn't a big wedding. They went to the preacher. But the best man gathered up all Otis's friends the night before and took him to the bar. Had this pretty gal dressed all skimpy to dance for them. I think the poor man was so nervous he didn't appreciate it."

"Took a lot to get Marva to agree to marry him. He thought she was going to stand him up," Glenda said.

"The next morning, he was ready to go to the church two hours ahead of time."

"Church was right down the street. What was he going to do there all that time?" Glenda asked.

"He didn't have a clue. He was wearing out that rug pacing and worrying James's nerves."

Everybody chuckled.

"Uh-huh. James had to give him a nip to calm him down. You know I don't go with a lot of drinking, but that fool needed it."

"I thought he was a bit tipsy when he arrived," Glenda mused.

"We had to do something to keep him together. Lord, I miss that man. He was a good man," Holly said.

Glenda's and Cecily's eyes turned glassy.

"A good father, too," Cecily said.

"You were just a baby then. I kept you and Delilah during the ceremony. And my daughter thought she was supposed to be part of the ceremony."

"She was funny and looked just like a doll," Glenda said. "The preacher would tell Marva 'repeat after me' and Delilah would stand and repeat right along with her. You were a cutie," Glenda said.

"Short of popping those legs, I couldn't get her to shut that mouth up."

"Then Cecily decided she wanted to stand at the altar with Otis."

"And he told them to come on up there with them."

"That man loved children," Glenda said. "Shoulda had a houseful of them. Cecily was the apple of his eye."

"She was that."

"Good thing you had a good heart or else you would have been spoiled rotten," Glenda told Cecily.

"It's nice that Marva found someone good after she left here," Pauline said.

"To find two good men in a lifetime is a blessing," Holly said. Cecily's biological father had died when she was two.

"Time passes," Glenda said, taking a napkin to dry her eyes.

Holly gazed at Delilah. "Oh yes," she said. "It does."


The next evening David and Delilah told Kendall they were getting married and asked how he felt about living with them.

"You want to adopt me?"

"Yes, we do," David said.

"Wow! I'd get to stay with you all the time?"

"You would."

"I can sleep in that coup?"

"The cupola," David said. "No. You'll have your very own bedroom."

"And you can choose the color," Delilah told him, to his delight.

"Great!"

They had completed the paperwork and some of the interviews for the home study. In the meantime they gained permission to register Kendall in the local school so he could begin school on the island in the fall.

He worried his lower lip with his teeth. "Do you think I'll fit in the new school?"

"You already have a couple of friends. You'll make more once you begin school," Delilah assured him.

One weekend when David kept him, Delilah roused Kendall to take him shopping for school clothes, knowing she'd be too busy closer to the date school opened. Her mother's warning slipped to the back of her mind. Perhaps David should be shopping. But then he might not get the things Delilah thought the boy needed for school. No, it was better that she shopped.

"We're going to hit the stores today, sleepyhead." He and David had slept in sleeping bags in the cupola again.

Kendall groaned and pulled the covers over his head.

"Oh, no, you don't," she said, yanking them back and whacking him with the pillow. He laughed, dodging her and looking like a wiggling bundle in the bag. "I'm not doing all the grunt work while you play on the beach. Let's go, buddy." She ruffled his hair as he emerged from the sleeping bag.

After breakfast, they rode the eight o'clock ferry to the mainland and drove to Staples, Wal-Mart, and Target for notebooks and other supplies that were on sale. Colored pencils, ink pens, poster boards. Delilah loaded the cart with everything he could possibly need and more.

"What's the use of living on the beach if I'm not going to enjoy it before school starts?" Shopping was beginning to lose its appeal.

"You'll have plenty of time to enjoy it after the shopping," Delilah assured him.

After the supplies, they went to the mall to shop for clothing. Delilah was a shopper and made quick work of their purchases, but at two she called it quits and they left for the island. Kendall sent up a shout.

They picked up Reggie on the way home. The boys shot out of the car, and were heading to the beach when Delilah reminded them to unload. As soon as the unpacking was done, the boys changed into swim trunks and finally headed to the beach.

Delilah couldn't think of a better life for kids than the beach on a hot afternoon.

David called, on his way to the hospital to make his rounds.

"Looks like your day was busier than mine."

"It was pretty full. Tomorrow, to Kendall's disgust, we'll be shopping again after church. He needs a whole new wardrobe."

The one thing David hated to do was shop, so he commiserated with Ken.

"Your mom and dad make it home okay?"

"Mom called last night. They enjoyed their stay."

After they disconnected, Delilah made dinner, then she called the boys in to eat. She ate a little snack. She'd wait for David for dinner, but by the time he arrived it would be close to Kendall's bedtime.

So far he was fitting in as if he'd lived there forever, except he wasn't quite as mischievous as most boys were. He seemed cautious, giving her worried looks now and then, especially when he thought he'd done something wrong.

After warning the boys to wait before they went back in the water, she worked on the proposal.

Delcia stopped by later on with Ranetta and the baby for a tour of the house.

"Before the kids return to school, we're inviting everyone over for dinner, probably Labor Day weekend," Delilah told her.

"Just tell me what to bring."

"I love to cook. So just bring yourself. They let you get away from the campground?"

"It's an absolute zoo. But this is Ranetta's first year in school. I'm taking the week off to spend time with her. I can't believe my baby is growing so."

"Pretty soon, you'll be saying the same thing about college."

"Oh, please. This is bad enough. By the way, tomorrow Cecily and I are taking the kids to the campground to play. Is it okay if I take Kendall?"

"He'd love it. Thank you for including him."

Delcia gave her a strange look. "You're family. Of course you'll be included in family activities."

Delilah felt a warm glow. "Thank you."

# Chapter 10

Holly arrived at Cecily's house a week before the wedding.

"Mama, you never took this much time from work in an entire year in the past, much less in two months."

"I took what I needed. I've been loyal to my customers my entire working career. I can take time if I need it. But you are going to bed, young lady. You can't get married looking ten years older than you are. What have you done to yourself?" Holly said in horror.

"We finished the proposal last night and I turned it in this morning. I always look like this after I turn one in. The good thing is, now my time is my own, but I still have things to do."

"Not today you don't. I'll take care of the emergencies. You are going to bed for the next two days and that's an order. I may have worked hard but I was never a fool."

Delilah couldn't believe her mother was actually

angry. But she didn't have the energy to argue. "Don't start on me, Mama."

Holly briefly closed her eyes. "Go to bed," she said quietly.

Well, she did need time to recuperate, Delilah realized. Her exhaustion was making her paranoid. On her way from Moore's she thought somebody was following her. She'd accelerated, dashing around corners trying to evade as if she were part of some chase scene in an action movie, only to witness the car turning on a street toward Beauford. Feeling like a fool, she drove to the ferry. She was losing her mind. For once her mama was right. She definitely needed sleep.

Delilah slept for fourteen hours. She got up long enough to take care of necessities and she was back in bed. Her mother had taken the phone, even her cell phone, and her car keys. She couldn't talk to anyone, couldn't drive anywhere. And since her parents were staying in the guest room in the new house, David was staying on the mainland. Without a phone she couldn't talk to him.

Forty-eight hours later, she felt human again. And although she worked like the dickens that week, she certainly got those eight hours of sleep each night. Her mama saw to it.

After the second day, her mother gave her the phone back. Good thing too, because furniture started arriving early in the week.

\* \* \*

Delilah made the bed in Kendall's bedroom and ran her hand over the spread to straighten out a wrinkle. And that was where David found her. He leaned against the doorjamb and watched her brisk movements.

"I don't think you can get that room any cleaner," he said.

Her head shot up, a scream forming on her lips. "When did you get in?"

"A few minutes ago. Talked to your parents."

"I guess I have to think of something for dinner."

"The Andersons invited them over. They're having both sets of parents over tonight. Give us a moment to ourselves before the craziness."

She sat on the lone chair. "Yes, the rehearsal dinner's tomorrow night and then . . ."

"You're all mine."

"Oh yes."

"So what do you want to do on our last night of freedom?"

"Sorry, but my mind's gone to mush. Not a single clear thought will emerge."

"You've done a lot the last six weeks. I feel guilty. I've had it easy with work."

"Yes, you have. But that will change. Are you and Louise all situated?"

"Yes, our offices are combined. All of her patients have been notified. We've made up schedules for the hospital rounds. She's holding up to her role in the partnership. But she always has been fair."

Delilah caught the admiration in his voice and felt a twinge of envy. "Well, that's good," she said.

"That's the least she could do after you saved her butt."

David wrapped an arm around Delilah, held her close. "No need to get catty. Women," he said, nuzzling her neck with his lips.

"Women nothing," Delilah said, but melted when he started kissing the anger away. After all, Louise had been in that office with him all day while she'd worked like a locomotive preparing for their wedding.

"Come on. Let's go snuggle on the deck off that nice master bedroom you've decorated so prettily. Don't think I didn't notice."

"That's good of you."

"I see it's going to take a lot to get you mellow tonight."

"You've got your work cut out for you, mister. You've been neglecting things lately."

"Let me make up for my oversight without delay."

Carter drove the Robertses from Baltimore on Monday. He and Delcia drove them to Delilah's cottage the following day. The couple appeared to be in their late seventies.

Delilah extended a hand, but the older woman enveloped her in her arms, then held her at arm's length. "Aren't you the prettiest little thing I ever saw?" she said, making Delilah blush.

"Thank you."

"You've made my son a very happy man. It's about time he found a nice young thing."

Delilah smiled and was enveloped in Paul's arms.

"He tells us you write books," Nadine said as she escorted them into the house.

"I'm trying anyway."

"That's good because I like to read."

"When I get it published I'll send you a copy."

"You do that. Lord, I couldn't climb these stairs every day," Nadine said when she reached the top. Instead of the cottage, Delilah took them into the house. For the very reason that the stairs were too much for them, David had not elevated the guest cottage.

She fixed glasses of lemonade and let them rest before she gave them the tour.

David arrived hours later. There was a distinct difference between his mannerisms with the Robertses and Howard. He definitely treated these people as parents.

"You've done a fantastic job on this house," Paul said.

"You better thank Delilah for the decorating," Nadine said. "I know my son didn't decorate."

Everyone laughed.

Rehearsal dinners were usually held the night before the wedding, but this one was switched to Thursday night. David's mother's family arrived earlier that day. Their mouths were pressed together like wrinkled prunes. She immediately detected that they didn't like her one bit. One of the aunts seemed approachable. But most of the lot . . . there wasn't much to say for them.

It was late Friday and Holly had left with Mrs. Anderson an hour ago. Delilah knew David's bachelor's party was tonight, but she was going to chill and get pretty for tomorrow—the big day. Her heart gave a little leap at the thought.

Just as she sat down to her dressing table, the phone rang. Delilah started to ignore it, but it could be David or the social worker.

"Delilah, could you come over here?" Cecily asked.

Delilah panicked. "What is it? Everything's ready for the reception, isn't it?"

"Of course. Everything's on schedule."

She breathed a sigh. "I'll be right over."

Cecily's shop was always busy, so she went to her room to hunt for something to wear. Her mother had left a simple lime green sundress on the bed. Delilah grabbed it and pulled it on, shoving her feet into dainty white sandals.

Outside, the wind was whipping. A storm was brewing tonight so Delilah left her car window down and let the breeze flow in. She drove by hikers once she turned onto the lighthouse road. She was grateful that David's house was situated on a quiet side of the island.

Nearly all the parking spaces in the tea shop's lot were full. Luckily someone was leaving and Delilah pulled into that slot and went inside.

"Oh, Cecily's upstairs in the Cove," the young hostess said.

Delilah climbed the majestic stairs of the Victorian house. All the banquet room names reflected the water. Once she reached the Cove, she frowned at the closed door.

She knocked and waited. When she didn't get a response, she knocked again and heard a faint "Come in."

Strange. The door should already be open, she thought as she opened the door slowly. She wondered if it was her imagination or if she actually heard a response after all. The room was dark. She pushed the door wider to look around when suddenly the light popped on and a crowd emerged.

"Surprise!"

"Oh my gosh. I can't believe it." Her heart was beating fast. "I can't believe you did this."

Cecily hugged her and led her to a chair. Many of the women she'd met since moving to the island were present. Her mother and father were there. Her dad was uncomfortable, the only male in a crowd of women.

Delilah moved about the room greeting everyone.

After fifteen minutes, Ryan came to collect her father. He looked very happy to leave for some male entertainment.

Halfway through the evening, Sasha approached her. "You've got your work cut out for you if you're going to win the approval of that side of the family," she whispered, of David's mother's prune-faced family.

"Good thing they don't live close by," Delilah said.

But later on one of his great-aunts approached her. "I'm so pleased to meet you," she said. "David has told me how smitten he is with you."

"The feelings are mutual," Delilah assured her. She wished she'd worn something a little more appropriate. Half the back was cut out on her dress and this woman's dress clutched her throat and hung nearly to her feet. The heat was so intense

Delilah couldn't stand to be buttoned down, but had she known she was coming to her own wedding shower, she'd have suffered.

"I can tell that," his aunt said.

"We were so pleased to finally discover what happened to his mother all those years ago, even though the outcome was painful. It's the not knowing that really tears you up. Not knowing whether she suffered, or what became of her."

"I can't begin to imagine what you all suffered."

"I'm telling you this because I know his family seems overbearing, but they have good hearts. A little too unbending and too rigid at times, but they will come around. They don't want to lose what's left of their daughter."

Delilah touched her hand. "I'm looking forward to getting to know you. Thank you for coming to my party."

"We wouldn't have missed it," she said.

His was the most confusing family she ever encountered, but she guessed you could never have too much family no matter what they were like.

Someone knocked on the door. Cecily opened it.

"I have a package for a Ms. Delilah Benton, soon to be Mrs. Washington. I was told I could find her here."

A handsome man with dark chocolate skin entered carrying a huge package. Delilah thought it was a little late for delivering packages.

"She's over there," someone said, pointing to her.

The man saw her sitting on the middle of the couch. "Are you Ms. Benton?"

"Yes," Delilah said.

"I was told to open this package for you. May I?" Delilah shrugged. "Sure."

He peeled off his jacket. "It's hot outside. I'm sweating like you wouldn't believe."

But he didn't stop with taking off his jacket. He started unbuttoning his shirt. Music started playing in the background.

Delilah smiled, then the man unbuckled his pants, and her eyes went huge. She knew he was a male stripper.

The women tittered, urging him on. They were clapping and stomping their feet until he was standing before her with nothing but skimpy briefs.

He had a body to die for.

Everyone was oohing and ahing at his fine, fine body.

And then he was dancing. He had moves Delilah hadn't seen before.

Before he finished, he kissed Nadine on the cheek.

Nadine brought her hands to her cheek, smiling. "You've got this old lady's heart tripping. I'm going to need a pacemaker after this."

The crowd roared with laughter, but Delilah noticed the horror on the faces of David's grandmother and the rest of the women from his mother's family.


David hadn't expected a bachelor's party. He was even more surprised with the inclusion of a belly dancer. His dad, sitting beside him, watching the sway of hips of the skimpily dressed woman, seemed to be enjoying the show more than he.

"One thing for certain," his dad said, "it's hard to find a woman more beautiful than your bride."

The crowd in the back room of the bar was getting rowdier by the minute. Liquor was free and plentiful. Since the island was small, no one was refused entrance.

Howard leaned across David and tapped Paul Roberts on the knee. "Enjoying the show?"

The older man slapped his thigh. "She's a sight for sore eyes."

"Mom's going to give you a licking for tonight," David said.

His dad whooped. "This is worth it."

Later, David stood talking to Carter. They both sipped on beer.

"Still not too late," Carter said.

"Thanks for the party. But nothing takes the place of Delilah."

"If you thought residency was tough, loving Delilah is going to be the most difficult thing you've ever done."

"Any relationship that's worth anything takes work. But in the end it's worth it, isn't it? Aren't you happy, Carter?"

"Of course I'm happy."

"Well, be happy for me."

Carter shook his head. "You really love her, don't you?"

David nodded. "Yes, more than anything. I've finally found someone who fits me."

"Come on, let's enjoy the party. I'm getting your straitlaced self drunk tonight. Forget that beer."

* * *

The day arrived. Delilah dressed in the house.

"Isn't she pretty, Mrs. Benton?"

Tears came to her mother's eyes. "Gorgeous. Absolutely gorgeous."

"Oh, I have to check on something." Sylvia disappeared, leaving mother and daughter alone.

Holly took Delilah's hand. "Be true to yourself first, daughter. Always value yourself and work as a unit with your husband. Remember, you're more than surface beauty. You have a huge, giving heart, Delilah, so much so that you'll let yourself be taken advantage of. Most of all, be happy, honey. I love you."

"I am, Mama. I am. I love you. Thank you for being here for me."

Her mother hugged her. "I can see you are," she said, but Delilah could see that she was also worried. This summer, Delilah glimpsed not the taskmaster, but the warm woman her father must have fallen in love with.


"Damn it, what did you slip me last night?" David said to Carter. He felt like hell. His head was splitting. "Shit, what time is it?"

"You haven't missed the wedding," Carter said. "You're just not used to drinking. You're just a baby."

"Forget you." David rummaged around in the cabinet for aspirin and swallowed it with a glass of water.

Paul came in. "You boys better not let your mama hear you cussing and fighting or she'll wash your mouths out with soap."

Carter checked the hallway. "She's not near, is she?" You didn't mess with Nadine.

"I look like hell," David said. "Delilah's going to run in the opposite direction."

Carter snorted. "You wouldn't be so lucky."

"You boys cut it out," Paul said. "You'll get some color back by the time you eat and the headache goes away. Delilah's a good girl."

Carter grunted.

"Be happy for your brother."


When David's gaze fell upon Delilah in her long white gown, her beautiful shoulders bare except for the train that kissed her shoulders and flowed gracefully behind her, his breath caught in his throat. He'd never been much of a romantic, but that such a marvelous woman was marrying him, and thought he was great too, well, life couldn't get any better, could it?

As Delilah walked up the long church aisle on her father's arm, her footsteps padded by a red runner, she felt like the princess in a fairy tale.

Little Ranetta stood next to Sylvia in her beautiful white dress and matching shoes with her delicate basket of rose petals.

Kendall stood beside Carter with the pillow and ring. They wanted to make him a part of the wedding.

But David . . . her love. David stood at the front of the church beside his brother. It was a portrait worthy of the cover of *GQ*, she thought as the photographer snapped photos.

David smiled.

Carter frowned.

Two handsome men, but David won the competition by a mile.

If Delilah weren't so nervous she would find some humor in it all.

"Be happy, daughter. I'm giving you my most precious possession," her father said before he handed her to David. "Value her."


As Delilah mingled among the guests at the reception, she realized every family was different. David's mother's family was stodgy and disapproving. His foster parents, the Robertses, were a warm and happy couple. No wonder David and Carter learned to love and flourish. The Andersons were supportive. Her own mother was busy watching that everything went well. For once Delilah wished she would take it easy and enjoy, but that wasn't her mother's style. Her father was laid-back and enjoying the event.

She often wondered how complete opposites managed to fall in love. Until, that is, she realized that she and David were opposites, too. He was calm and steady to her frenzied rushing. He was the saint and she was the wicked one. At least his brother and some of his mother's family thought so.

But Delilah wasn't going to think of that at her wedding reception. Marriage was what you made of it, and hers and David's was going to be one to write home about.

\* \* \*

David lifted Delilah and carried her across the threshold. Laughing, Delilah linked her arms around his neck. He kissed her.

"You're all mine now to do with as I wish, Mrs. David Washington."

"Hmmm. You've had too much to drink," Delilah said, shaking her head at his foolishness.

"Not too much. I made sure of that."

He carried her through the sitting room and deposited her in the center of the bed.

Delilah brought him down on her. Seeing the desire in his eyes ignited an answering yearning in hers. A delicious quiver ran through her. His lips touched hers and his hands ran down her sides, fanning a flame through her body.

"Baby, you've got too many layers," he whispered, his voice deep with longing.

It took only minutes that felt like hours before they were both lying naked against the cool sheets.

"Thought this night would never come. You've driven me crazy by making me wait," he chided.

She ran her tongue over her lips. "Had to give you something to look forward to on your wedding night."

David leaned forward, pressed his mouth to hers. Her lips softened under his, and he agonized with need for his wife. His wife. He searched her eyes with awareness of possession.

As her hands touched him, stroking him frantically, David thought his desire would spiral out of control. Her mouth opened under his. He tasted the sweet honey within. She caressed every inch of his body, she stroked him to the edge of madness.

The moans escaping Delilah sounded foreign as

his hands, his mouth, his body drove her wild. She wanted him.

"Now, please," she whispered.

David gazed into her eyes, a cloud of longing flowing through him. Never, in his entire life, had he seen a woman as beautiful as she. Never had he wanted a woman as much as he wanted his wife.

He slid his chest down her body, watching the play of emotions on her face. The friction of skin against skin ignited her even more.

He touched her intimately.

"I want you to enjoy this, baby. You are so beautiful, Delilah."

She was aroused to a fever pitch. When his tongue touched her intimately, Delilah thought her hips would buck off the bed. He caressed the inside of her silky thighs, causing her legs to spread wider. She grasped at his shoulders, anything, anywhere she could touch—until finally, he dragged himself up her. He teased her to the brink of insanity.

"You're driving me crazy. Please, David," she pleaded.

He gently stroked her breasts, slid his tongue over her nipples, then gently clasped them between his teeth. The contrasting textures drove a trail of fire down her throbbing body. His touch became a mixture of pleasure and pain.

David had never known he could derive so much pleasure from pleasing someone else.

When he entered her, Delilah was overcome with pleasure so intense and raw it left her completely vulnerable. He thrust in and out and the fullness of him inside her was unlike anything she'd ever felt before.

He whispered sweet words to her. Their bodies moved as if they were made only for each other. The sensations rose so intensely that she screamed as a tornado ripped her from her moorings and carried her on a path she couldn't control.

When she cried out, David felt his own control slip. Her legs gripped him, heightening the sensations, his thrusts quickened until a powerful moan escaped him and he closed his eyes as he felt himself sliding down a slippery slope of pure uncontrollable satisfaction.

When he opened his eyes, he found hers searching his. He lowered his body to hers and kissed her with pride of possession.

His wife, he thought. She was his.

Delilah the temptress. His temptress.

# Chapter 11

Both David and Delilah were returning to work tomorrow. She was going back part-time to help them find a proposal manager who was willing to relocate.

One of the things she liked most about her new house was the pool and exercise room on the ground level.

David had furnished the exercise room. Delilah had the music blasting as she sweated from the workout. She pushed herself to do two more sit-ups. No pain, no gain, she told herself. Especially after she'd seen David's muscles as he worked out across from her.

A hand reached down to tickle her side.

"David. What are you doing?"

"Trying to interest my wife in another kind of exercise."

"I'm sweaty."

"So am I." Deft hands peeled her clothes off.

Time passed slowly while they made wonderful

wild love to each other. Then they both ran up the stairs like kids and showered together. God, she loved that man.

Their honeymoon had been restful after weeks of craziness.

Delilah was glad to get out of the overlong meeting with Redcliff's staff. Essential management from Redcliff and Moore's met with the proposal managers to discuss the possibility of another joint project. They were working together on a collaborative effort. They met on Redcliff's site this time, in their impressive conference room. Delilah had ridden over with Stuart.

"I have a meeting with Norman," Stuart said, reaching into his pocket. "Take my car back to the office. I'll call for someone to pick me up."

"No need for that," Katherine Day said. "I have some company errands to take care of. I'd be happy to drop her off." Katherine was Redcliff's full-time proposal manager.

"Thank you," Delilah said. "Could you point me to the ladies' room first, please?"

"Down that hall to the right. I'll meet you in the car."

Delilah had been holding it for the last hour of the conference and she couldn't wait another moment.

When she finished, she rushed downstairs. Katherine was waiting in the car. The driver, waiting behind the wheel, reached for the door handle at the same time the motor started. Delilah was no more than thirty feet away when it exploded.

The impact knocked Delilah off her feet. She flew through the air and landed on her backside. It seemed as though she was having an out-of-body experience. Everything was moving in slow motion. It seemed the car would never stop exploding. Flames leaped into the air. And then she heard sirens. Somebody was standing over her, asking where she was hurt. She tried to respond but her mouth felt as if cotton balls were stuffed where her tongue should have been.

When Delilah woke up in the hospital, Carter was standing beside the bed.

"You gave us a hell of a scare," he said.

It took a moment for her thoughts to focus. "What on earth happened?"

"Do you remember anything?"

"Only the car blowing up. It was horrible. I saw the people . . . Oh God!" She covered her face with her hands.

Carter stroked her arm. If she were in the right frame of mind, she'd think it ironic that someone who absolutely hated her could be so tender.

"You're okay now," he assured her.

"Where's David?" Delilah asked.

"They're trying to locate him. I was already on the mainland when I got the call," he said. "What were you doing in the limo?"

"We had a meeting at Redcliff's this morning. I was catching a ride back to my office."

"So the bomb wasn't meant for you."

"A bomb?" What else could it be? she thought, seeing the answer in Carter's eyes and envisioning the bodies on fire in the car? Carter was asking her a question. She tried to concentrate.

"Has anything else strange happened with this company?"

Delilah shrugged. Her head was groggy. She couldn't think straight. "Not that I know of."

"Sir?" The nurse came into the room. "I'm going to have to ask you to leave. She needs her rest."

Delilah tightened her hand around Carter's. For some stupid reason, she didn't want him to leave.

"She's had quite a scare," Carter said to the nurse. "I won't tire her out. I'll sit here quietly." Carter looked as if the nurse would have to drag him out to get him to leave. There was a brusque attractiveness about Carter that had some of the nurses whispering behind their hands. The woman regarded him for a moment, nodded, then left.

Delilah was deeply grateful he stayed. She was afraid to close her eyes for fear of seeing the people in the car.

David rushed in ten minutes later.

"My God, what happened?" he asked.

Before she could explain, Carter said, "I'll talk to you in the hallway."

David kissed her tenderly before he allowed himself to be dragged off.

As soon as they cleared the door, Sylvia burst into the opening. "Girl, you scared the hell out of me. I had stopped smoking and now I've started up again." Her hand was shaking and Delilah smelled cigarette smoke on her breath when she hugged her.

"I lived through it. That counts for something," Delilah said.

"Well, the others weren't quite as lucky."

"Did you know them?"

Sylvia nodded. "I've worked on a couple of proposals with Katherine. We didn't get the contract, but she was a nice person. It wasn't her. It's that damn company she works for that's crazy." Sylvia eased into a chair as if her legs couldn't support her any longer.

"I'm not supposed to be here, but I couldn't stand not seeing you."

"Thanks, girl."

"You're going to have a whopper of a bruise on your face. It'll fade though. Eventually. At least the skin isn't broken."

"Give me a mirror."

"Don't go crazy on me. Your beauty is still there. Don't worry. David isn't going to stray."

The men came back in five minutes.

Carter touched her hand. "I'm leaving for a while, but I'll be back," he said.

Delilah nodded.

Carter kissed her on the forehead, then headed for the door. Before he cleared it, Delilah called him back.

"You asked if anything strange had occurred."

"Yes?"

"I don't know if it means anything, but Stuart, he's the owner of Moore's, his brother-in-law was murdered recently. They found his body in the sound."

"Do they know who did it? Or why?"

She shook her head. Pain shot through her skull. "I never met him. He was missing before I began working there."

"What was his name?"

"Stan Hamilton."

"I knew him," Sylvia said.

"Why don't you tell me about him on our way out?" Carter asked.

Sylvia squeezed Delilah's hand. "I'll be back later on, girlfriend. Marcia said she would visit you after she gets off from work."

"Thanks for stopping by."

David looked so worried that Delilah lifted a hand to caress his cheek. "I'm okay," she said.

He closed his eyes, briefly, and lowered his lips to hers. "It was too close," he whispered. "You are never going back to that company."

"Moore's had nothing to do with it."

"I don't care. Too many people are dying at that place."

Delilah reached up to touch his cheek. "I'm fine."

The police came by to question Delilah, but she wasn't any help. No, she didn't see anyone in the vicinity of the car before it exploded. She remembered focusing on getting there because she was holding everyone up. Then they asked her if she heard anyone leave. Again, she didn't see anything. She was too busy flying through the air.

"Sorry, I can't be of much help."

The next day, she checked out of the hospital.

Holly Benton arrived on the island an hour after Delilah. Delilah and David were fighting about her returning to Moore's.

"I won't be returning any time soon. Not until I heal at any rate. I'm fine, David." But, although nothing was broken, it seemed every muscle in her body ached.

She felt guilty that her mother was taking yet another week off from her beauty shop.


A week later, Delilah felt almost like new and her mother returned home.

Delilah covered a bruise on her cheek with foundation and brushed powder on her face.

Kendall had moved in and Delilah towed him to the mainland to finish shopping for school clothes.

"I thought we'd finished all that. I've got lots of jeans," he whined.

"Almost. You need more shirts and a suit for church." She didn't really need him to shop, but he was too young to leave alone. A devoted shopaholic she might be, but after school began she wasn't going to shop for months.

She wished someone would open a small department store on the island.

The island stores were geared toward the tourist trade, not the bare necessities. The island wasn't quite large enough to warrant a Wal-Mart and she did miss the creature comforts that now forced her to ride the ferry to the mainland to shop. Living on the island required planning ahead. No more quick trips to pick up items.

They dashed from store to store until several bags dragged from their arms. "Do you like your clothes so far?" she asked.

"Yeah, they're pretty cool," Kendall said, with

the air of a male who'd had enough. "Ready to go home now?"

"I guess we can call it a day," she said as they walked out of the shoe store with a couple of pairs of sneakers and dress shoes.

Delilah was going to have to get the boy started in Sunday school and in youth activities at the local church. All the responsible things her parents involved her in. Keep him pointed down the straight and narrow road, although life wasn't so simple any longer.

"Let's stop by David's office and get him to take us to dinner."

"Will we get home too late to go to the beach?"

"Yes, but it's in your backyard. You can play on the beach anytime. I'm not cooking tonight."

Kendall shrugged. "Guess I can play videos until he's ready."

Once they began the everyday routine of having a child around, David saw the difference between being a full-time father who participated in raising a child and one who'd shirked the duty. Seeing the fear that he'd felt as a child mirrored on Kendall's face brought back some of the insecurities that had been buried in the back of his mind since he was a kid and his adoptive parents died.

"What's the problem, son?" Howard asked. "Looks like you have the weight of the world on your shoulders."

The man David never called father stood at the

door of his office. It was quiet. The machines had stopped running. The patter of voices had ceased. The staff had left for the night, leaving him with only the silence.

The stillness seemed out of place in the usual movement of the office.

The man whose hair resembled his own. The man whose genes were clearly responsible for his height, his weight, his build. David had probably gained his desire to become a doctor from both his father and his mother.

"Son. What does that really mean these days?" he asked.

Sommars sat across from David in the office chair.

Sometimes when Howard called him "son," he wanted to lash out at him. He'd never done a thing to give him that privilege.

"I knew we'd have this talk one day," Howard continued. "I didn't think it would take this long."

David studied the diplomas on the wall. "I think people use the term 'son' too loosely. I remember at baseball games the coach would say, 'Great work, son. Great hit.' Or a father with the Boy Scouts would say, 'Son this or son that.' You call me son, but those men, with whom I only spent snatches of time, had more right to call me son than you do."

Howard's gaze dropped to his hands. "You've refused to talk about your childhood in the past. Do you want to talk about it now?"

David inhaled a deep breath. He never broached

the subject of his childhood to anyone in great detail. "You know most of it. Some nice people adopted me, died, and I passed through a couple of foster homes before I ended up with the Robertses. They were great. End of story."

"There are a lot of pages covered by that very abridged version you just gave me."

"You married your high school sweetheart. You always knew you were going to marry her."

"Yes," Howard said. "I did."

"Then why did you go to bed with my mother?"

Howard Sommars glanced at his tie, raked a hand down it. "Did you plan to marry Delilah before you went to bed with her?"

"Delilah isn't pregnant with my child."

Howard sighed. "It wasn't planned. Your mother was an amazing woman."

"You've said that on more than one occasion."

"She was a brilliant physician. Your talent comes from her. I see a lot of her in you. We were residents. They work you like hell."

"I went through it, too, remember?"

Sommars nodded. His green eyes looked as if they were gazing into the past.

"That night . . . it was a particularly grueling shift we'd just finished. There had been a terrible bus accident. We worked for hours trying to save people. Lost a few, saved more. Well, anyway, my place was closer to the hospital than hers. She had much farther to drive and it just wasn't safe as tired as she was. I told her to crash at my place. The plan was innocent enough. She slept in the bed, I slept on the couch.

"We crashed for about ten hours. Neither of us

awoke in the night. The next morning she pulled on one of my shirts and we cooked breakfast together. God, was she beautiful. All brown skin with her hair falling in wild disarray around her shoulders."

"Wasn't beautiful enough for you to marry."

Howard chose to ignore the snide remark. "Well, anyway. That's when it happened."

"Between the bacon and eggs?"

Silence stretched.

"What happened next?" David asked.

"In a couple of months our residency was over."

"So you came to North Carolina to join your father's practice and marry your high school love, and my mother left to give birth to us."

Sommars nodded.

"And you never once thought to use protection, or that since you hadn't, she could have conceived. You never asked."

"I thought that if she had, she'd have said something."

"Six months later, six months after you screwed my mother, you married your high school sweetheart who was waiting patiently for you back home."

Pain chased Howard's face. "You weren't a virgin when you married, son."

"I didn't leave any little babies behind to fend for themselves, either."

"How do you know?"

"I know. I don't just screw women and send them on their way." He looked at his watch. Standing, he said, "Delilah's waiting for me."

"You have a lot of hidden anger we haven't begun to touch. Let's deal with it so we can put it behind us. First of all, you're a pediatrician. How many pregnant teenagers come into your office?"

"You and my mother weren't teenagers. And my mother shouldn't have delivered your babies in a stranger's house alone. You can't write a prescription that will cure forty years of whatever in ten minutes."

From the hallway Delilah listened to the painful conversation. She'd hoped to have dinner with David before he made his rounds. As she listened to his voice she fought the tears that sprang to her eyes. She wanted to leave so that he wouldn't know that she knew his pain. At the same time she wanted to do something . . . anything to lessen it.

As he and Howard walked out, they were surprised to find her in the reception area.

She forced a cheerful expression she was far from feeling.

"Hi. Kendall and I thought we'd have dinner with you before we left for the mainland." She approached David and kissed him lightly on the lips, looped an arm around his waist. "Hi, Howard. How are you?"

Howard mumbled something. At the same time, Kendall finished his video game, and sent up a cheer. It seemed so out of place in the gloomy atmosphere.

"Is he ready yet? Oh, you're here," Kendall said.

"I'm ready. But I don't have to make rounds tonight. I'll have dinner with you."

"On second thought, I took out ground beef for

spaghetti. It won't take me long to fix it," Delilah said, although cooking was the last thing she wanted to do after a day spent shopping. But she sensed David didn't want to be around people and she wasn't going to force him.

"I thought you weren't going to cook," Kendall said.

"I changed my mind. I can fix some mean spaghetti."

He shrugged. He seemed to like most of the foods Delilah prepared. But spaghetti was one of her easiest meals.

On the ferry, David left the car and stood at a secluded spot at the railing. Kendall stood down the railing talking to some kids his age. One thing about the ferry, it was easy to make friends quickly.

David let the wind blow on his face. Somehow it seemed to bring a measure of peace, especially with the added pleasure of having his wife beside him. Her arms were looped around his waist. He wondered if she had heard any of the conversation between Howard and him.

He purposely kept Howard and his past from his mind and focused on Ken. Ken was still having problems adjusting to Delilah and him. As much as he'd wanted David to adopt him, he couldn't trust that it had actually finally happened to him.

Delilah was a real trooper and he was grateful for her.

When they arrived home, David helped Delilah prepare dinner and after they ate, Ken played for a while until it was time to prepare for bed. They both tucked him in and then it was the two of them.

Sometimes they showered together, but that night David showered while Delilah read Ken a story. And now he sat on the deck off the master suite while she prepared for bed.

He was surprised when she massaged his shoulders.

"Something's bothering you."

He reached up to clasp her hand.

"I don't understand myself sometimes," he said.

"Does it have anything to do with your conversation with Howard?"

"You heard?"

"Yes," she said. "Do you want to talk about it?"

"I don't know." He was silent a moment. Then he said, "I don't understand why the past bothers me now. I'm forty, for God's sake. My childhood is years behind me."

Delilah moved to stand beside him. "But the feelings have been buried. You've never actually dealt with them. You didn't talk to anyone. And now going through the process of adopting Kendall has brought some of those fears, some of those feelings back. Have you ever talked to anyone about them?"

"No. I was lucky. I had great adoptive parents and once I'd finally settled with the Robertses, my life has been good. Rich with love." He kissed her. "I have nothing to complain about."

"What about the years before you moved in with the Robertses? What about those years of suffering, insecurity, and anger?"

"I never thought that dealing with Ken would

bring up all these deep-seated issues I had filed in the back of my mind."

"Are you sorry you suggested we adopt him?"

"No. My past helps me understand better what he's going through. I even understand how a man and woman can get caught up in the moment and forget protection, common sense, and everything else when he was hot to get her into bed." David chuckled a humorless laugh. "God knows it happens enough with you.

"It's just Howard knew he wasn't going to marry my mother. He knew he was going home to marry his sweetheart at the end of his residency. If he knew her at all, he more than likely knew that she had a family who was strict and unbending enough to choke a horse. She shouldn't have been on her own delivering two babies with no family, no one who loved her. I wonder sometimes what was going through her mind?"

"She made that choice, too. It wasn't one-sided," Delilah said softly. "She was strong. Black women have had to be strong. Your mother knew she was on her own and she did what she thought she'd have to to keep her children."

"I have to believe she planned to keep us."

"Of course she did."

"The lady who kept her things said she wore a wedding band and that she'd said her husband had died."

"She wouldn't have done that if she'd planned to give you up for adoption. And even if she'd planned to give you up, she would have made sure you were with a loving family who desperately wanted you."

"Life isn't always easy, is it?"

"No."

He'd lived on one motto to get him through the rough years. Don't look back, because there wasn't a damn thing he could do about it. Now his goal was to make Ken a whole, functioning person.

He was grateful for his family. He finally had the family he'd longed for. Carter might not trust Delilah, but he did. She might not be perfect, but neither was he, even though she called him "the saint," which he absolutely hated. What man would prefer to be a saint rather than a hot-blooded man who stirred his wife in ways no other man could, in ways that she remembered weeks or months later?

Carter came by the house the next day. As soon as the doorbell rang, Kendall burst out of his room to answer the door.

"Uncle Carter. Are you going to take me back to the campground with you?"

Carter looked at Delilah.

"Absolutely not. You have to finish the work I gave you," she said.

"But I only have a few days of summer left."

"And you're going to be prepared when you return to school."

Kendall looked at Carter for help.

"Sorry, pal. Mother's rule."

Delilah had given Kendall math problems to do just to strengthen his skills before school started. He didn't even pretend not to hate it.

"Back upstairs, buddy. And don't come out unless you need help or you've finished."

Kendall's retreat upstairs was much slower.

"And I better not hear that music until you've finished."

"What good will that do? He probably has the TV turned down low."

"He doesn't have a TV in his bedroom."

"Smart woman."

"May I get you a cup of coffee or lemonade?" Delilah asked. "I made blackberry lemonade."

"Lemonade sounds good," he said. "Then sit out on the sunporch with me."

Delilah fixed the drinks, but Carter carried them out.

"I'm fine now, you know," she said, sitting on the couch opposite him.

"I know. It's just . . . well, you had me worried."

"Thanks for your concern."

He frowned after her. "You aren't at all what I expected."

Delilah tilted her head. "What did you expect?"

"Someone shallow."

"What gave you that impression?"

"You're so pretty. And you flaunt it. I've talked to the people at Moore's. Everybody's impressed with how hard you work. Your actions don't portray a powder puff."

"A woman can't be pretty and smart?"

"Many are smart, but they use sex to advance. From what I've gathered, you don't do that. Your work speaks for itself."

"I think you've complimented me for the first time."

"I have." He leaned back in the chair. "I really

came to discuss the bombing. Norman Redcliff has many enemies. The man's a total ass. He doesn't go any place without his personal bodyguard. And the guard always checks the car and starts it before Redcliff gets anywhere near it."

"I didn't know that."

"A lot of people think he has a guard because he's vain, but it's for safety reasons. I don't understand why Stuart does business with him. Nobody at the company likes him," Carter said.

"Stuart doesn't like him either, but he needs to expand in order to save his company. His company isn't positioned to handle the larger contracts alone, so he subs. Usually he takes a portion of the sub and Redcliff takes a portion. He's only using Redcliff until he can go it alone."

"The police believe the bomb was placed there for Redcliff, but a couple of things bother me."

"What?"

"Well, for one, his personal bodyguard was conveniently off that day. He did have a doctor's appointment, I checked that. But according to the bomb people, the bomb was probably placed where it could be easily detected if only the new driver had checked under the hood."

"Why do you think he didn't?"

"That's the question, especially since his regular bodyguard always checks the car before he starts it. It doesn't make sense that that information wasn't conveyed to the replacement driver, does it?"

"That's not something someone would easily forget."

"I was told this guy was a screwup sometimes."

"If danger was involved, why use a screwup when lives are involved? And do you think Redcliff would ride with someone incompetent?"

"The word is, he was the only driver available."

"Convenient. That poor man and Katherine. I feel so sorry for their families. What a horrible way to die."

"Yeah. And Redcliff has the nerve to bitch about being sued."

"Their families deserve whatever they get, although money can't replace a loved one."

Carter rubbed the bridge of his nose. "I don't have a good feeling about this. Stay alert. Call me if you have the least suspicion, even if you think it's stupid and it embarrasses you."

"Okay. Thank you, Carter."

"If you have any problems, call me. All right?"

"Yes. I . . . I really appreciate this."

"Stop saying that. You're family," he said. "Maybe I misjudged you. I should have waited until I got the chance to know you before I made a conclusion on the type of person you are. But for what it's worth, I think you're good for David."

"He's good for me, too."

"A perfect match, then. There's nothing you can do but sit tight and wait. We're working on this. Take care, Delilah." And then he left.

She never thought she'd hear Carter say he thought she was good for David. Never. She thought he'd be fighting her every step of the way. That he'd be giving her snide looks and remarks at family gatherings, trying to protect his younger brother. Would wonders never cease?

Delilah crossed her arms in front of her as if ward-

ing off the cold as flashes of the bombing came
back to her. Goose bumps spread on her arms, not
from the temperature, but the fear that chilled
her.

# Chapter 12

Delilah had originally planned a huge cookout for Labor Day, but Glenda persuaded her to let Emery and her take everyone to the point on their boat. It seemed the point was Ryan's favorite hangout for fishing.

The day was warm and windy. A storm was brewing farther south. It was still more than a week away. They were waiting to see if it would go out to sea before it reached the North Carolina coast. Luckily, today the seas were calm.

Carter and the men unpacked the chairs and coolers and carried them to the shore, making sure they put the cooler with beer next to them. Soon after, they extended fishing poles into the water.

As soon as they docked, the boys sprinted to the mudflats and gathered oysters. The girls played on the beach, picked up seashells, and swam.

The women walked the island exploring and generally lazing about.

This time, Sasha was with them. Usually she didn't participate in this side of his family's events. Not because she didn't want to, but for the most part David kept the families separate. After the talk with Howard, he seemed to be loosening.

Carter had asked David if he wanted to invite her, and for once David asked her when he saw her in town. David still had mixed feelings about his father's family. He wasn't comfortable with having Sasha here. But her divorce had finalized and she was having problems getting her life back together. Boy, they were quite a family.

He glanced at his wife, overcome with emotion. The bombing brought home how fragile life really was. That morning, she'd fretted about wearing a swimsuit because all the bruises hadn't completely faded. It would take months for her natural color to fade in. Bruises or not, he loved her.

Delilah was applying sunblock to her shapely legs. She passed the bottle to Delcia, who applied some on Ranetta.

She was being a real trooper in putting up with the emotional stress from adopting Ken. To her his name was Kendall. He imagined most mothers called their children by their given name. Nicknames were reserved for fathers and friends.

But contrary to what Carter believed, marrying Delilah had been one of the most sane decisions of his life. He was mostly surprised at the change in Carter toward her. She'd won him over.

"We're starving over here. When do we get to eat?" Cecily called to the men.

"Those buckets look empty to me. Have you been fishing or pretending?" Delilah asked.

"I think they've been pretending," Delcia said.

Sasha inspected the buckets. "They've got some little baby ones in there."

"Baby ones!" Carter almost hopped out of his seat in outrage. He picked up the biggest fish in the bucket and held it up like a trophy. "You need glasses."

"That's the only sizable one in the bucket. You're supposed to throw back the scrawny ones."

"Just for that, you're cleaning them, Dr. Sommars."

Sasha started waving her hands back and forth. "Oh no. The one that catches it cleans it."

"Just an excuse for women to be lazy," David said.

She snatched his hat off and whacked him with it. "You've married a throwback here, Delilah."

"Just for that, he deserves to be dunked."

"Oh no. If I get dunked, you get no fish for dinner."

"We're going to do it anyway." The four women didn't even try to pick him up, but they dragged him, hat, clothes, and all, into the cold, tossing water. He grabbed Delilah and dragged her under with him. Pulling her to him, he kissed her. Sasha made gagging sounds. He captured her and dragged her under. When he let her go, she came up sputtering.

"That's what you get for trying to dunk the stronger species."

She pushed him back to land on his backside. "Sexist."

Sasha looked truly happy for the first time in a

very long while. Suddenly David was glad Carter had asked him to invite her. It was time that he began to accept that side of his family—in his heart. After all, they shared biological fathers. Even though they were raised separately, there was that unbreakable link between them that the past couldn't change.

Several hours later when the kids were well fed and hyper from sweets and food, Delilah showed them new dances. David laughed at the comical picture they made trying to imitate her.

"Thanks for inviting me. I had a wonderful time," Sasha said.

David linked his hands behind his back as they walked the shore. "You're very welcome."

"I know that I've been down lately and I haven't been very much of a sister, but I hope to make it up to you."

David inhaled the sea breeze. "You don't owe me anything. But I'm glad you enjoyed yourself. How are you coping without Randall?" he asked.

"I should have left him years ago. He was just in the marriage, not contributing to it. I guess it took a catastrophe to wake me up."

"And now you're free and open to the good things that will come."

"I'm not even looking for a man right now. I've had enough for a while."

"That's what we all say and feel for a while. That's how I felt after Louise."

"If I'm as lucky as you the second time around, then I'll be truly blessed."

"Yes. But you're blessed anyway."

"I feel like such a heel. What have I got to complain about compared to you? I mean I grew up with my parents. I always knew I was loved."

"I've got nothing to complain about. Life could have been a lot worse." His brother stole a chocolate popcorn ball Delilah made for the kids. She was chasing after him. His brother. The one who thought Delilah was the worst thing that could ever happen to him. His change of heart—well, one of David's worries was that the people he loved would be at each other's throats. He didn't relish a life of battling between the two.

"I have a lot to be thankful for," David said to his sister.

"Dad loves you, David. I think he's hurting because he doesn't know how to reach you. The two of you are alike in some ways. You're both closed. You feel things deeply within, but you won't talk about them."

"Yeah, well."

"Think about giving him a chance, even if you have to fight it out first."

"You can't always take back hurtful words."

"It's better to clear the air. Gives both of you a chance to heal."

In his heart, David knew Howard didn't really do anything different from millions of other men. He went to bed with a woman. Didn't know she was pregnant. Went on with his life. But it was hard to accept this stranger as his father.

"He's a stranger," he said as if to confirm it.

"You've known him for three years. Try to think about the good things you know about him."

By the time they were ready to leave, the kids could barely hold their eyes open and the mothers were convincing them to pick up their toys and round them up.

By bedtime that night, Delilah was so exhausted she could drop, but she couldn't help reflecting on her day. She distinguished her life between two times. Before Coree and after Coree.

Even with all the emotional upheavals, life was slow on the island. There was family time, quiet time, time for loving and reflecting.

And then there were Kendall and David. When David had changed all his financial accounts to include her, she felt guilty for not working. She'd always taken care of herself. It felt odd having someone take care of her. Buying her food, clothes. When Delilah bought clothes the other weekend and wanted to pay for them herself, David wouldn't let her. The money wasn't his, he said. It was theirs. And then he'd forced her to hire a service to clean once a week.

Delilah wasn't accustomed to those luxuries. But he'd said she'd have her hands full with Kendall and him. If she were working, who would spend hours at the school? Who would have enough energy to help him with homework after school?

Millions of women worked outside the home and performed those duties. She felt she was given a rare opportunity to accomplish her goals of writing and to make a comfortable home for her family. If she did those jobs to the best of her ability, wouldn't she have accomplished something?

"Have you sent anything out yet?" David asked. Her head rested comfortably on his shoulder.

"I mailed out a proposal in June to four publishing houses. I haven't heard anything yet."

He kissed her on her head. "You will. You're a very talented writer. Everybody takes vacations during the summer."

"Is this love speaking?"

"Well, of course. But I also read something you left out."

"You aren't supposed to read it until I finish."

"Why not?" he asked.

"Because I usually have to polish it."

"Next time I'll know."

Silence reined. "Did you really like it?"

"Yes."

"But it's romance. You guys are squeamish about romance."

"Honey, you know by now I'm not frightened by a little romance. As a matter of fact, I read a love scene. I've been waiting to try some of those moves on you."

"Oh yeah?"

He tipped her chin, kissed her. Then he shifted, sliding his nimble fingers under her nightgown. "Oh yeah."

For the next two weeks, Delilah saw very little of her husband. Often David arrived home after Kendall was in bed. Kendall was always asking about him. He'd hoped to spend more time with David.

Delilah volunteered one morning a week in Kendall's classroom. That was when she discovered Kendall was supposed to bring in money for a class trip.

"Kendall, why didn't you bring the note to me asking for money for your trip?"

He shrugged.

"Your teacher told me about the trip to the aquarium in October. How did you pay the admission fee? Did you get the money from David? I haven't seen anything on it."

He looked at his shoes. "I didn't want to worry you about the money."

"Honey, it's our responsibility to pay for what you need. How did you pay for it?"

He shrugged. "With my lunch money."

"You went all day with no lunch?"

"I fixed a peanut butter sandwich and took it with me."

"Kendall, don't hide papers from me. I know I can't take the place of your real mother, and I will always support you in remembering her and loving her. But I'm your mother now. I love you. David and I will provide you with the things you need. Do you understand?"

He nodded, but Delilah knew she had a long way to go in getting him to completely trust her.

"Would you like to sign up for the soccer team?"

Kendall bit his lip. Then he said, "Reggie's dad signed him up."

"But do *you* want to play?"

"He says it's lots of practices and games. I don't know. Do you have the time?"

"Of course I do sweetheart. I'll sign you up tomorrow." Delilah ruffled his hair. "Go wash up and have your snack. It's macaroni and cheese."

Macaroni and cheese was his favorite and Delilah wiggled the first smile out of him.

Delilah rubbed lotion on her shoulders. David was sitting up in bed reading some medical journal.

"Kendall is doing well so far in school. I talked to his teacher today."

"Wonderful," David said with a distracted air.

Delilah plowed on anyway. He spent most of his time away from home. He had to talk about family sometime.

"I think it's important we keep up with his classes to make sure he's adjusting well in his new school and in new surroundings."

"He does have friends, you know. He played with Reggie most of the summer. He met another kid at Carter's party."

"The other good thing is Reggie's in his class. That works out very well."

David nodded.

"He spent his lunch money on the admission fee for a field trip because he was afraid to ask me for it. He actually hid the papers from me."

David put the journal aside.

"He's still adjusting. He doesn't feel completely comfortable yet. It takes time. It was a while before I trusted the Robertses," David said.

Delilah rubbed lotion on her legs and capped the bottle.

"I realize that, but I think he needs more. You've been pretty busy lately. This is your weekend off. I think we should do something together," she said.

"Make him feel more like a family. He's always asking about you. What do you think?"

Delilah waited for David's response. When more time passed than should have, she said, "David?"

She turned around in her seat. David had fallen asleep. She was wired up and couldn't sleep if she tried. So much for being newlyweds.

Delilah had noticed early on that David came home tired most nights. She spent most of her days alone and one morning at Kendall's school helping the kids with the computer math program. She craved adult conversation. She wanted to snuggle in David's arms and talk a little while.

Delilah finished her nightly ritual and flipped the lights out. She would try to be an understanding wife. After all, he'd just moved Louise into his office. Wayne just left the practice and Louise brought her patients with her. It would take time to adjust to the added patients. She could understand that.

She took the medical journal out of his hand, laid it on the bedside table, and pulled the sheet up to his chest. He didn't even move, poor thing. He worked so hard.

The good thing about this, Delilah thought, was it wouldn't last forever.

Sunday morning Delilah gathered her brood early for church. She prepared breakfast and started on dinner. She was chopping onions when she realized she was acting just like her mother used to. Holly would start Sunday dinner early that morning before they left for church.

An hour after she rose, she heard the bathroom shower go on. David was up. She fried bacon and mixed the pancake batter and set it aside. Then she climbed the stairs and roused Kendall.

While the men dressed, she fixed the pancakes and eggs. The scent of the food must have brought her brood downstairs.

She set the table in the sunroom where the bright light streamed in.

"The weather is so nice I'm going to open these windows," she said.

It seemed she was the only chipper one this morning. David immediately grabbed the Sunday paper he hadn't had the chance to read yet and sat in the corner chair.

"Could you carry the platter of pancakes to the table, David?"

"Oh, sure." He set the paper down and gathered up the pancakes and pitcher of fresh-squeezed orange juice.

"Are you all alive over there?" Delilah asked when Kendall dropped into the seat.

"Barely. Something smells good," he said around a yawn.

They sat and ate, then Delilah told Kendall to get dressed for church. While he dressed, David read the Sunday paper and Delilah stacked dishes in the dishwasher.

After the service, Delilah was talking to Delcia and Cecily when Marcia approached them.

"Hey, Cecily, Delilah," she said.

"How are you?"

"Good, good. I hate to break this up but I'm in a hurry. Delilah, do you have a minute?"

"I have to get home. I'll see you later," Cecily told Delilah and walked away.

Marcia and Delilah walked toward the car.

"What is it?" Delilah asked.

"The accountant at Redcliff and I are friends. We eat lunch together sometimes. Well, on Friday, she started asking questions about you. It seemed suspicious because she doesn't even know you."

Puzzled, Delilah asked, "What kind of questions?"

"Like did you know Katherine? Did you hang out together? He thought that Katherine might have given you some confidential corporate correspondence."

"Hmm. What did you tell her?"

"I told her she should ask you. I don't get in your business. Although I know neither one of you would have done anything like that. The folks at Redcliff are crazy. A bunch of paranoid fools. They make everyone sign confidentiality documents, which isn't a bad thing, because there is a lot of industrial espionage. With the government handing out these A-76 contracts, everyone wants their piece of it."

"Would you be willing to talk to Carter about this conversation?"

"Why?"

"It's just . . . I've got a bad feeling about the bombing and I'd like you to tell him what's going on. He's become very protective."

She shrugged. "Is he here?"

"He went to the campground right after the service. I'll have him contact you."

"It's easy enough for me to stop by the camp-ground. Gives me a chance to see Mark." She rolled her eyes heavenward. "He's been a real fool lately because I haven't agreed to marry him. That man's going to make me break down before I want to."

"I thought you were in love with him."

"I am. I just didn't want to leave my parents and immediately move in with a man. I wanted some freedom first without complications. We're still pretty young."

"You've got the rest of your life. If you're not sure, no sense in rushing into things."

"It's not that I'm not sure. I love him. I just want to live alone before I take that big step."

"Take your time."

Marcia looked at her watch. "I've got to go. Have a good one."

"Thanks for informing me."

"Sure."

Delilah rounded Kendall and David up.

"Drive by the campground on your way home, please," she said to David.

"Any special reason?" David asked as he steered the car behind others leaving the church.

"People at Redcliff's have been asking questions about me. Marcia's going to talk to Carter. I want to get his take on it."

"Are you sure you're safe?"

"Why wouldn't I be? I don't know anything. I just wish I knew what's going on. Maybe the bomb was meant for Katherine. But what could she know to make them want to kill her?"

"Maybe I can tap Louise's brother for some information. He works security at Moore's, but he could know some of the guards at Redcliff."

"That's a good idea, although Louise is the last person I'd want to tap for anything."

David threw her a wry glance. "You're being catty."

A trifle peeved. "She and you both promised you'd work less hours after the two of you joined forces. That hasn't happened so far, so I'll be catty all I want to be."

"Are you having a fight?" Kendall said, sounding nervous in the backseat.

David turned into the campground driveway. "No, we aren't. We're just having a slight disagreement."

"Mom and Dad called it fighting."

"No different from arguments you have with your friends," Delilah said, turning in her seat to reassure him. But he was twisting his hands. "Don't worry, Kendall."

"Can I play the videos?"

"Pull your jacket off and get ice cream or something. You still have on your good clothes."

Delilah dug into her purse and pulled out a five. "Forget the ice cream. As much as I hate to say it, play a video game or something that you won't get dirty with."

"Thanks."

"Don't be long. It'll just take us a few minutes."

"I won't."

They talked with Carter and Marcia. When Marcia rushed away David told Carter about Louise's brother.

* * *

When David and Delilah left, Carter called Wadell.

"Hey, old man."

"Who're you calling an old man?"

"If the shoe fits . . . Anything more on Redcliff?" Carter asked.

"Not yet. The man's hated for sure. He's gotten some very large government contracts. He's pretty new in the business, but his company's growing at a much faster pace than most start-up companies. It's leaving Moore's in the dust—and most of the others for that matter."

"I'd like you to do a background check on a Katherine Day. She was the woman in the car when it blew up. And while you're at it, do a check on the driver too. Hold a minute." Carter dug his wallet out of his pocket and retrieved a slip of paper with the name of the driver. "They might tie into this somehow."

Carter hung up. Delcia was standing at the office door. She came in and closed the door.

"What's going on?"

"Somebody at Redcliff's been asking questions about Delilah."

"Still? I thought you had established that the bomb wasn't intended for her."

"I haven't established anything. We don't know anything yet."

She looked worried. "Do you think she's in danger?"

"I don't think so. They've had plenty of time to . . . I do think there is a connection between Stan, who worked at Moore's, and Redcliff, though."

"Moore's is his brother-in-law's company. You think he would betray his family?"

Carter tilted her chin, kissed her lips. "It wouldn't be the first time one family member betrayed another."

Delcia sighed. "Will we ever get to the bottom of this?"

"Yeah. I'm not going to have this mess going on in my family. We'll get to the bottom. And that's a promise."


Later that night, David closed the door to Kendall's room. The boy was fast asleep. He and Reggie had played pretty hard before Marcia picked Reggie up and Delilah made Kendall shower and prepare for bedtime.

David went to the master bedroom. Delilah was on the deck standing at the railing. Soft music played in the background. For late September, the weather was just a little nippy.

Delilah had wanted him to spend the entire day with Kendall and her, but he'd promised Howard a game of golf. She was the one who wanted him to forge a closer relationship with Howard, yet she'd screamed like a fishwife before he drove off.

He made it home in time to spend an hour with the boy. But Delilah's shoulders had remained stiff. He had some serious making up to do.

David clasped his hands around Delilah's waist, snuggled her close to him. He swirled a tongue around her earlobe.

"Still mad at me?" he asked.

"Yes."

"Forgive me?"

"I'm thinking about it. You don't spend enough time . . ."

He dipped his head and kissed her neck, turned her around, and kissed the words away. When she started to melt, he knew it was working.

"David . . ."

He worked kisses down her chest, to her breasts, clasped a nipple gently between his teeth.

"Hmmm . . ."

"We . . ."

He slid his hand up her thigh, touched her intimately, worked a finger inside her panties, stroked soft skin.

"Damn you!" He felt those hot hands caressing him, lifted her, and took her to bed. Maybe he wasn't there twenty-four-seven, but he was there now and he pleasured her body like never before.

# Chapter 13

"Can you help Kendall with his homework?" Delilah planned to write after Kendall's game while David spent some time with their son.

"I have to go in to the office. Can't you help him?"

Delilah looked up from the metro section of the paper. "I thought this was your weekend off."

"I had to switch with Louise."

"I see. Why didn't you say something before? Did you consider that I might have plans?"

Exasperated, David said, "Why didn't you tell me you had plans?"

"It's beginning to feel like you're the father with none of the responsibility of raising a child. All the parenting has fallen on me."

"I help too."

"Not much."

"Tell you what. I'll have next weekend off. I'll help with the homework then."

"How nice," Delilah said, her voice dripping with sarcasm.

David set the front page of the paper on the table. "Are you in one of those moods?"

"Why do I have to be in a mood to need some help with raising Kendall? He has a game this morning. He'd like you to attend some of them. I'm turning into the carpool lady. I take him to practice. I pick him up. The least you could do is attend some of the games. Or consult me before you and Louise change your schedule."

"Next weekend I will be at your beck and call." He glanced at his watch. "I'm going to be late if I don't get moving." He leaned over to kiss her. She evaded him, but he planted one on her cheek.

"Don't think that sex is going to fix this, David," she shouted after him.

"Come on, baby. Don't be that way. My patients need me."

"So does your family. I don't think I'm being unreasonable."

Delilah fumed for a moment, then gathered up the dishes. She saw a flyer earlier about an apple orchard. Perhaps Kendall would like to go with Marcia and Reggie after the game.

She called Marcia and they agreed to ride to the game together.

"Picking apples seems boring to me," Reggie said.

Delilah glanced at him from the rearview mirror. "Just wait until you try my apple Betty. You'll change your tune then."

"She's a great cook," Kendall said loyally.

But once they got to the orchard, the complaining ceased. They climbed ladders between playing with other kids. They ended up with a bushel of apples. Kendall must have seen someone in Donnie's group before because he was watching them closely.

"Do you know them, Kendall?" Delilah asked.

He shrugged. "Don't know."

"Why do you keep watching them?"

"Delilah?" someone called out.

Delilah turned to the voice.

Derrick was striding toward them with a giant smile. "I thought that was you over here. Where's David?" he asked, halting in front of her.

"Working as usual."

"Yeah. Louise is pulling long hours, too."

"How's the job? Things still working out with you?"

"Yeah. I've enrolled in the community college." He chuckled. "Louise's doing. Says I have to think of my future beyond this security job. But so far the pay's decent and guess it's time I stopped wasting my time and straighten up as Louise would say. Big sisters can be nags."

Delilah laughed. "What brings you here?"

"Came with a friend and his kids. His wife wanted everybody from under her feet. He was talking on the cell phone to Marcia during the soccer game. Said she was coming here afterward, so we thought we'd give it a try." He regarded the bushel of apples next to Delilah. "His wife told him not to bring more than a handful of apples back because she wasn't canning them. But his mom likes to can stuff, so we're going to take her a bushel."

"I'm going to make some desserts and bake them

with pork. There are a thousand and one ways to use apples in cooking," Delilah said.

"I cook enough to get by. That's why I can't save anything. I eat in Cecily's place and Wanda's until I run out of money, then I hit Louise's kitchen." He rubbed his flat stomach. "I'm no cook but I love to eat."

"It's not showing so far," Delilah said.

"Yeah, well, I work out a lot."

Delilah kept an eye on Kendall as he continued to pick apples, but he kept watching the other group, too. Not that anything was wrong, but every time Kendall looked that way he frowned and she wanted to know what was going on.

"Looks like your chief of security came with you."

"Donnie and Percy's just tagging along. Donnie loves to cook. When he comes to cookouts, he always brings something good."

"He's done well for himself at Moore's," Delilah said. "How long have you known him?"

"Just since I started working there. I wouldn't mind having his position. I wouldn't need to attend community college if I did."

"Nothing takes the place of an education."

He moaned. "You're beginning to sound too much like Louise."

"Let me stop. I don't want to sound like an older nagging sister."

"They carry a powerful punch," he said. "She disowned me for a while."

"Oh yeah? Why? Just tell me it's none of my business if you don't want to talk about it." Delilah didn't want him to think she was getting in his business, but he had brought the subject up.

"I don't mind. I had some gambling problems a while back. Just about sent her into bankruptcy before she got me into Gambler's Anonymous. It worked. My favorite was the horses. I can't go near a race track."

"I'm glad you turned your life around."

"Yeah. Me too."

"We picked a whole basketful of apples," Kendall said. "Can we go home now? We want to get in the pool before you start making me do homework or watch something on the Discovery Channel."

Derrick rubbed Kendall's head. "She actually makes you watch stuff on that channel?"

"The History Channel, too."

"Hey, sport. We all suffer at your age."

"That's for sure," Kendall said.

"Thanks for the support, Derrick. Let's hope he'll appreciate it when he's older," Delilah said.

Kendall rolled his eyes heavenward. "That'll be forever," he said.

"See if Marcia's ready," Delilah said. "Good job with the apples. Thanks." Marcia was talking to Donnie.

"Check you later," Derrick said.

"You too." He walked toward his group.


One of David's patients had died. When he drove home, he didn't recognize the smell of spices and apples in the kitchen. All he wanted was to be with Delilah and lose himself in her arms.

"You know, as much as we aren't supposed to become emotionally involved, you can't help it when children are involved. They're tiny and helpless and they look to adults for guidance."

"And as much as you want to you can't heal all of them. But you help many, many more than you lose." Delilah linked her arms around him.

"That doesn't help much when you lose one."


A week later, Kendall was pressing Delilah's nerves to the breaking point. It seemed he did everything he could to get on her nerves. They had both been at their wits' end by the time she sent him to bed. He stomped off to his room. She let him stew for ten minutes to calm down. She was on her way to his room when David arrived.

David took one look at her tense features and knew something was wrong. He gathered her in his arms, nuzzled her neck.

"Been quite a day, hmm?"

"And then some. I was just on my way to Kendall's room to talk to him. I don't know what got into him tonight."

"Why don't you take a long shower and relax? I'll see to him."

"I'll get your dinner out fir—"

"I can get my own dinner. Run the water and let the tension out."

He walked with her toward the stairs, where they parted, she to the suite and he to climb the steps to Ken's room.

The light was spilling into the hallway. Ken's hands were behind his head as he stared at the ceiling.

"What's up?" David said to the boy.

Ken sat up. "Nuttin'."

"I guess it's been a pressure-cooker day for both of you."

Ken shrugged, his stubborn chin jutting in the air.

David sat on the side of the bed. The fear in Ken's eyes was palpable. David ruffled his hair. "Want to talk about it?"

Ken shrugged again.

"She's been a little tense lately."

"I guess I was bad. She's mad at me."

"No, she's not angry with you. She's just not herself right now."

"Are you going to have to send me back until things get better? Do I have to pack all my things? Even the new things she bought for me?" His eyes were worried, his lips pinched to hold in roiling emotions.

"This is your home, regardless of what goes on. You're not going anywhere. We're a family," David said.

His eyes widened. "I get to stay?"

"Just like Delilah and I get to stay, so do you. That's what families do. It's never going to be perfect, but it'll be as close to it as humanly possible."

David ruffled the boy's hair. "You're stuck with us, kid."

The worry began to lift from Ken's features.

"You might want to go give her a hug tomorrow morning. Give her a little time to calm down first."

"She's mad at me."

"Worried. Not angry." David glanced at the book on the nightstand. "Let me read you a story."

* * *

Instead of dinner, David peeled off his clothes and got into the Jacuzzi behind Delilah, letting her head fall against his chest. He ran a hand over her arms and tucked it against her waist. Nuzzling her head with his chin, he said, "Feel better?"

"Lots. Did you square things with Kendall?"

"Yes. He was just worried that we were going to send him back."

"I know that's one of the things we're to look out for, but what gave him that impression?"

"He doesn't need a reason. Fear has nothing to do with logic. He's just not completely comfortable with us yet."

"It will take time. I don't care how perfect we want things to be, life gets in the way."

"We'll get through this. Don't give it another thought." He grasped the bar of soap and rubbed it into his hands. Then he began to massage her body with the slickness of soap. He wanted to comfort her, wanted her to feel warm and protected. At least give her some small measure of peace of mind for a little while.

The next morning after breakfast, Kendall had apologized to Delilah and given her a huge hug. It felt wonderful. She never realized how comforting a hug could be. Life had taught her to weather her storms alone.

She prepared strawberry pancakes topped with maple syrup, whipped cream, and fresh strawberries.

"A special treat just for you," Delilah told him when he sat at the table.

"Thanks," he said. "My mom used to fix it like this."

"And did you like them?"

He nodded and dug in. "A lot."

Delilah was surprised to see Carter at her kitchen door before she even called him.

"It's a devil of a morning. Got any more of that?" He pointed to the cup in her hand.

"Sure."

He eyed her china cup and saucer with disdain. "And not in one of those delicate sissy cups. Give me a mug."

"Men." Delilah pulled a huge mug out of the cabinet and made it the way she made her own, with the chicory her mother, born and raised in Mississippi, used.

"Sugar, cream?" she asked.

He shook his head.

"Where's the slugger?"

"Out roaming with Reggie."

"Good. We can talk in peace."

She handed the cup over and he closed his eyes on the first swallow. "I might just detour here every morning unless you give us that recipe."

She shook her head. "Give you an excuse to visit," she said, taking a seat across from him. "What brings you here so early? You must have telepathy. Saved me a call."

"What happened?"

Delilah told him about the body. "That was in June, I believe. He said he saw two men throw big garbage bags into the sound. Do you think it could have been Stan they tossed in?"

"Could have been." Carter took out a tiny note-book and scribbled.

"Would you like breakfast with your coffee? Or biscuits or something?"

"Whatever's handy. Got pulled out of bed before the crack of dawn to fix a broken pipe at the campground."

When Delilah got up to fix his breakfast, they talked of inconsequential things like Delcia and the children, the campground, follies with the tourists until she set a heaping plate in front of him.

After his first bite, he said, "You're going to make it hard for me to run you off."

"I'm doing my best."

"I don't know how some of Redcliff's security force got clearances. The limo driver had a record a mile long."

"Redcliff is paranoid about security. He's scared to death that some of Moore's employees might cause them to not get a contract."

"Well, it might be the pot and kettle throwing punches."

Carter stood. "Do you think he recognized Kendall?"

"I don't know. Do you think he's in danger?" The bustling wind swept her hair all over the place when they went outside. Although Delilah didn't see the boys, she heard their voices in the distance.

Carter hugged her. "Try not to worry too much. I'll do what I can."

She nodded. But it was impossible not to worry.

"I talked to Marcia earlier. Told her I was taking the boys to the campground. They can play in the arcade, swim, eat hot dogs and sodas until they pop. Then you and David come to our house for dinner tonight. Okay with you?"

"Sure."

"You go back in and take it easy. I'll rustle them up."

"Thanks, Carter."

"You're welcome, sis."

Before Delilah could react to his statement he was strolling toward the sound of the children's voices.


Late that night, the silence of the night was disturbed by Kendall's heartrending screams. Delilah jumped out of bed, David behind her, and sailed down the corridor to his room. She flipped the light on.

"Kendall? What's wrong, honey?" She crossed the floor to him.

When he didn't respond she shook his shoulder lightly until he awakened.

"You were having a nightmare."

Tears were running down his face. Delilah gathered him into her arms.

David reached out a hand and caressed his back.

"You want to talk about it?" David asked.

"You were gone. And I was all alone again."

Delilah smoothed his hair. "We're right here, sweetheart. We aren't going anywhere."

Kendall was ashamed of himself for showing weakness. He hadn't meant to say anything.

"Yeah, I know," he said, but his stomach was doing flip-flops. He knew that nothing was a sure thing. His mom was gone and so was his dad. And he knew Delilah and David could leave just as easily. And his world would turn upside down again.

Drying his eyes, he pulled away from Delilah's soft arms. She was sweet-smelling. She always smelled sweet.

At the beach today, Reggie had asked what he was going to do when David and Delilah had children of their own. He wondered if they'd send him back.

"I'm okay now," he said.

"Do you want to talk about it?" David asked him again.

He shook his head. He was a kid. Adults always made decisions for him. He wasn't going to let them know he was scared. He already felt ashamed for hollering out in his sleep and crying like a baby. In the last year he'd learned to keep his feelings to himself.

"You know you can talk to us if you're worried about something. That's what we're here for," Delilah said.

*Yeah, sure.* He wanted to be as perfect as he could be to make sure they kept him. He wasn't going to go complaining about every little thing to give them an excuse to get rid of him. "Yeah, I know," he said with a smile, hoping he sounded convincing.

When Delilah and David returned to their bedrooms, David was still frowning.

"What is it?" Delilah asked.

"Just thinking. There are lots of things going on in his mind that he isn't talking to us about. I want him to feel comfortable talking about his fears."

"It'll come. We'll be patient."

"Yeah, well, I'll try to talk to him again tomorrow. I could just see him thinking. He's holding it all in."

When they got under the covers, Delilah snuggled up to him. The feeling he had was beyond words, but he wanted Ken to feel that kind of security, the love too. And he couldn't relax knowing that that little boy down the hall was worried that any moment the rug was going to be pulled from under his feet. He wanted his little boy to feel comforted and loved.

By rights Ken should have had a charmed life. He lived with his natural parents who loved him. His existence had been an ideal one until his father died and shortly thereafter his mother.

David's mother died at the very beginning of his life. Perhaps the unfortunate incident could be explained as "things happen." Whom could he blame? His father? His mother? The overworked night that put the two together after healing the sick, sending off the deceased? An occurrence that threw two lonely people together for a much-needed respite— a need that out of the bad, something good happened?

Maybe his mother's family was overly strict, and he could certainly tell that by the way they acted around him. His grandparents acted as if he were a pariah at times. He was considered a blight on the family honor and name. But it was his mother's choice whether to tell his father that she was pregnant. She chose not to. She might not have had to go it alone. She might not have had to be among strangers.

There was so much in life that was unexplainable. The only reasonable thing he could say about it was, things happen.

Sunday afternoon, Howard drove to the island. He talked to Delilah, did the grandfatherly indulgence with Ken, then asked David to take a walk with him along the beach.

David obliged. It was cooler that day.

"I know you blame me for what happened to you."

"I don't. I think I was just letting off steam that day. I know my mother could have informed you that she was pregnant. She should bear the responsibility for not telling you and for not leaving some information of who she was and what to do with us in the event something happened."

"She was a good woman."

"You've told me that. I'm sure she was."

"No parent wants his or her child to suffer what you have. There's nothing I can do about the past, but I hope—I pray—we can share a meaningful relationship in the future. I'd like you to know more about your family, about your background. Do you have a problem with that?"

"No. Knowing you won't take away from the relationship I share with the Robertses. I don't have a problem with knowing you."

Delilah spent two hours at school supervising Kendall's fourth grade class in the computer lab. Today they worked on math problems. She stayed until lunch. Then she stopped by a dress shop in town. She'd hoped to get some work done on her book before Kendall came home from school.

But when she drove into the yard, an unfamiliar car was parked there.

She left her car and walked around the house looking for the car's owner. But no one was there. She hoped tourists hadn't just parked in her yard to spend a day on the beach. She loved the isolation, but that remoteness could very well bring danger.

She shrugged and went into the house, taking the time to make sure the door was locked, and set the security alarm. Five minutes later, when she was in the process of stashing the breakfast dishes in the dishwasher, the doorbell rang. Turning the water off, she dried her hands on a paper towel and walked to the door. Through the glass pane, she saw Keith standing on her porch.

She opened the door with an angry gesture.

"What are you doing here?" she asked him.

He flashed one of his charming smiles. Didn't he know it no longer carried the weight it once had?

"Can't I at least come in?"

"We've said everything we needed to say. I got my last check, thank you." She started to close the door, but he put a foot in the opening to stop her.

"I need to talk to you. You've really bought a beautiful place with your bonus. I'm impressed."

How she arrived at the house was none of his business. "You should be."

"Come on, let me in."

"Keith, I'm working. I'm not interested in anything you have to say. Let's not waste each other's time."

He nudged her back. "Just five minutes. That's all."

Finally she stepped to the side so he could enter. "Go on through to the sunporch." He followed her to the kitchen and she pointed him toward the porch.

When he continued on, she poured two tall glasses of iced tea and took them with her.

She drank half the glass before she spoke again. When she looked up she noticed Keith's glass was still full.

"Why did you come?" she asked him.

Keith leaned both elbows on the table and rubbed the bridge of his nose. For the first time she took a close look at him. He looked as if he'd lost weight, as if he'd aged.

"I know we didn't part on the best of circumstances, but I'd like you to come back to work for me."

Delilah was shaking her head before he completed his sentence. "I can't."

"Look, Laurie and I broke up. That's not a problem anymore."

"And you think that makes everything all right? Because she left your sorry behind?"

"It's not just me. It's the other workers at the company you should think about. Besides, with the money you'll make on proposals, you could buy a dozen houses like this one. Let this be your vacation house."

"There are plenty of proposal managers who

can work for you. I'm married. I can't come back. Even if I wasn't married, I wouldn't. You can't treat people like trash and expect them to come crawling at your beck and call."

As he slumped in shock, he seemed to shrink before her eyes.

"Married!" He looked at her ring finger. Delilah just then realized she'd taken off her rings to do the dishes.

"Yes, married. In August. To a wonderful man. I can't help you."

"Who is the lucky man?"

"You don't know him. He's a pediatrician who has a practice in Morehead City."

He seemed to let that digest. "We haven't won a bid since you left."

"I'm sorry." She really was. Just because they didn't work out, she didn't want his company to fail. Although she didn't get along with most of the office staff, she liked some of the workers in other departments. "There are many qualified proposal managers out there. Do some interviews and hire one."

"They won't take a cut in salary the way you did."

"I wish I could help you. But I can't. And I really have to finish the dishes so that I can get some work done before my son gets home from school"

"You have a son?"

"My husband and I adopted."

"So you have your life all planned out," he said.

"It's working well so far."

In another five minutes, Keith left. After the way

he had treated her, why did she feel so bad that his company wasn't doing well? She really shouldn't give him another thought. But she thought of the workers she'd grown to like. For their sake she hoped it survived.

Delilah grabbed the mail and spotted a letter with the return address of one of the publishing houses she'd mailed her manuscript to. Her heart sank. Bad news. If they wanted the manuscript, they would have called her. They wouldn't have mailed a letter. Reluctantly, she opened it. They'd rejected the manuscript.

She tried to tell herself the same thing she told her friends who had received rejections. That someone else might buy it. But the pep talk didn't make her feel any better.

When she got into the house, the phone was ringing.

"How are you, ma'am?"

Delilah smiled. "Sorry, I'm not buying anything today."

"You don't know what I'm selling," David said. "How do you know you don't want it?"

"What are you selling?"

"Your most fervent dream."

Well, she'd just lost one dream, temporarily, anyway.

"And what might that be?" Delilah asked, in the spirit of fun.

"A thirty-second conversation with your husband."

"That long? Let's pull out the drums."

"We're picky, aren't we?"

"You're cheap."

He laughed. At least she felt better, Delilah thought.

# Chapter 14

Delilah was definitely feeling more like a mother and less like a woman lately. With Kendall, the house, and trying to squeeze in writing time, little time was left for her. So she was looking forward to attending the benefit and dinner with David and to engage in adult conversation. The benefit was on Friday night and since David was unable to return to the island to dress, he had carried his tux to the office with him that morning.

Carter and Delcia were doubling with Ryan and Cecily. Delilah caught a ride with them to David's office. Once they arrived, they all rode the elevator up to David's office.

Earlier Delilah had told David she felt as if she'd been married eighty years instead of eight weeks. He'd promised her a weekend out. Kendall was spending the weekend with Carter and Delcia so that David and she could enjoy some time alone—maybe feel like newlyweds for once. Honestly, at this point she didn't have a clue what a newlywed felt like.

When Delilah opened the office door, David and Louise were standing in the middle of the floor. Louise was fixing the tie to his tux.

"Oh, hi," Louise said as everyone filed in.

Delilah saw red. It looked so innocent, but she'd been chasing after kids half the day. And she wasn't feeling reasonable. Knowing that, she kept her mouth pressed together.

"Be right back," David said when Louise finished. He disappeared in back.

"My car is in the shop and I arranged to go with David to the benefit. I had completely forgotten that he drives a two-seater. I should have rented something, but I just couldn't get away today. Delilah, would you mind terribly going with your friends?"

Delilah looked at the woman as if she were crazy. She couldn't believe her husband, who had barely taken her any place since he married her, actually expected her to be a fifth wheel.

Carter waited for the air to explode. He could see the tension riding Delilah in waves. Could see it building for weeks, which was one of the reasons he and Delcia offered to take Kendall for the weekend.

David sauntered in carrying a wrist corsage.

"Tell you what. I'll find my own ride. You all go ahead." Delilah turned to the group who stood as if rooted to the spot. "Thanks for dropping me off. I'll just use the phone in your office, David."

She shrugged out of the jacket.

The jacket, which stopped a couple of inches above her knees, made the outfit look discreet and respectable. Perfectly appropriate for the escort of the keynote speaker. But without it . . . well, there were thin strips of fabric that crossed at about every inch and a half starting from just above midthigh to her hips. She definitely wasn't wearing any underwear.

In the end, Louise rode in Carter's car while Delilah rode with David. David may have given a rousing speech, but Delilah didn't hear any of it.

After the event, when David parked the car on the ferry, Delilah opened her door and went to stand at the railing. The temperature was very cool, the wind whipped the air and waves, but she couldn't sit in that car with David for one second longer.

"Delilah, I know you're angry."

She turned her back to him. "Is the word 'livid' in your vocabulary? You lied to me."

"I didn't lie. I didn't tell Louise I'd take her to the benefit."

"Forget the benefit. You haven't held up your part of the bargain. I'm the one who's raising Kendall alone while you're off playing games with your partner." She spat the word like a blasphemy.

David sighed. "I'm not playing anything with Louise. How can you believe something like that?"

"What the hell was she doing tying your tie?"

"That's ridiculous. She said it was crooked and just straightened it."

"What gives her the nerve to think I'd go to a formal function with someone else while she rides with my husband?"

"I was as shocked as you," David said. "She never even asked me."

"Don't do this, David. Don't play stupid with me. I know she wants you back. You hired her on so that you could work fewer hours, so that you could spend more time at home, but you don't work fewer hours. You don't spend more time at home. I'm not raising Kendall alone. I don't even know if I want this marriage anymore."

"What the hell are you talking about? Just because we're having a few problems you're giving up on the whole marriage?"

Delilah turned away from him. "It's not what I expected it to be. All I know is I didn't get married for this."

She walked off from him, farther down the railing. He watched her a moment before he followed.

"Go away from me. I don't want to be around you."

"Delilah—"

"Just go away. You're never there anyway. Never. Just . . . just go away."

"It's not just you and me we're dealing with. There's Ken to consider," he said quietly. "We can't—"

"Is that why you married me? As a caretaker for Kendall? You love him. You wanted to adopt him, but it wasn't fair because you work fourteen-hour days. I was handy."

"That's not true. I wouldn't marry you for that reason."

"Well, you did. Because all I've been is a mother to Kendall and easy sex for you when you fall into the house at odd hours. And a damn dog sitter for your dog, which has turned out to be the best part of this whole ordeal. At least she's there for me to talk to."

The occupants of Carter's car watched David and Delilah at the railing. Even from a distance in the low lights, things did not look good.

"I wouldn't want to be in your brother's shoes right now," Ryan said.

"I don't know what the hell's going on in his mind."

"One thing. I know it started before she got in the car. She was not herself when we picked her up," Cecily said. "But she didn't want to talk about it."

"Maybe this thing with Louise has been building up for some time. I told him not to take that witch in his partnership," Carter said in disgust.

"Louise can't do any more than he lets her," Cecily murmured.

"She can tear his marriage apart," Delcia said. "I wouldn't have your ex working in the campground, I tell you that. And I told Delilah so, too."

Ryan groaned. "You should have known better than to bring this up."

"When did this get to be about me?"

"Uh-oh. It's getting worse. She's walking away from him," Ryan said.

"My brother knows how to find trouble. Wish I could help him, but there are some areas where a man just has to stand up to the pressure and handle it on his own."

"Well, it's about time you felt that way. You can be too interfering at times," Delcia said. "I thought you learned a lesson from my father."

"I don't interfere."

"Ha," both Delcia and Cecily said.

After the laughter died, Cecily said, "She's hurting. I don't know what it is, but she's hurting. Delilah rarely talks about things that really trouble her."

"I've got a feeling he's getting an earful now," Carter said.

Delcia scoffed. "As well he should."

"I'll tell you one thing," Ryan said. "As mad as she is, I'd put a lock and chain on her."

Carter nodded. "Sister's about to run buck wild."

"How can you say something like that? She's given you no reason to think she isn't trustworthy," Delcia said.

"That was in the past. She's been cooped up too long and she's going to spring free like a jack-in-the-box."


David was livid. Did Delilah think he would walk away from his responsibilities on a whim? He tended children's illnesses. That required time. He gave as much time as he could to his family and resented her saying that he used her.

She hadn't spoken to him since they left the ferry. And after the way she'd railed at him like a fishwife, he didn't have a thing to say to her. Especially about an argument that started with something as stupid as Louise helping him with a stupid tie.

\* \* \*

The plan was that Delilah and David would spend the night at home instead of the hotel. Delilah had the maid come in to clean from top to bottom.

She didn't want to even see David. She changed into jeans before she disappeared into her office to write. Only she was too upset to get anything done. The rejection letter weighed heavily on her mind. She tried to read over notes, but she'd read an entire page and couldn't tell what was on it. Her creative juices were dried up, and no matter how hard she tried to tell herself that even *New York Times* best sellers received rejection letters—many received more than one or two rejections. Some received twenty-five before the rare publisher appreciated their work.

Flipping off the computer, Delilah went to the bar and poured herself a glass of wine. She looked around the beautiful house and realized she was happier in the tiny cottage when she thought David truly loved her.

With drink in hand, she went out on the patio and listened to the night creatures, the crashing waves, and the whistling wind.

She heard David come out behind her. She just wanted him to go away. They might as well have kept Kendall for the weekend. At least he'd be a buffer between them.

David went back inside. A moment later she heard the Manhattans' "Nites Like This" drifting outside and soon David floated outside with it. He stooped on his haunches beside her chair. It was when he wiped her cheeks that she realized tears were drifting down her face.

He stroked her chin. "Delilah," he whispered softly. "We can work it out. Whatever troubles you . . ."

"It's not just me."

"I'm sorry I hurt you. I love you, more than anything. I'd erase your pain if I could." And then he pulled her into his arms.

She pushed away from him. She knew she'd melt with the first touch of tenderness, which was why she didn't want to be anywhere near him.

"Sex isn't going to work this time. You used sex the last time I was angry. We can't solve our problems with sex, David."

"Okay, I'm all ears. Let's talk." He plopped down into the chair.

"I feel like I don't have a life anymore," she began. "When I was working outside the home, I worked long hours, but there were breaks. I could take a few days off to regroup. It seems now it's an ongoing ordeal, with no break in sight. And it's not just that. When was the last time we went out to dinner, to a club, a movie—something for just you and me? I love Kendall, but I need some downtime."

He pulled her back to sit on his lap, wrapped his arm around her. "I'm sorry I've neglected you."

"It's not just me. We're neglecting us. Remember what I said I wanted out of a marriage? You said you wanted the same thing."

"I do."

She was so hurt. He was supposed to be her ship in the storm. And as she floated into his arms, all the pain of the rejection, of too many evenings alone, the loneliness converged.

"Oh, baby," he said. "Why didn't you tell me? I don't care what else is going on, you're first in my life. I love you."

"Damn you, David. I can't let you do this."

"Do what? Love you?" he said, stroking her face with his fingers.

"I'm not going to melt with soft music and sweet words and have everything go back to the way it was tomorrow."

He framed her face with his hands. "I'm all yours the rest of the weekend. Ken isn't here. We've got the house to ourselves. Don't waste it, Delilah. I want to be with you."

Setting her on her feet, he stood, lifted her into his arms, and carried her into the house. With sensuous songs humming in the background, he kissed her with a passion that left her breathless and wanting more. He touched her body in ways that aroused her desire to a fever pitch. He stroked her with strong, yet light strokes.

"Dav—"

"Lie back and enjoy," he whispered. "Let me love you. Baby, let me guide this." And he did. Oh, did he!

He turned her on her stomach. She never knew a kiss behind the knee was so amorous. He planted a kiss on her back, then stroked her with his tongue. With an unhurried pace, he showered her with tender kisses, he stroked, he drove her to the brink of madness.

When he was doing such delicious things to her body, how could she think of anything except how incredible it felt?

He finally turned her onto her back, one knee on

the bed beside her. "Are you enjoying yourself?" he asked softly, his whispery breath brushing her skin.

All Delilah could do was moan.

His amazing chest and shoulders were bare and Delilah reached out and touched his hard body.

"This is for you," he whispered, and moving up her body, he slowly lowered his mouth to her breast and suckled. Ran his hands between her legs, replaced fingers with his mouth. He loved her slowly. He loved her sweetly. He loved her completely.

Delilah was ready. Oh, she was more than ready. Her breath gasped in little puffs of excitement. He continued to stroke her, and with slow, oh, so gentle loving, brought her to an explosive orgasm.

Giving her barely enough time to breathe, much less rest, he hovered over her for agonizing moments, then was pushing himself into her, and she encased his amazing size and length. For a moment he hovered still, giving them both a chance to enjoy the fullness. Then they moved to the frenzied pace of lovers who grabbed for every inch of stimulation—until they both climaxed so violently they were left gasping for air.

Some time later, it felt like forever, he rolled off her and gathered her into his arms. They lay side by side, completely sated, arms and legs entwined.

An hour later, David held Delilah in his arms. She felt complete in some ways, but knew problems were still on the surface waiting to erupt, because although they could bring each other complete sexual satisfaction, lovemaking couldn't solve the other problems.

But for now, Delilah kissed his chest. In his sleep, he snuggled her closer until finally she drifted off to sleep.


Sunday morning, in an effort to soothe Delilah's ruffled feathers, David told her he was taking them to the Fall Festival after church. But Delilah had gone stubborn. Sex didn't fix their problem. Instead of talking about it, they'd made love until the wee hours of the morning. But Delilah didn't know how to broach all the problems that were plaguing her.

If he didn't want to spend time with her, then she didn't want to be with him, either. She knew she was acting silly, but she was so emotional at that point she didn't even try to stop herself.

But once they were in church the preacher started talking about forgiveness, and with David looking like he didn't have a clue, she couldn't hold on to her anger. She decided to join them in the family outing. Then later on she got angry all over again for giving in.

As angry as she was, Delilah loved David. Perhaps she was expecting too much. Expecting perfection, which didn't exist.

How did you bring up an argument when you only wanted to close your eyes and believe that everything would be okay? And you knew very well that the problems that plague a relationship that day would plague the relationship the next day and week after that if changes weren't made, if compromises weren't formed.

She wasn't going to be his doormat.

* * *

Delilah was taking a lunch break from her writing when she realized she hadn't been to a play or hit happy hour since she got married. Perhaps she and David could do the dating scene Friday night. Wouldn't that be fun?

She dialed his office. He was seeing a patient, so she left a message for him to return the call.

She fixed a salad and topped it with chicken left over from the night before. The phone rang.

"I heard I'm wanted." David's husky voice warmed her heart.

Delilah dropped into the chair. "You're always wanted."

"What's up?"

"I'm inviting you to go out on a date."

"Hmmm. Sounds naughty."

"I'm thinking I'll meet you at your office. We'll go to happy hour, then a play. How does that sound?"

"Great. Who'll keep Kendall?"

"A sitter, silly. I'm sure I can find one even on Coree." Men, Delilah thought, were so clueless.

"Sounds like a winner."

"Tomorrow night?" she asked hopefully.

"Let's see. Can't do."

Delilah wanted to bang him in the head with the phone, but she kept her cool. "When will be a good time for you?" she asked patiently.

"Let me get back to you on that. Okay, sweetie?"

"I'll be waiting."

And Delilah waited—a solid week—without a word from David, until she finally called Sylvia.

"Rescue me."

Sylvia laughed. "From what?"

"Girl, I'm going stir-crazy. I have to get out of this house. I don't feel like myself anymore. I don't want to go out with another mother sopping up noses. I need some fun, girl. Help!"

"I'm with you. But what about that handsome husband of yours?"

"Oh, please. He's got me sitting around this house like I'm some old woman. I've had enough. So we'll start with happy hour?"

"Right down my line."

"A play. A new one is onstage."

"Even better. Maybe a little clubbing afterward. I'll pick up the men while you look married." She spoke to someone in the background. "Marcia says hi."

"Invite her to come with us."

A pause, then, "She's game."

"All right," Delilah said. "I'll get the tickets for tomorrow night? Okay with you?"

Another pause. "It's a go."

"I'll pick you up after work. Tell Marcia to call me with the name of a reliable sitter for Kendall. Not like the single days. Can't just pick up and go anymore."

But Delilah didn't need the sitter, although she took the name and phone number anyway. Delcia offered to keep Kendall overnight.


"It's almost three in the morning. What are you going to tell David?" Marcia asked as Delilah drove up the path to her house.

"Nothing."

"But you didn't tell him you were going out," she said, more worried than Delilah. Delilah wasn't concerned at all.

"So? He doesn't give me a play-by-play of his days, either. Why do I have to act like I'm some kid?"

"You *are* his wife."

"Who he's neglecting," Delilah said. "You better not say a word either, not even to Mark. There are no secrets among those men."

"My lips are sealed."

Delilah stopped the car in front of Marcia's run-down white clapboard house spotted with peeling paint. "Thanks for going."

"I had a ball." She opened the door. "See you at the game tomorrow if you're still alive."

"Where the hell have you been? I've been worried sick about you!"

Damn if David didn't look good in jeans, T-shirt, bare feet, and outrage.

"You didn't see my note?" Delilah asked, heading for the fridge for a bottle of water.

"It didn't say anything about you being out half the frigging night."

Delilah snatched up the note secured to the fridge with a lighthouse magnet. Pointed a finger. "Says right here I'll be late."

With water in hand, she bounced down the hallway with dancing steps. She hadn't danced like that in—since before marriage. Darn, it felt good getting out again.

Angry steps pounded behind her. "Late is nine or ten. You're a married woman."

"Married. Not dead, sweetie." In the bedroom, Delilah threw her purse on the bed. Pulled off her earrings and dropped them into her jewelry box.

"I said I was working on getting an evening off to take you out."

"Okay."

David frowned. "That dress is too tight. A married woman has no business going out like that without her husband." He'd started to say without him, but she had asked him over a week ago and he hadn't had the time.

"Uh-huh." Delilah shimmied out of the dress, even threw in extra hip wiggles, and tossed it over the chair.

David saw red. Damn it, she didn't have on a stitch under the scrap of fabric except for that excuse for underwear. Here he was busting his ass every single day trying to provide for his family and she's out doing God knows what with . . .

"Who did you go out with?"

"Why did I have to be with someone?"

She sashayed into the bath, turned the shower on, and slipped out of her thong, presenting him with her curvy backside and long shapely legs.

"I called Kendall," David said, trying to get a grip on his temper. She'd neglected the boy. Before the thought completed itself, he knew she hadn't.

"That's nice." She slipped into the huge shower that contained enough heads to water a lawn.

Leaving the bathroom, David stormed to the bar, poured himself a drink. Woman was trying to drive him crazy.

*   *   *

Delilah peeped around the corner of the shower and smiled as David stomped out. Some of the tension that had built up and was making her crazy had seeped out. She hadn't felt this good in a very long time.

After her shower Delilah smoothed lotion on her skin. Opting for subtlety, she spritzed perfume into the air and walked into the scent so she wouldn't smell as though she'd bathed in it. Forgoing underwear, she slipped into a skimpy nightgown and casually strode into the bedroom.

With a shot glass in his hand, David was pacing.

"I promised Delcia I would pick Kendall up early tomorrow. I have to sleep fast. He has a game at nine."

David frowned at the liquid left in his glass. "I think I can attend this game."

"That will please Kendall." Delilah slid beneath the covers. "Aren't you coming to bed, sweetie?"

She was playing one of those women's games on him. He knew it. David didn't believe for a moment she had been out with another man. But she looked in the mood for sex. He had started to say they needed to talk before, but then he'd be playing a scene switch of a previous experience. He remembered how he'd smoothed her ruffled feathers using sex. That crap wasn't going to work with him.

Except, what the hell could he do? How could he complain? Heck of a position to be in. He was going to get this mess under control. She wasn't going to play with his head.

He wasn't sleepy, but he set the glass down, dragged off his jeans and shirt. Tossing them aside, he slid beneath the covers. Her subtle scent wafted over to him and he found himself reaching for her. He'd let her have her little vengeance, he thought. For now. He was man enough to handle this.

"I have to spend more time with Delilah," David said to Howard. "I don't know about the sitter she hires. Just a teenager." Not only had she gone out Friday night, but when he returned early the next day from playing golf with Howard, a bubble-gum-popping sitter was at the house with Kendall. Delilah came strolling in, happy as you please, seven hours later.

"Kendall isn't a baby, David. But if you're worried, what do you think grandpas are for?"

David directed a glance at Howard. He never really thought of the older man as a grandfather.

"If Delilah wants to drop him off before I arrive home, it's no problem. The housekeeper lives in the cottage in back. She'll keep him until I get there or you can drop him off here. The nurses will keep him busy. Either way works."

"We'll do that. Thanks."

"No need to thank me."

They walked on in silence.

"My partner's son just finished his pediatric residency. He thought about opening his own practice, but it isn't something he really wants to do. He prefers to work in a practice already established. If you're interested, I can give you his number."

"I'm interested. Although he's not going to come in as a partner."

"He realizes that. He'll have to work his way up."

"Louise and I both want a third person, but most of all it will give me more time at home."

"You're still newlyweds."

"Yeah." David glanced at the sky. "The hurricane went out to sea. The weather is supposed to be really good this weekend. Probably the last good one before the cold sets in. Could you spend it with us? We're having a cookout. The Andersons will be with us. Some friends. So will Sasha."

Howard couldn't mask how surprised he was. "I'd love to."

"Drive over after work Friday."


First thing Friday morning, Delilah beat a path to the dock for fresh fish, but this time she had them filleted. The same man who had sold her the fish in June waited on her. "You having a party or something?"

"Tomorrow. Stop by if you have time. Bring your family."

"Will do. My wife wants to see that fine house. I see it from the boat sometimes."

Delilah was surprised he knew where she lived, but it was an island, after all.

He handed her the package already packed in ice. She didn't have to ask him any longer.

"See you tomorrow," she said.

On her way home, she stopped by the video store for videos for the kids. Kendall had given her a list. She'd shopped for groceries at the mainland on Thursday.

She spent the rest of the day making salads, various flavors of lemonade, desserts, popcorn balls, brownies, and other snacks for the kids. Delilah prepped the food for the grill before she went to bed. This was her first function in Coree and she was pulling out all the stops.

She used her outdoor kitchen. Having the handy fridge outside was a bonus.

Sylvia arrived at the crack of dawn. Ryan dropped off Willow Mae early that morning, but she was a crafty old devil. She'd already cooked enough to feed a platoon. She was getting ready to prepare for the second one when he dragged her out of the house and deposited her on Delilah's doorstep.

By three everyone had arrived, even more than had been invited. The yard was so full it seemed practically the entire island had landed on their doorstep.

Even Mark and Marcia seemed to put their arguments aside to have a good time. Delilah was talking to the fisherman and his wife when Mark called everyone to attention.

"Ladies and gentlemen. A moment of your time please." When he had everyone's attention he said, "Marcia has finally agreed to marry me."

Cheers and claps erupted.

"Finally wore her down," Harry called out.

Delilah wove her way to the couple and hugged Marcia. She and Mark had separated.

"I'm happy for you, girl."

"What happened to your needing some time alone?" Sylvia asked.

"I've had some time alone," Marcia said, looking over at Mark. "It's time."

* * *

If the old maxim "action talks louder than words" was an indication, then Delilah's decision to quit being the doormat worked. True to his word, David began to spend more time with both Kendall and her. They'd begun to have family activities that included the three of them. Kendall was in seventh heaven spending more time with David. And Delilah enjoyed time with them as a family and separate private time with David.

Delilah had also settled into the routine of writing. From the time she got married, she'd taken care of Kendall and David, her writing relegated to the back burner. But if she was serious, and she was, she realized she had to put it first. Now she didn't do the dishes, didn't do laundry or anything during the day. As soon as Kendall's bus pulled away from the curb, she disappeared into her office and wrote. Except on Wednesdays, when she spent the mornings in Kendall's class.

On this particular Wednesday, there was an afternoon activity. Since the field day lasted most of the afternoon, Kendall left school with her a half hour early.

"I'm in the mood for some ice cream. How about you, Kendall?"

"Oh yeah."

In the past he rarely asked for anything. Gradually, he was becoming more comfortable with asking.

Another storm was brewing. By now, Delilah was accustomed to them and thought this one would probably go out to sea just like the last one, so she wasn't too concerned as they headed to the drugstore.

This was one of the few places she'd visited with an old-fashioned soda fountain in the drugstore. Delilah splurged on a double scoop of butter pecan and Kendall ordered a double scoop, one chocolate and one peach.

"Yours look good," Kendall said.

"Want a lick?" she asked.

He nodded. She handed him the cone. He took three licks.

"Which is better?"

"Yours is a close third."

"That's why you took three licks, you scamp." Their playfulness was nonsensical, but what did it matter if they were having fun? She took his cap off, whacked him with it. Laughing, he danced back, almost lost his ice cream trying to evade.

"Careful." She ruffled his hair and plopped his hat back on his head. He straightened it into position.

He was loosening up, she thought. She'd grown to love him. He was her son now. She wanted to hug and kiss him, but he hated for her to show affection in public. She casually placed her arm on his shoulder, anyway and pulled him close. When he didn't shrug it off, she was hopeful.

The tourists were gone and Coree had turned into a sleepy little island. School hadn't let out and barely anyone was walking the streets.

When she stepped off the sidewalk between the dry cleaner's and the drugstore, powerful arms grabbed her, dragging her back farther from the street. She tried some of the self-protection tricks she'd learned, but a gloved hand covered her mouth and nose. She wanted to tell Kendall to run, but she was fighting for breath when she noticed Donnie was pulling on Kendall.

Her eyes widened. What was he doing? Why was he here?

Dear God, don't let them hurt her son. She clawed at the hand, but she was losing consciousness. She tried to gain her feet, but the man was dragging her so fast she couldn't get purchase on the ground and found herself flailing about.

Finally he stopped at a car. Donnie opened the trunk and taped Kendall's mouth. He held on to him with one hand as if he were weightless.

"If you scream, I'll break his neck," Donnie said.

The man uncovered her mouth. Delilah gasped in several breaths of air. "Why are you doing this, Donnie? Please let my son go. Take me."

"Can't do." There was no remorse in his eyes.

"Why?" She tried not to let the fear in Kendall's wide eyes keep her from thinking. She had to save them. They were going to kill them. She knew it.

They heard a loud crack. Someone was in the alley in back of the shop to empty something in the garbage can.

While the men's attention was diverted, Delilah charged into her attacker. His head slammed against the wall and she screamed at the top of her lungs. For a moment Donnie stood still as if he'd been shot with a stun gun. She head-butted him in the stomach, grabbed Kendall, and sprinted down the alleyway, screaming the entire time, hoping that, since it was a small town and not a large city, she would draw attention.

Three men ran to the opening of the alley. One had his cane in the air ready to strike.

"What's going on?" one asked.

The old man with the cane braced himself on the building, holding the cane like a sword. "What you running from?"

She felt a pull on her arm. As Kendall turned around, so did she. The alley was vacant. And they skidded to a halt. Breathless, Delilah said, "Somebody tried to kill us."

"Nobody's back there now."

The two brawny men went to check, but the men had disappeared.


"The man with the gun dumped the garbage bag in the river," Kendall said.

They were in the police station. Delilah had called Carter after the men from the alley escorted them there.

"When was this?" Carter asked.

"It was in June, right after school closed," Delilah said. "Kendall and some friends were playing near the river in Morehead City and he saw someone dumping a big garbage bag in the river."

"How many men?" the officer asked.

"Two. One was picking apples the day we went to the orchard, remember?" he said to Delilah and shuddered.

"I remember." Delilah didn't think anything unusual about Kendall watching Donnie then. Donnie was an imposing man, a striking figure. Many people watched him. And he was a killer.

She shook her head. Such mannerisms. He seemed so nice, too. Sylvia would be heartbroken.

Delilah clutched Kendall's hand again, lavishing

kisses and hugs on him after the incident. She'd embarrassed him. People were watching, he'd said. But Delilah didn't care. He was hers. And she'd come too close to . . . She didn't want to think it, couldn't think it without bursting into tears, and that would frighten him even more.

"I knew I'd seen him before," Kendall was saying, "but I couldn't remember where. He was wearing a hat when he picked apples. He wasn't wearing one at the river. He looked different until I saw him in the alley." He looked at Delilah. "I lost my ice cream."

"We'll get you another one," Carter said.

"They won't get off this island," the officer said. "We have officers at the ferry checking every car that goes on and some are combing the island."

# Chapter 15

"Two guards will be with you all the time," Carter said to Delilah.

Four guards from Wadell's security company arrived hours after the incident. Working in twelve-hour shifts, two slept in the guest cottage when the other two were on duty.

Even now, a more sophisticated security system was being installed in both the house and cottage.

"Poor Kendall. This was such a fright on top of everything else. Are our lives ever going to be the same?" Unable to settle down, Delilah paced the floor.

"Of course," Carter said emphatically. "You have plenty of protection. I know these men, Delilah. They're retired SEALs. No one is going to get past them."

Delilah nodded, watching a thin tree bend with the building wind. She was so worried about Kendall.

Her nod was obviously unconvincing because Carter asked, "Do you want me to stay?"

"You have your own family to take care of. We'll be fine."

"With the guards here, you don't need me. If you did, I'd stay."

"We'll be okay, but there are still some things I don't understand. Why would Stuart's chief of security kill his brother-in-law? There has to be some connection to the project."

"The Morehead City Police are questioning Stuart," Carter said.

"None of it makes sense. And then there's Katherine. She worked for Redcliff. How does she fit into the equation? It's all connected somehow. It has to be."

"Once they talk to Moore, they'll start placing the puzzle pieces together."

When she continued to look shaken, Carter looped an arm around her shoulder. "Come on. Let me do the worrying."

"Yeah, right."

"I'll be checking on you."

Delilah nodded. And then he was gone.

David was rushing out of the office when Howard stopped him.

"I need a word with you," Howard said.

Irritated, David turned. "Can it wait? I have to get home."

"What's wrong?"

"Someone attacked Delilah and Ken today."

Howard took a step back. "Attacked? Are they hurt?"

"Luckily, no."

"Does this have anything to do with the car bomb?"

"We think so. Except they weren't really after Delilah. It was Ken they wanted." Impatiently, David glanced at his watch. He wanted to make the next ferry. "What did you want?"

"Get home to your wife. If the storm stays on course, it will hit this area."

"That's the last thing we need right now."

"Is there anything I can do?" Howard asked.

"Carter hired some guards for protection."

"It's that bad?"

"Unfortunately."

"If you all need to move out, my home is available."

David nodded and rushed out.

As he waited on the ferry, wishing it could travel the speed of a catamaran, David considered a major drawback to living on an island. Access wasn't easy in an emergency.

David crushed Delilah in his arms as soon as he stormed into the house. "Thank God you're okay."

She hung on to him like a limpet. He closed his eyes and rubbed his cheek against her head. He could have lost both of them today. "You mean everything to me, Delilah. Everything."

"We're okay, thank God."

He hadn't been able to take a good breath until he reached home to be sure that she was all right. Still he pushed her to arm's length and perused her. "Did they hurt you?"

"No. Both of us are okay." The tentative smile

she offered revealed just how worried she was. He gathered her into his arms again, trying to reassure her.

"Where's Ken?" he asked.

"Washing his hands. I fixed a snack, his favorite, hoping he'd have an appetite. He's pretty shook-up."

Kendall dragged his feet as he came out of the bathroom.

David held out a hand. "Come here, son."

Ken walked slowly toward him. David rushed forward, met him more than halfway, scooping the boy in his arms, and squeezed him tight. "You know how much I love you?" he said.

Kendall's eyes widened. "You do?"

"Of course I do. You're my son."

The warm image of father and son brought tears to Delilah's eyes as she watched the display of emotions on Kendall's face turn from weariness to uncertainty to relief.


Carter returned two hours after David. "Where's Ken?"

"Upstairs with one of the guards. They're watching a video."

They sat at the kitchen table. Delilah poured him a cup of coffee.

"They found Donovan Jarrett," he said.

"Where? They've arrested him already?" Delilah asked, hopeful this nightmare was over.

Carter shook his head. "In the marsh. He had a bullet in his head."

"A . . . Oh my word!"

David put his arm around her shoulder.

"Did they search his house? Find any information?"

"They searched, but haven't found anything useful so far. Delilah, do you still have access to Moore's computer system?"

"Probably. I have access to both Moore's and Redcliff's. I'm supposed to do preliminary work on a proposal they plan to bid on, but because of all this trouble I haven't started yet."

"Could you log on to their site?"

"Sure." He followed her to the den where the family computer was located. "I ended up on a secure site at Redcliff's once, one I shouldn't have had access to, but I was using Stan's password, not my own, at that time."

"Why didn't you tell me?"

"There was no connection to me."

"Do you think you can get back in there again?"

"I can try."

Delilah logged on to the Internet and used her password to get into the Moore's computer system, then Redcliff's. It took her a half hour to make it to the site she'd gotten in before.

"Here it is."

Carter took control. As he scanned through files and pressed the limits of access, she realized he knew a lot about computers.

He worked for a couple of hours before he ran off some pages and came downstairs.

"Did you find anything?" David asked.

"I believe," he said emphatically, "Redcliff is a front for a terrorist organization."

"Terrorist!" Delilah's hand went to her throat.

"They're only pretending the bomb was for Redcliff. I think it was really for Katherine. She must have something on them. With Stan's murder, her murder would look suspicious to the government and they would have to take a closer look into Redcliff and Moore's. Redcliff doesn't want to draw that kind of attention. If you're bidding for part of a Homeland Security contract by keeping things low-key, who's to question?"

"So right now, as far as anyone knows, they're still after Redcliff, the hated owner of the company," David said.

"Why would they kill Stan?" Delilah asked.

"You said he was a computer whiz. I'm guessing that since he had access to their computer, he did some snooping. Computers leave trails. He probably discovered they were involved with terrorists."

"Do you think Stuart's involved? Could he have his own brother-in-law killed?"

"I don't know yet." He looked outside. "You have fifteen minutes to pack your bags. Change into dark clothing, preferably black. Wear sneakers or hiking boots if you have them."

"I thought we were safe here with the guards." Delilah looked even more troubled.

"Where are you taking us?" David asked.

"I have to move you to a secure location until this situation is cleared up. By the way, your Donnie used to work for Redcliff. Tells his guards it was hell working there, which was his reason for applying for the position at Moore's."

"So you think he was spying for Redcliff," David said.

"I think so. Could have been either one."

*  *  *

David held Delilah tenderly in his arms as they traveled through the night, but her tense muscles were a sure sign she was worried. So was he—for his family. He loved this brave, beautiful woman.

They traveled in two SUVs, the one in front with three guards serving as a reconnaissance vehicle. Delilah sat in the middle because Kendall insisted on a window seat. Another guard rode in the front seat with Carter.

They tried not to frighten Ken any more than necessary, but he wasn't stupid. Someone had already tried to kill him. The equipment Carter asked him to hold occupied him. Night-vision goggles. Carter even let him look through them once, but wouldn't let him keep them on just in case he needed them. He said they couldn't take the chance of the batteries going out.

David knew that Carter had a gun in the shoulder holster hidden under his jacket.

Since David was bent more to the medical than the physical, even as kids, Carter had felt he had to protect him. And here he was again taking his brother's family to safety. Delcia and the kids were staying with Ryan until he returned.

There wasn't a spec of blood between them, but it was this tie, this sharing of pain without being asked, and pleasure, too, for most of their lives which made the two of them brothers.

"Thanks, Carter," David said, clapping a hand on his shoulder.

"No thanks needed, bro."

David tightened his arm around Delilah. With the wind whipping around them, they drove from the ferry, traveling the lonely stretch of highway. The farther they drove from Morehead City, the more Delilah relaxed. To her, distance gave them safety.

Carter was worried. More worried than he'd been on missions overseas. This was his brother—his family. And the info in the files sent chills through him. The U.S. had many enemies. Infiltrating the biochemical area of Homeland Security was a coup for any terrorist.

The road was dark and lonely. Worse than in the city where one could achieve anonymity.

The first car was more than half a mile ahead of them. Suddenly a boom shook the car. The force was almost powerful enough to overturn them and Carter wondered if they'd been hit until he saw a tree burst into flames behind them. A car was gaining distance on them. "Jesus!"

"Hand me the goggles," Carter said, and cut the lights and donned the night-vision goggles. Hitting the brakes, he swerved right. The car bumped over a ditch and it felt as if they were driving on railroad tracks, then into a cornfield. The stalks beat against the sides of the car.

"What's wrong?" Kendall asked.

Delilah touched his shoulder. "Shush."

Kendall leaned forward, watching the darkness through the windshield. Out of the side windows they glimpsed only cornstalks. Limbs lashed against the car. A thick one broke the glass.

Using his cell phone, the other guard roused the guards in the other vehicle and told them they were going for cover.

"Antitank gun?" the other guard said.

Carter floored the SUV. "Yeah," he responded, checking his rearview. "We've got to get out of here."

The guard was talking to Wadell on his cell phone. "We're thirty miles west of Morehead," he said. "We're going to ground. Got separated from the first car."

Carter kept his eyes on the field, praying they wouldn't get stuck. He swerved to the left. "It's going to hone in on the heat in the engine."

Carter hit the brakes and they came to an abrupt stop. "Get out!"

Delilah unbuckled Kendall's seat belt, then her own. Carter had switched the inside lights off so they were working in the dark. David hopped out, dragging her and Kendall with him.

"Are we going to die?" Kendall asked.

"Not tonight, buddy." Not if he could help it.


Delilah wanted to ask where they were, but wouldn't disturb Carter's concentration.

"Start running," Carter said. "We'll catch up."

As Carter and the guard headed to the back of the SUV, Delilah grabbed Kendall's hand, and the three of them ran through the dried stalks in the opposite direction of the burning tree. The ground was surprisingly soft, but it was dark as heck. They couldn't see two feet in front of them.

David pushed her and Kendall in front of him. Not uttering a word, Kendall ran silently beside her. Delilah wished she could assure him that everything would be okay, but right now the important thing was to keep moving.

She was shocked to see a gun in David's hand.

She didn't know he knew how to use one, had never seen one in the house. It wasn't something they had ever discussed. It went to show how much they still had to learn about each other.

"Pick up your speed," David said.

Delilah forced her legs to run faster. Stalks were hitting against her, making it harder.

Suddenly they cleared the cornfield and were in the open. A dog barked in rapid fire. That's all they needed, to get mauled by a dog while dodging terrorists. But the dog was tethered by a chain somewhere close. They could hear as it pulled to the full length, leaning its strength into it.

"Keep going," David said.

Delilah didn't know if she could run any farther. This was not like exercising on the treadmill in the basement.

Kendall stumbled, bringing them both down. David tripped over her.

"You okay?" he barked.

With David's help, Delilah hauled herself up, picking Ken up as she went. "You okay, sweetheart?"

"Yeah," Ken said, winded.

They were running again, and had almost made it to the trees when they heard a huge boom.

"Carter!" David and she said together as their steps slowed and they looked toward the sound.

"The SUV?" she said. Fire exploded in the air. The dog was yipping even louder, but nobody turned the light on in the house they passed.

"Yeah," David said, clearly worried about his brother. It felt as if they'd been running for hours, but it had only been a couple of minutes.

Footsteps pounded behind them.

"Keep moving," Carter said. He looked weird in the night-vision goggles. The other guard was only a step behind him.

"Thank God you're okay," Delilah said, winded by both exertion and fear.

"Move!" Carter repeated. Although the emphasis was in his voice, his pitch was low.

He meant business. No time for pleasantries, she thought as they moved into the trees. The dog continued to bark, giving away their location.

Her mind flashed back to the night when she'd defied David and gone out with her friends. They had stopped by Phases. About eleven of Moore's employees and four of Redcliff's were there. Donnie was included in the bunch. So were Percy and the always friendly Derrick. She wondered if all three men were embroiled in the conspiracy.

Danger certainly had a way of putting things in perspective. Right now she wished she were home on one of those boring evenings waiting for David to arrive.

Rapid-fire pops exploded the silence. Carter shoved them into the shelter of the trees, turned around, and started firing.

Kendall screamed. Delilah covered his mouth with her hand.

"Are you hurt?" she asked him.

He shook his head, but he was shaking in her arms. If they made it through this they were going to have to get him some more therapy.

Delilah had Kendall pressed against the tree. David was pressed against her back as he fired off shots. Her heart was pounding her to death. The muscles in her legs screamed, but with bullets whizzing around them she didn't feel it.

David put in another clip and continued firing. Suddenly the tree exploded just above them. They moved just before a blazing limb fell to the ground.

Screaming, Delilah and Kendall were shoved behind David and into the shelter of a huge tree large enough to be several hundred years old. It looked as if someone was reloading again when suddenly a scream rent the air and something exploded in the top of some trees several yards to the left. The man who had fired lay prone on the ground, the gun resting on his torso.

A lifetime passed before they heard sirens. It seemed that half the police cars in the state were arriving to surround them.


The first face Delilah saw when they came out of the forest was Percy Wright.

Fear stopped her in her tracks. He was dressed in jeans and a T-shirt under a windbreaker. He was talking to two men in business suits. He and Donnie were friends. He looked up and saw her, said something to the men, and approached her.

"Are you all right?" he asked, looking her over carefully.

"Yes," she said slowly. "What are you doing here?"

He reached into his breast pocket and flashed his badge. "Special Agent Percy Wright with the FBI."

Suddenly Delilah was freezing. Still on that adrenaline rush, she must have started shivering because David peeled his coat off and wrapped it around her shoulders. His shoulder holster stood out in stark relief. Delilah had Kendall tucked up against her side. For once he wasn't trying to get away from her.

Percy was talking to David, but Delilah couldn't comprehend a single word. David was an impenetrable force beside her that kept her standing upright.

Carter dialed the number to Ryan's home. Delcia picked up the phone as if she were guarding it.

"It's me," he said. "We're okay."

"Thank God! There was a news flash that police from several counties had been called west of Morehead City. It's a big story, but no one knows exactly what's going on. Just that there had been some explosions. A couple of casualties."

"Redcliff's men," he said. "Seems like we have the law enforcement from half the state here." Carter knew it wasn't exactly true, but there were more police cars than he'd ever seen in one location.

He heard Delcia talking to someone in the background, then a rousing cheer. For a moment he couldn't hear anything above the noise.

"Sounds like a party going on there."

"Everybody's here, Mom, Dad, Willow Mae, Harry, Mark, Marcia, Sylvia, Glenda, Emery . . ."

"Jeez. Half the island came over."

"Feels like it. Are you coming home now?" Her voice was shaky.

"Still have to get these troops to safety until they find Redcliff. I'll be back tomorrow. Stay safe, baby. Kiss my babies."

"Carter?"

"Yeah?"

"I love you."

His voice softened. He relaxed for the first time since he left the island. Family was the glue that made his life meaningful. "I love you, too, baby."

Norman Redcliff was apprehended sooner than anyone expected. He was at home packing up to go on an extended trip out of the country. The FBI had taken over his company, combing through computer files and paperwork. It turned out that Katherine had stumbled on to a file on the terrorists.

"I'm so glad Moore's was exonerated," Delilah said.

Sylvia sighed. "It's still hard to swallow that Donnie was spying for Redcliff. He was such a fine-looking man. So mannerly, so nice. I really thought our relationship was slowly building to something special."

"You wouldn't have thought so if he'd held a gun to you, and if you saw the way he handled Kendall. You don't want to know the real Donovan Jarrett," Delilah said. "Trust me."

"I'm so glad you're okay."

"All of us came out of it safely, thank God."

"Are you going to have problems with adopting Kendall because of this?"

"No. They know Kendall saw the body being dumped, although he wasn't aware of what it was. He was inadvertently in this even before we tried to adopt him. We kept him safe even in the face of danger."

"If you were with any other family, none of you would have survived."

"I don't even want to think about that. There's a beep on the other line. Let me call you back."

"I have to go anyway. Take care."

Delilah flashed for the other line.

"May I speak to Delilah Benton, please?"

"This is she," Delilah responded, wondering who would be calling and didn't know her married name.

"I'm Christine Porter with . . ."

Delilah clutched a hand to her heart. It was one of the publishing houses she'd sent her proposal to.

"We're very interested in your novel. But we'd like to do a three-book series. Could you send me a proposal for the series?"

"Yes." The rest of the conversation was muddled. The only thing Delilah really heard was that they were interested.

As soon as they disconnected, Delilah stood up and shouted.

David and Kendall came running from various parts of the house.

"What's wrong?"

"They made an offer for my book!"

David picked her up and swung her around. "Wonderful."

Kendall frowned, not knowing what all the excitement was about.

"Your mother's going to be a published writer," David said. "And we're going out to celebrate."

A half hour passed before they settled down and Kendall went upstairs to dress. Delilah and David were in their suite.

"You could write a story about what happened to you," David said.

Delilah shuddered, then thought about it. "Maybe one day. Right now it's still too fresh." She changed into a pair of black slacks. "Do you think Kendall will be okay after everything?" she asked.

"He seems to be adjusting."

"He knows we love him, that we'll do anything for him. I think he's feeling better about us at least."

After lunch, they played a game of miniature golf at the campground.

"I won," Kendall said.

David glared at him. "No, you didn't. You pushed the ball in with your hand. Not allowed."

"The wind drove it in. I was a mile away."

"In your dreams. Put that ball back."

"You're just a sore loser." Kendall backed up laughing trying to dodge David.

Game forgotten, David chased him, while Kendall darted away stumbling over his laughter.

*What a pair,* Delilah thought.


Later that night, after their lovemaking, David held Delilah in his arms. "Honey, about that night when you came in at three in the morning."

"What about it?" Delilah asked.

"Where were you?"

Delilah's smile was sultry, and mysterious. "No need to worry, sweetie."

Dear Reader,

I hope you enjoyed reading about Delilah and David. Delilah was such a striking character in *Lighthouse Magic* that she begged for her own story. There had to be something redeeming about her. She isn't my typical heroine, but I had fun developing her.

Readers like you help me to continue working with the craft I love. Thank you so much for your support and for so many kind and uplifting letters and E-mails.

My next novel is scheduled for publication in late 2005. I invite you to visit Seattle, Washington with me. See you there.

I love hearing from readers. Please visit my web page at www.erols.com/cpoarch, or write me at:

P.O. Box 291
Springfield, VA 22150

With warm regards,
Candice Poarch

# About the Author

Raised in Stony Creek, Virginia, national best-selling author Candice Poarch portrays a sense of community and mutual support in her novels. She firmly believes that everyday life in small-town America has its own rich rewards.

Candice currently lives in Springfield, Virginia with her husband and three children. A former computer systems manager, she has made writing her full-time career. Candice is a graduate of Virginia State University and holds a Bachelor of Science degree in physics.

# ARABESQUE 10th ANNIVERSARY
# GREAT ROMANCE CONTEST WINNER

## Denise Hayes DeLapp

## Avid Arabesque Reader and North Carolina Native!

Denise Hayes DeLapp, a school teacher, avid Arabesque romance novel reader, and native of North Carolina, is the winner of the 2004 Great Romance contest.

An only child, DeLapp currently cares for her ailing mother, two very active children, and her husband Reuben at their home outside of Raleigh, North Carolina. DeLapp says that reading Arabesque romance novels is "my addictive leisure-time pleasure." She adds that "with an active family life, I often find myself reading into the early hours of the morning."

DeLapp's own life reads like the pages of an Arabesque novel. She met her husband while visiting friends on a trip to Winston-Salem, North Carolina, and they grew close over a two-year, long-distance relationship. Overcoming obstacles and life's challenges together, they recently celebrated their sixteenth wedding anniversary.

A graduate of Broughton Senior High School and North Carolina Central University, DeLapp has always loved the written word and reads approximately 40 Arabesque novels a year. "It's like a latte that you just *have* to have. Especially my favorite author Rochelle Alers," says DeLapp. "I get consumed with the intense passion that her characters experience!"

Denise Hayes DeLapp will donate the Arabesque books she receives as part of her Grand Prize package to a transitional home for women and Shaw University's tutorial program. "I've enjoyed reading Arabesque novels, and it's a wonderful blessing that I get to pass these uplifting novels along to others in my community," concludes DeLapp.

**Arabesque was proud to conduct this nationwide Great Romance contest honoring the avid readers of the Arabesque imprint now celebrating a decade of soulful romance. For a complete list of contest winners, please visit us online at www.BET.com.**